HAIL THE NEW AGE

HAIL THE NEW AGE

MIKE CHINN

PROLOGUE

Even a wealthy, rowdy port like Scan Leroth has to stop and draw breath sometime. Sit back and take stock of the numbers of deaths and injuries – both natural and not so natural. Count how many merchants have been fleeced, and how many have done the fleecing. See how much misery and pain it's squeezed out of potential joy. Scan Leroth has a vast capacity for the latter, maybe more than any other city in the Ramini Republic. Even so, there comes a time – at some point after the last revelling sailors have gone face-first into the gutter or staggered back to their berths, stripped of every last *dinari*, before the morning tradesmen start to erect their pitches and the night trade has retired or is busy elsewhere – when silence falls. Usually somewhere between three and four in the morning. Even the streets closest to the harbour are empty, with not so much as a carriage in sight. Few cabbies would care to be about at such an hour, in such a quarter of the city. Anyone could be hidden in the lightless door-recesses: watching, waiting.

And on what felt like the coldest night Scan Leroth had suffered for years, someone was waiting in a shadowed doorway. Hidden as much by a long overcoat and wide hat as the darkness, a tall male figure rubbed at his hands, blowing on them occasionally. Pale clouds of chilled breath hung in a cloud about his head. He was tempted to stamp his feet, too, and would have done so if he wasn't certain the noise would carry too far across the black silence and give away his position. He had heard more than one passing voice earlier that evening, before the streets had emptied, half-seriously complaining some vengeful wizard must be having a spiteful joke, the cold was so unseasonal. The idea had amused the hidden figure. Few appreciated that dragging the temperature down, even by so much as one degree, used more power than any sane Chrysomancer would care to waste. And the mild discomfort of a few citizens was of no interest to them. Freezing men don't throw lumps of coal at a cat just because it's annoying them.

The multiple clatter of hooves on cobbles echoed along the crooked street, sharp and clear. The watcher tensed and drew back even further into the shadows. Less than half of the street's oil-lamps were lit, but he wasn't prepared to take chances. Assume nothing. The driver might be deaf, dumb and blind – but who could say what his fare might be able to sniff out, or sense.

The cab rattled into view and pulled up directly opposite a house. It was a plain, two-wheeled carriage, dragged by a skeletal, sway-backed horse only a few days away from the glue factory. It was absolutely remarkable in its commonality.

A lone passenger stepped out. He was stooped to disguise his height, wrapped in an ankle-length overcoat, with a tall, gleaming hat tilted to shade his features. He muttered something to the cabby, barely raising his face, and went indoors. The cabbie whipped up the disinterested horse and it pulled away.

Silence chased away the echoes.

All of the houses in this corner of Scan Leroth had once been the homes of prosperous merchant-chandlers – before fashion had dictated they move on. Each building was narrow-fronted and several stories high. Ground rent had once been so exorbitant, keeping the buildings' footprint to a minimum had been the only way even the wealthiest families could afford them. Now, they were, for the most part, derelict, used by seamen too sick or old to find berths, the cheapest doxies, tramps, and sometimes mysterious men on late-night assignations. The silent watcher would have bet it wasn't some amorous tryst. Not unless the newcomer enjoyed his sex mixed with a liberal dose of cockroaches.

Then again, he knew those with the most money tended to have the most perverse tastes.

There was a noise to his left – the faint rasp of cloth on brick. Although he couldn't see anything, or anyone, his right hand twitched to a knife hilt inside one of the overcoat's pockets.

"It's me," a voice hissed from nowhere.

The watcher's hand relaxed its grip, wary fingers still caressing the hilt. The voice may have been familiar, but that didn't mean he would know whoever was using it. Mimicry was an easy talent.

A second figure clotted out of the cold air and joined the watcher in his niche. He relaxed, just a little. "Taking a chance, aren't you?"

The newcomer rolled back his coat's huge collar, exposing a mournful face. He was shorter than the other, and apparently many years older. He smiled, as far as his dour face was able. "I kept my back to the wall. No chance of losing my way."

"I didn't mean the loss of vision!" The younger man sounded irritated. Useful as invisibility was, anyone casting such a glamour over themselves also lost their own vision. Only a fool used it, except over short or very familiar distances. He nodded towards the house across the street: the one the cab's passenger had entered. "What if they've got a crystal scanning the area?"

"Calm yourself." The older man pulled a small, milky pebble from his pocket. A tiny chunk of abaston. The gold threads which normally interlaced the stone's surface were invisible in the darkness. Not a trace of luminescence showed. "I checked. There's not the tiniest scrap of abaston within a mile. No abaston stone – no wizard."

It was a well-observed fact that although one might find a crystal without a wizard, there was no such thing as a wizard without a crystal. Much more likely to see the President walking the streets of the Capitol naked.

"Then what are they up to?" The younger man didn't sound any more mollified. "Meetings all over Scan Leroth, always under cover of darkness, always covert. Only supporters of the old regime would need – or want – to act so clandestinely. Even if there's some new, non-magical political group emerging that we don't know about, there'd be no need for all this. The Philosophic Party's hardly likely to fear any real opposition just yet – at least from mundane sources – too much the hero of the War." He rubbed at his face. His fingers were trembling. "But if it's not the Chrysomancers, who is it?"

"If we knew that, we wouldn't be here, would we?" the older, mournful-faced one muttered. "Gods, but I wish I could have a smoke!"

"I'm damned glad you can't." The younger one gave silent, heartfelt thanks that being on observation meant he was saved from the filthy stuff the other habitually put in his pipe.

They continued to watch. The house remained dark and unreadable.

Eventually, the older man sighed. "We're going to learn nothing out here. We'll have to go in." A moment later, he became almost transparent again. All that remained was the faintest scratch of his coat buttons on brick and the hint of condensed breath against the night. Eventually, even they faded.

The watcher tensed again. This would be the chanciest part. A dozen armed men charging across the street was hardly subtle. Casting a glamour of invisibility over the squad would only end up with one half bayoneting the other once they began colliding with each other under the spell's blinding influence.

He drew his knife free of its sleeve and waited. Scan Leroth seemed to be holding its breath.

A whistle blew. Figures swarmed from hiding and ran at the house, the watcher with them. All were draped in long coats, floppy hats covering their heads and faces. Each carried a short carbine with bayonet fixed. Unnaturally silent, they charged across the street. The first three reached the shadowed door and kicked it open without pausing. The hinges snapped silently. The watcher followed them inside, his knife ready for any hint of ambush.

The rooms were small and irregularly shaped. Many of the walls had long ago slipped from vertical. The floors and ceilings sagged. Shadows and dust were everywhere.

Dark figures ran up a warped and creaking staircase. The sound suppression glamour had already failed. There was shouting from above, a single shot. A vivid, blinding flash threw the ground floor into silhouette, leaving a seething purple blot across many pairs of eyes. Almost immediately, an explosion followed. The entire house quaked. Chunks of wormy timber and ancient mortar rained down in powdery ruin.

More men rushed up the stairs.

The older man stood behind the younger, now cloaked in dust and thinning skeins of smoke. His mournful face looked even more downcast.

"So much for your crystal!" the younger one snapped. He sounded edgy.

The other drew out his piece of stone again. It still registered no trace of activity. "That wasn't abaston power." He sounded like a man who'd just been convinced the sun didn't rise in the morning.

"And it wasn't blasting powder, either."

The older man continued to stare at his abaston fragment, as though any moment it would have a change of heart. The stamp of boots down the stairs heralded the armed men returning. He stopped glaring at his stone and raised his sour face.

"Anything?"

The one closest to him looked grim, angry at being cheated of the chance to kill whoever had been responsible. "Nothing." He spat out a wad of gritty saliva. "Might I recommend we evacuate. Everything above this floor is likely to collapse any moment."

"Agreed. Get your men out, Sergeant. We'll join you shortly."

The sergeant hesitated. "I strongly urge you to—"

"You have your orders. We'll take responsibility for ourselves."

The armed man paused a moment longer before nodding curtly, ordering his men out. Once the stairs were clear, the two remaining began to ascend warily, the younger in the lead. The steps had creaked before, now they groaned in pain.

There was little to be seen on the next floor up. Whatever had caused the flash and explosion, it had taken everything with it. Nothing aside from the floor and walls were left, and they looked scorched and weak. A fine, grey dust covered everywhere. It rose in irritating clouds with each footstep.

"Thorough," remarked the mournful-faced man, stepping off the groaning stairs.

"Was it suicide, or something to cover a retreat?"

The younger man took a step, his foot plunging straight through the floor. Only the other's grip on his arm stopped the rest of him following.

He slid his feet onto a firmer surface. "Maybe we'd better do as our friend suggested and leave." His voice had the merest quiver to it. Sweat had run thin channels down the dust masking his face.

Somewhere, timber cracked.

The other nodded and started to turn. He paused, seeing something at his feet. He bent and picked it off the dusty floor, then led for the stairs without a word. Behind the pair came a series of tortured wooden shrieks.

Neither of them wasted any time going down the steps. They took them three at a time, ignoring the shrieks of protest.

Outside, the older one made straight for the nearest street-lamp. Just as he reached it, there was a rattle of staccato explosions. The younger one turned, watching the house fall in on itself like a rotten tree. The buildings on either side staggered briefly, losing pieces of themselves onto the ruin, but they held. For now. A thin cloud of acrid dust ballooned across the street. Echoes died, and silence once more settled over Scan Leroth.

Spitting out flakes of grit, the younger one joined him in the lamp light. He craned over his companion's head, trying to see what the short man had found. He was holding it up against the light, frowning ponderously.

"What do you make of it?" He dropped a fingernail-sized oval of stone into the other's hands. The younger man held it up to the light.

It was a familiar milky stone, chased through with golden filaments, but a profile had been carved into it. A cameo. It looked vaguely familiar.

He handed it back. "Abaston stone, after all. A pretty old piece, judging by the face carved into it."

"Several centuries, quite possibly," admitted the other. "And totally drained of all power."

"No wonder you couldn't detect it." He still sounded tense, irritable.

The older man pulled a dented hip flask out of his coat and handed it over. The younger one took a long drink, sighed, and handed the flask back.

Holding the piece of stone close to his dour features, the short man frowned at it. "Just a pretty bauble, now. You recognise the face?"

The other wiped sweat and dust from his eyes. "Menelik XIV, isn't it?" His voice no longer shook; he was cool and calm. "The last King of Steatal before the Chrysomancers conquered all of the Ramini kingdoms. That bauble's an antique."

"You think so? Look again." He held it up, angling it so that the light from the street-lamp cast well-defined shadows into the carving. "Abaston's a very soft stone, not much good for cameos. Yet, look how sharp the cuts are."

It was obvious once attention had been drawn to it. All of the edges were clear and brilliant. There was no sign of wearing.

"You see the problem?" the short man said. "The likeness of a king who died before even the Archimandrite was born, on a piece of exhausted abaston from about the same period." He paused, wanting the other to fill in the rest, to say out loud what he was thinking.

"Yet carved recently," his companion obliged.

CHAPTER ONE

You can't fake death. Actors roll back their eyes, hold their breath and whiten their faces with arsenic rinses, and just look like they're sleeping off a particularly brutal hangover. Death isn't something you can mistake, not once you've seen it. And I was looking at it three times over.

I was in a small kitchen – not a place you'd normally expect to find three dead bodies, not human ones, anyway. The place was spotless: walls scrubbed white; floor clean enough to eat off. Even the sunlight lancing through the only window didn't dare have a single dust mote floating in it. The air was sharp with the tang of bleach. Normally, I wouldn't mind eating anything that was prepared here. But today, the menu was off.

The corpses were huddled behind what some parochial chef probably called his work-surface. Anyone else would have called it a counter: narrow, barely waist height, and just wide enough to hide three dead stewards from someone who wasn't looking very hard.

I sighed as I bent down to look closer. I didn't relish having to examine each body carefully. Seeing death so many times doesn't mean you have to get used to it. Maybe I'm the sensitive type.

Their orange and gold tunics had acquired a fresh crimson trim that didn't match. Judging by their wounds and the rips in the fabric, each one had been stabbed from behind – straight through the heart.

Maybe someone hadn't liked the service? Someone who could slip a knife between the back ribs and nail the heart first time: a real artist.

They all still had their pocket watches. One even had a sizeable purse of silver tucked inside his blood-soaked tunic. So, robbery wasn't the motive; at least, not a straightforward one. But they were all missing one item and it was not something you'd expect a regular steward to have about them. No one would ever notice the loss, no one but me, anyway. I'd handed each one over personally, four days earlier: a security pass, signed by the President himself.

I got to my feet, towelling my hands on a handkerchief. I tossed it among the dead. No disrespect – after all they were, had been, colleagues of mine – but it wouldn't do to start my journey carrying a bloodstained wad of cotton. I'd have enough problems without that.

I took one last look at the bodies, wishing I could remember their names, and slipped out of the once pristine kitchen, as carefully as I'd entered, through the back door.

Outside it was deserted but not so quiet. There was a distant, undulating murmur – coming from what I expected was a very large, excited crowd. They'd be round the front, admiring Professor Entissodamo Alva's latest marvel, or giving the impression they were. There was no reason for anyone to be skulking round the back of the building. Except me, and I reckoned I had a damned good reason. Judging by the disturbances in the gravel covering the ground, someone else thought they did, too.

It hadn't rained for two days, and the gravel was white and dusty from the summer heat. But there was a neat trail of darker impressions where someone had walked, disturbing the stones, exposing their damp undersides. Recently, too.

Going in or coming out? I wondered.

I've never wanted to follow in anyone's footsteps. Instead, I slunk along the wall, trying to look unimportant and insignificant; like someone who always crept around the backs of old coaching inns. A devotee of pre-Republican architecture. But I knew there'd be at least one person who'd be looking out for me. I was guessing three.

Not that it would actually be me they'd be on the alert for – I'm not that vain. They'd be alert for someone who was so unmemorable, so likely to disappear in a crowd of two that their simple ordinariness was notable. Blending in is one of the things I do – just like whoever killed the three stewards.

As I rounded the side of the old inn, the noise increased in volume. I could already see some of the spectators craning their heads to look over anyone thoughtless enough to be in front of them. Men in their best suits and tallest hats. Women in new silk dresses, waists as tiny as their bustles were exaggerated. Children, happily waving tiny flags, not knowing or caring whose flag it was, just thinking it was pretty. It was our new flag, of course: the black, red and blue flag of a reborn Ramini Republic. The flag of the post-war Philosophic Party government. The symbol of reason and science. Everything the Chrysomancers never were and aren't.

I almost wished I had one of my own.

I slipped into the crowd with the ease of practise. I didn't cause so much as a ripple. No one was there to look at me. Dressed as I was in a worn black suit and scuffed boots, I imagine most did their best to pretend I didn't exist, or held onto their purses and pocketbooks a little tighter – just to be on the safe side.

I weaved my way through the cheering mass, dodging flags and the occasional over-enthusiastically swung stovepipe hat. I couldn't see him yet, but I knew Professor Alva was out there somewhere, at the crowd's focus, preening and lapping up every ounce of worship. It was strange not to be able to spot the other cause for all the hysteria – Alva's latest invention. It was big enough. But somehow the jostling mass of overawed humanity masked it – until I burst out at the very front of the crowd and stood less than three yards away.

It looked so much bigger in reality.

Alva's locomotive engine and train. A steam-powered contraption which hauled passenger-carrying carriages along steel rails. A steel, iron and brass monster that President Thinos seemed to believe was the future. A future that had, so far, almost bankrupted the country.

The *Novandik*. The New Age.

The locomotive engine wasn't much to look at: a massive box on wheels, with a row of windows under the curved roof, giving 360-degree vision to the driver. In the sun, they seemed to be gazing blindly outward – not a good metaphor for the journey ahead. And from the front end, like a set of jutting, stained teeth, was a slatted plough arrangement. As I understood, it was some kind of fender to throw wildlife off the rails. At least the locomotive engine was colourful: a gleaming vermillion, polished like a mirror so the sunlight bounced off it, with intricate gold lining on every flat surface with enough room to cram it on.

Hard to imagine that hidden away under such a generally unremarkable wrapper was the steam-powered engine presently giving the Chrysomancers – our former not so benign masters – apoplexy.

Attached to the rear of the box-shaped *Novandik* was a large, cylindrical tank, also painted and lined out in vermillion and gold, containing several thousand gallons of water for the boiler. It had Professor Alva's personal sigil, also in gold, sprawling across the tank's surface. Just in case anyone might forget who the brain behind the whole endeavour was.

Behind it trailed three long, bulky vehicles which seemed to have been based on standard stage-coaches – stretched and widened by a crazed builder who hadn't known when to stop. Each ran on two swivelling, six-wheel trucks to support their outrageous size and weight. Open balconies were fitted at each end – marked out with the fanciest wrought iron steps and rails. Baroque entrances to the strangest journey of your life – or your last. The vehicles were painted in the striking colours of our new flag, a scheme which some pencil-pusher likely imagined would look patriotic, but in the end just looked like it had been done by a child with no sense of colour.

The first carriage was Alva's own, easily identified since it had the fewest windows – especially in the sleeping section – even more black, blue and red paintwork, gilded balcony ends, and the name *ALVA* on a massive oval plaque on its side. The second was for passengers like my good self, and the third was mainly a mobile kitchen and wine cellar.

Bringing up the rear was another box – an ugly black mass of planks just as large as the passenger carriages, but with none of their pretensions. Even the boarding platforms had the simplest of railings. Maybe they had run out of blue and red paint by the time they came to decorate it, or they saw no sense in wasting artistic effort on what was little more than a mobile barracks.

Looming in the background was the old coaching inn chosen to be the first staging post of this new form of transport. It was a ramshackle, three-floored monstrosity that had started out as a half-timbered drinking den and been added to over the next three or four hundred years as its importance increased. Extra floors, new wings, a couple of cupolas – with flags, naturally – in local stone, or brick, the original crazily leaning black timber and lime walls all but buried under the extensions: an architectural chimera. As Scan Leroth became the major port of the east coast, the need to feed and board passengers had become a local industry. Coaching inns had sprung up across the city, fighting to be the biggest, best, or just the closest to the piers. I think this particular eyesore was chosen by Alva, or the government, because it was the most venerable. It certainly wasn't for the rooms or service. I knew it had once been called *The Archimandrite's Rest*. Now it gloried in the title of *The Rail-Road Inn*.

It was gratifying to note someone had spent as much effort thinking up a new name as they had painting the place. They still hadn't changed the old sign over the arched entranceway.

While I was admiring the rail-road train, trying to imagine what it was going to be like living on it for some time, I became aware that I was also being watched. A blue-uniformed figure was standing on the steps of the second passenger carriage. A woman, judging by the way her tunic fitted in all the right places. Although blue-lensed spectacles masked both of her eyes, I was pretty sure they were locked on me. I grinned back, waved in my friendliest manner, and started walking along the train's length. The woman didn't so much as twitch. My first impulse was to pull out my security pass. Then I thought better of it. I had the distinct feeling that suddenly reaching for anything inside my coat would be unwise, for me. It seemed smarter to wait until I was much nearer, when I could do everything slowly and clearly.

Up close, she was no less severe: ramrod straight, arms folded into the small of her back, eyes still invisible behind the blue lenses, the planes of her face rigid and unforgiving. Unattractive features on what was otherwise an attractive, blonde woman – one dressed in a gold-braided Internal Bureau uniform, with the insignia of lieutenant-commander. I must have been having a slow day because it took me far too long to figure who she – it – was.

"You'll be *Gosigné* Batrix," I said, keen to show I'd at least glanced at my brief. Batrix the heteromorph. A Switcher. The last of its kind, which, despite all appearances, was neither a woman nor a man. One of the Chrysomancers' peculiar little jokes. And contrary to the law and spirit of President Thinos's revised Constitution – working, quite illegally, for the Internal Bureau.

"I am Bureau Lieutenant-Commander Batrix." The voice was as stiff as its bearing. I could feel the hidden eyes taking in my less than best suit – which seemed shabbier in contrast to the crisp blue uniform. "Who – or what – are you?"

The heteromorph wasn't making it easy for me, but then I've always had a problem with Switchers. They remind me of the past too much. It wasn't her fault – I was self-aware enough to realise that – and, hard as I tried, I couldn't help thinking of the creature as a her, at least from a distance. Maybe it was a convenient habit, one all of us at the Seminary had fallen into.

"Wilonek Scilli. You should be expecting me." This devastating news failed to move her, so I reached for my pass. She stiffened even more – if that was possible – her fingers flexing, as though they were itching to close around some kind of weapon and try it out on me. I slowed to the speed of molasses in winter. Hooking out the pass between two fingers, I handed it over.

She raised one long, delicate hand and took it. Opening it slowly, she took the best part of my lifetime to read it. Eventually, she folded the pass shut and looked at me.

"This could be a forgery." She said it slowly, in the tone of a teacher.

"Of course it could." I was growing tired of her attitude. "Why don't you check it?"

That produced a reaction I wasn't expecting. Her head flicked back as though I'd slapped her. After a moment she regained her icy composure and stared at me harder than ever. Much more of this and I'd get bruised.

"You are happy for me to do so?"

"Would I have said so otherwise?" Things fell into place with a click so loud I'm surprised Bureau Lieutenant-Commander Batrix didn't hear it. I remembered a note attached to her file. She had an almost pathological hatred of all things magical. Quite perverse, under the circumstances. To check my pass, she'd have to use the simple charm which the Bureau had issued her. It was almost comical: the use of supposedly illegal methods by a creature who loathed them, a creature that should have been destroyed by law. I bet the Director had a really good laugh when he'd decided who to detail for this mission.

"In fact," I said, enjoying myself again, "I insist."

As though she was expecting it to hold a venomous snake, she slowly reached into a pocket in her tunic. She produced several pieces of paper, each no larger than my thumbnail, pinching them between fingertips like they were about to bite. One would have my name on, printed in tiny, neat official copperplate – a slip that had been magically linked to my pass the moment it was signed and sealed. She took a while to find the right paper, she was holding them so gingerly. She eventually pocketed the rest, opened my pass again, and – with the expression of someone about to bite into a fruit that may be rotten – pressed the slip of paper against the presidential seal.

Nothing startling happened. Wisps of colour drifted up from the seal, gradually coalescing into a flat image: my face. Or at least, the one I was wearing at that moment. Accompanying the picture, two words came out of the air: "Wilonek Scilli." If I'd ever wondered what dead leaves would sound like if could talk, my curiosity had been satisfied.

Batrix handed my pass back.

"Happy?" I asked.

She looked anything but. "I am satisfied, *Gosigné* Scilli."

"Good." I dropped the pass back into a pocket. "Because I have excellent reason to believe there are three people on board this rail-train who intend to assassinate President Thinos."

CHAPTER TWO

I have to admit, I was disappointed when Batrix didn't leap into action. She just stood, pointing those blue lenses at me.

"And what leads you to believe this?" she asked, almost offhand.

I nodded towards the end of the rail-train, towards the inn. "Three bodies back there. Men who were assigned as stewards on this trip. Whoever killed them clearly wanted to get on board. I believe they intend to assassinate the President when he makes his speech in half an hour."

In fact, I had no real idea if they were actually on board, or even why – other than it probably wasn't for the general health of the remaining passengers. But it seemed as good an answer as any. I wanted the heteromorph kept busy, scouring the entire rail-train for a trio she might never find, as far from me as possible.

"You have proof of this?"

I resisted the urge to grab her by the pristine collar and shake that spotless tunic until the next full moon. "Other than three bodies hidden in a kitchen, no. Perhaps you'd prefer to wait until they shoot Thinos?"

She paused again. I wondered if it was just her or a standard Switcher reaction. The few I'd come across hadn't seemed quite so reluctant to act – not that I'd stayed around them that long. Like I'd said: they make me uneasy, knowing that, originally, they'd been just a stir of chemicals in some Chrysomancer's cauldron. Who wants the stew you're served for dinner suddenly taking on shape and discussing the price of beef with you?

"You have no idea what they look like, I suppose?" she asked.

I grinned broadly. "That would take all the fun out of it, Commander. But any steward aiming a gun at the President during his speech might be considered a suspect."

"Would that not be a little late?" There might have been a touch of irony – but I doubted it.

"Then we'd better move, hadn't we?"

I thought she was going to pause for more reflection, but she surprised me by abruptly spinning and hauling herself up onto the carriage's end balcony. She glanced down before hurrying into the carriage itself. "I trust you are armed?"

I would have produced my brand new, five-shot Alva-patent repeater pistol – it was a beautiful toy, the barrel and cylinder carefully engraved with minute images of Alva's past inventions, although I still wasn't used to it – but she vanished too swiftly. So I left it safe and warm in its coat pocket. I was pretty sure there'd be plenty of opportunities later for it to help me act big and tough.

Batrix was standing in the corridor of the central passenger carriage, which ran down one side of the vehicle, leaving the rest for the small compartments to be occupied by the honoured guests. None were showing their faces just now, and for that I was modestly grateful. The carriage smelled of beeswax; all the wooden surfaces gleamed bright and new. It gave me a headache.

"What is your plan?" she asked, peering at me over her blue lenses. I couldn't help shuddering: the gesture reminded me of one made by a small, soft-spoken nun-tutor I'd known back at the Madrasaté Seminary, just before she beat me to a pulp.

I tried to shake the memory. "I thought I'd make it up as we go."

"I trust you will not take offence if I observe that that does not surprise me."

"You'd be surprised how much offence I can take." I pushed past her. Somehow her body contrived to take up even less of the corridor – no mean feat in someone so slight. "Any idea which of these is mine?" I waved a hand towards the compartments.

"The final one."

It seemed apt: the last one before the ugly black box carriage containing the troops. I made my way down the corridor, found the last door, and slid it open. I was impressed; even in good hotels I've stayed in worse rooms. I was a little amazed how much had been fitted in.

All the windows were hung with plush, deep red drapes. Against one wall, sat a broad leather sofa, one that I knew pulled out and converted into a bed. A large mirror faced it. Above the sofa, running the length of the wall, an overhead closet seemed to be the only storage space. A tidy table and chair were in the opposite corner, by the widow. There was something like a cupboard door below the mirror, and I pulled at it: a washbasin and stand smoothly unfolded themselves into the compartment. The remaining décor was as dark and rich as the drapes, and four gas lamps snaked out of the walls to offset the gloom.

"May we go now?" Batrix demanded from the corridor. I glanced back at her, willing her to stay outside.

"A moment more," I asked, heading for the overhead closet. I swung the curved door up, as if checking there was room for my extensive wardrobe. It was there – as promised – tucked at the back: a pint bottle, a faint blue luminescence shouting its presence in the closet's gloom.

I slammed the door shut, radiating indifference. "Right – let's find ourselves some assassins."

It was obvious Batrix desperately wanted to do something – most likely turn the rail-train upside down, have everyone parade alongside and present his or her credentials. Bureau people like to do things by the book – and what I already knew about Batrix was that if the book didn't already exist, she'd want to write it. I let her go off and do whatever made her happy. With her frigid aloofness, and the Bureau uniform no more obvious than the sun rising at midnight, I could have guaranteed the killers would remain invisible. Maybe literally.

What I wanted to do, more than anything, was to go back to my snug apartment and that tantalising bottle with its luminous contents. But I didn't. I held on, trying not to dwell on it, trying not to visualise it glowing in the closet like a signal fire at night. It didn't work. The more I tried, the more it insisted on dominating my thoughts. *Chavet* is like that. But at least I wasn't getting the cramps – they were still a few, blissful hours away.

I hung around on the rear balcony of the passenger carriage, watching the admiring crowd as it swirled and billowed around the rail-train. I turned back towards the coaching inn, wondering how long it would be before someone found the bodies. Well after the *Novandik* had pulled away from Scan Leroth, I hoped.

Some of the crowd glanced up at me – probably wondering just what I thought I was doing up here. Most ignored me; far more engaged in admiring the rail-train in all its garish glory. Women, men, a few children – all decked out in their finest clothes. The men in their tallest hats, the women in their most flamboyant bonnets. Most of the youngsters just looked bored, wanting to be back in their normal daywear and playing.

I still couldn't see Professor Alva, but I could hear him. His voice was a perfect echo of the man: puffed up, bristly, under absolutely no doubt as to his importance in the Ramini Republic's future. He had a short, round body which carried a self-esteem ten times his size.

Something above the inn's high-peaked roof caught my attention. For a moment, I thought it might have been one of the steward-killers taking up a position. But it was a movement in the sky above the rail-train – a misty, sinuous shape no bigger than a sparrow. But the lazy, almost arrogant flap of multiple wings gave away its real size. This was big – very big – and very high up.

I found myself reaching for my Alva repeater – even though if the thing had been in range, I'd have had more luck throwing rocks at it. It rose in a sky that had all the colour burned out of it, drifting assuredly across Scan Leroth and the inn. Its shadow – pale and vast – flashed over the crowd so fast they wouldn't have noticed. No one else saw it – not that I could tell – they were all engrossed in the *Novandik* and today's national hero as he harangued them from whatever perch he'd found.

I lost sight of it as the rail-train obscured my view, but I'd seen enough to know it was heading due west – straight for Scana Carsofi, which just happened to be the *Novandik's* destination, too.

I dropped my gaze – partly because the brilliant sky was pricking out tears – and found I was staring at the road down which President Thinos was expected. At some point in the last few minutes – whilst I'd been watching the skies – two rows of armed military had assembled and lined the road. Their muskets were grounded, each man standing stiff and proud in the red and purple of the Republican Infantry, steel helmets polished to an agonising brilliance. It was impossible to discern them as individuals any more than you could one heteromorph from a batch grown in the same vat – except the creation of heteromorphs was now a state crime, and what kind of government breaks its own laws?

I pulled out my watch. There were just eight minutes to go before the presidential address. Thinos would be on time – he made a point of it, as though shackling his day to a small timepiece somehow made him a better man than the wizards. I looked carefully about me once more. Nobody jumped up, waved, or identified themselves in any way.

I wondered if Batrix was having more fun than me.

As though conjured by that thought, she appeared at my shoulder: ramrod straight, hands resting in the small of her back. I wondered if they automatically returned there when not wanted.

"I have searched the entire train with the assistance of the chief steward. There is not one member of his staff he does not recognise, but there are three missing, as you indicated."

"Good to know you haven't been wasting your time." I was intrigued to learn the three replacements hadn't replicated the dead stewards' faces. That meant whatever they were aiming to do, it was likely a hurried job – with very little or no planning and preparation. It made me feel warm knowing how rattled the Chrysomancers must be.

"And I suppose you have been equally busy," she commented, her tone on the point of aridity. She glanced at the swirling multitude. "Examining the crowd for suspects, I imagine?"

"You'd be surprised how much you can learn just observing."

"I imagine perhaps I would—"

She was cut off by a thin shriek from the distance: a whistle. The crowd grew silent and more restless. Alva's self-promoting drone tailed away. The President was on his way.

I pulled out my watch again: two minutes to go. As I dropped it back in my pocket, I heard another shrill whistle as a steam-powered coach swung into the guard-lined road. Around a quarter the size of one of the rail-train carriages, the coach ran on four huge wheels –

the iron tyres rumbling and crunching along a road not designed for such punishment. The boiler and drive-chain were situated to the rear, steam and smoke billowing thickly. At the front, on a platform directly over the front wheels, the driver was steering the ungainly creation with what looked like a winch. As he spun it one way and then the other, the coach drifted from gutter to gutter, never quite hitting either. It was no way for the head of a country to travel.

The crowd drew back – either through respect or from doubt over the driver's skills. The coach wheezed and belched past, covering us all in grey, sulphurous smoke. But in spite of its ludicrous manoeuvring, the contraption reached the front of the inn at the precise moment, by my watch, anyway. I guessed they'd been rehearsing for weeks.

I'd imagined President Thinos would step down from the coach. But I'd reckoned without the grandstanding. He could give Professor Alva a run for his money. Swinging open the door, the President pulled himself up onto the coach's roof and stood there for a full minute, waving as the crowd applauded, yelled and pushed closer. Professor Alva's rail-train was forgotten; Ramini's war hero and saviour eclipsed it.

Thinos never failed to amaze me. He wasn't young, and his stick-thin frame was beginning to show the strains of presidency, yet he almost shone with vitality. His greying hair was a badge of distinction and valour, not age, and he radiated a charisma which gave him the presence of a man more than half his age. No wonder the crowd loved him. He was a natural leader, someone who wouldn't ask a soul to do anything he wasn't prepared to do himself. He rarely had to ask.

He was a true politician.

Even Batrix seemed smitten. She'd moved across the balcony and was already halfway down the steps to see better. Although it occurred to me that perhaps she was really hoping for a better view of the crowd, waiting for the assassins to show themselves. That was fine with me: I didn't want her noticing me leaving. I checked the crowd: everyone seemed to be trying to get closer to Thinos. I saw stewards' tunics, and guards' uniforms, as well as recognising the crowd of the great and good that Alva had invited along – they'd finally been flushed from whatever holes they'd been lurking in. Without exception, crew, passengers and onlookers had been squeezed into the inn's courtyard.

No, I had to correct myself, there were three exceptions, and I'd formed a pretty good idea where I'd find them.

I slipped back through the carriage door, along the corridor, and into the next carriage: Alva's own private one. I didn't have time to admire it – though I'd glanced through the plans a couple of years ago and I knew the professor had built himself a mobile palace.

When I reached the front of the line of carriages, I opened the door carefully, slipping my head through by degrees. The view of the locomotive-engine was partially obscured by the water tank, which probably meant I was also hidden. Taking the Alva pistol from my pocket, I slowly shifted myself across the balcony to look along the tank's left side. I saw nothing. Shuffling to the right, I checked down its length. I spotted three men in steward's uniforms, standing within ten feet of the *Novandik*, bent over something I couldn't quite make out. I'd bet a year's wages they weren't admiring the huge box's fancy paintwork.

There was a sudden eruption of applause and shouting from the rear of the train: Thinos saying something that had really pleased the crowd. I used the opportunity to slip down the left-hand steps to edge carefully alongside the water tank. Through the gap between rails and the tank's underside, I could see the lower halves of the three, and something of what they were clustered around. It was a piece of stone – abaston stone. Even at this distance I could see the gold veins pulsing with accumulating energy. It wasn't a sight that filled me with happy thoughts – especially as all I had was a gun. If I leapt out, waving the pistol, shouting "Put your hands up!" I'd be nothing more than a shadow on the ground a moment later.

I reached the front end of the tank, where it was coupled to Alva's locomotive-engine. Masked by another blast of applause, I crouched and swung myself under the heavy coupling and stayed. I needed to watch for a moment, see what they were up to and figure out if there was some way I could stop them, and still be smiling afterwards.

They were standing around the chunk of abaston stone, equidistant; one holding it, the others simply resting their left hands on the top. Their right hands were pointing at the *Novandik*. It was a formation I'd heard of, but never seen before: the Triad. One Chrysomancer – at least third *shakrat*, more likely second – would be attuned to the stone, the other two augmenting the power transfer, allowing three to channel the kind of power levels that would fry one man, from his nervous system outward.

There was nothing to see – no brilliant streams of light splashing off the locomotive-engine's sides, no dazzling sparks dancing from their fingertips, yet I could feel the build-up. It was like a pregnant storm, directly overhead, waiting for just the right moment to be born.

After a while, I thought I did see something, although I couldn't be sure. I could just be seeing what I expected: a distortion in the *Novandik's* side, a twisting, wrinkling, as though the wood, steel and brass sides were made from gold leaf. I even imagined I could see through the metal, to the actual boiler, pistons and drive shaft at the heart of the machine. But despite the potential for some real damage, I got a feeling that whatever they were doing, it wasn't a destructive mission. Rather, they seemed to be searching for something, using the Triad to draw something from the *Novandik*.

I hoped none of the crew were inside the locomotive-engine – with that kind of power bouncing off the fittings, you could easily loose something, like your life.

I wasn't left with much of a choice. Someone – or something – had to be shot. Preferably, the chunk of abaston stone. If you destroy that, the power's gone. Shoot a man, and the stone's still active. Even if I killed the one to which the stone was attuned, the other two would have enough juice left between them to leave me as a fond memory.

If I'd had a single shot pistol, that would have been no real problem – modern pistols are pretty accurate, and I'm fairly handy with one. But Alva's patented repeater wasn't so reliable, something to do with the chamber rotation. I might need all five shots to get it right. And facing a Triad you don't have the luxury of practice runs.

It had to be the stone. I came out from under the coupling and took up position on one knee. I rested my back against the coupling – the world might get unpredictable once I shot the stone. Thumbing back the hammer, I raised the repeater to eye level and sighted down the barrel. With a quick prayer to any of the illegal gods who might have been listening, I squeezed the trigger.

Everything happened very quickly. The abaston stone shattered perfectly, tiny chunks of power-charged shrapnel flying in every direction. This time, I did see the released energy: a rapidly expanding sphere of brilliant light. It was gone in a second – inflating to infinity – but as it passed, it tried slamming me through the steel coupling. I felt sure my spine had shattered. All that pain had to mean something.

The members of the Triad recovered with depressing speed – all except the one who'd been holding the piece of abaston. He was on the ground, screaming, blood running from his eyes, ears and nose. I could safely discount him.

But the other two spotted me in seconds, drawing their own pistols, and coming at me with impressive, if unsteady, speed. As I'd dropped my own repeater when the shockwave hit, I was served up to them on a plate.

The nearest reached me, swinging his pistol like a club. I ducked and it missed – just. At the same time I heard a gunshot, and guessed the second was taking pot shots. Accuracy be damned. It missed both of us, and I was left wrestling with his partner, and he was the kind who didn't want to waste bullets on a man when you can simply beat him to death.

He swung wildly, mostly missing, but when he connected, he more than made up for it. After three roundhouse blows to my skull, I was starting to wonder why we weren't retiring to our corners: the referee was ringing the bell loudly.

I focused long enough to see the next sledgehammer coming. I ducked, relieved to hear a yelp as my assailant slammed his pistol against the coupling. To take his mind off it, I clenched both of my hands together and swung them as hard as I could into his gut. He made a sound like a breaching whale and dropped to his knees, pistol falling. Taking the hint, I leapt away, locating my own repeater. I had just enough time to snatch it up before slugger got his wind back. From somewhere he'd found a knife – a long thin stiletto that shone from all the love and attention he'd lavished on it. I figured I'd found the knifeman.

There was another gunshot. It missed me, but the knifeman twitched to a halt, a patch of blood spreading across his orange tunic. He looked at me with a puzzled frown. I shrugged – after all, it was nothing to do with me. As his knees went, he spun in a slow pirouette, and hit the ground.

Movement snagged the corner of my eye, and I turned, raising my gun, expecting the remaining member of the Triad to be joining in the fun. Someone was stood inside an open door in the back of the *Novandik's* boxy shell. His ugly face grinned at me, and the repeater that had been in his own hand vanished inside his oily clothing so quickly I almost convinced myself I'd imagined it.

"Looks like you were having a spot of trouble there, son," he grinned. He withdrew into the locomotive-engine's interior and shut the door.

It's amazing how ugly guardian angels can be.

Chapter Three

After that, it was a simple matter of body disposal. My ugly little friend had nailed both gunmen. The first shot I'd heard had been him taking down one of them. The centre of the Triad, who'd been holding the abaston when it blew, had died of blood loss. There I was, stuck out on one of the flattest spots in Scan Leroth, with a couple of hundred cheering people about to come swarming back to watch our departure after the President's stirring final words, being observed by more armed guards than ants at a picnic. Half the muscles in my body were screaming in protest at how much they'd been abused. Was I worried?

My guardian inside the *Novandik* seemed in no hurry to come back out and give me a hand. I was left to drag all three bodies out of sight. In the end, I rolled them under the locomotive-engine, between the rails. Unless anyone was expecting three corpses to be there, or made a habit of checking between the wheels, they'd remain a secret until the train pulled out.

However, I figured there'd be enough interested parties in the admiring crowd to ensure that particular matter would be dealt with quickly, quietly and anonymously.

I dragged myself back on board, shoulders and back aching, head pounding, and made my way towards my compartment. The pull-down bed was inviting, seductive. I didn't have the strength to unlimber it though. Instead, I dropped into the chair by the window and allowed my eyelids to droop. My body began to rock gently, pain ebbing, cradling me slowly into sleep. I had no time to realise the train was in motion, pulling out of Scan Leroth, before I was deep under.

The big send off, and I was missing it.

गओ

I was dragged back to consciousness by an endless series of spasms playing skipping games with my guts: new pain for old. It was dark, and for a moment I thought I was blind. But it was only the night – I'd slept the day through. Past the contractions which were twisting my limbs and merrily tying knots in my lower intestines, I could feel the train's rhythmic movements.

An extra vicious spasm felt like a hole had been torn through me. I couldn't understand why there wasn't any blood. My skin began to wriggle, and I could swear the temperature of the compartment had dropped several degrees. So why was I sweating?

It was *chavet* withdrawal, of course – it had crawled up on me while I was asleep, all the better to give me no chance to anticipate it.

I dragged myself to my feet, but the contractions threatened to toss me to the floor. I needed to get to that bottle; I needed it like air. But there was no light in the room. No thoughtful steward had entered the compartment and lit the gas lamps. I couldn't see the overbed closet. I only had my memory to go on.

I lurched a little way across the floor, arms outstretched like someone badly acting out a sleepwalker. Then I remembered: matches. I had a packet of matches in my coat.

I stood in the centre of the compartment, fumbling for pockets with numb fingers that felt ten times their normal size. Eventually I found the matches and wasted three trying to get a light – breaking or dropping them. The fourth sputtered reluctantly to life, threatening to flicker out at any moment. The closet came into view, hiding coyly beyond madly dancing shadows. Stumbling towards it, legs heavier with each step, wave after wave of cramps knotting my body, I was convinced the closet was keeping pace with me. That precious bottle of *chavet* was getting no closer.

Then, my forehead slammed into polished wood. I'd made it. Dropping the packet of matches and fumbling for the catch, I managed to swing the door up and open. Inside, the *chavet* glowed cold and blue and unmistakable. I seized the bottle like a drunk. No matter how unfeeling my fingers, I'd never drop this.

I twisted off the top and gulped in a large mouthful, almost choking. Then it poured down my throat, soothing each cell and organ it passed, tender and apologetic, promising never to stay away again. The cramps eased; the compartment began to warm up. As a sense of normality returned to my mind, I realised the match was burning my fingers.

I dropped the match with a scream – still keeping a firm hold on the bottle of *chavet*. Thumb and forefinger weren't numb any longer; they were on fire with pain. I didn't care. I had the *chavet*, I was alive again.

After taking another swig, I put the bottle down on the small table, found the matches again and proceeded to light the gaslights the stewards had neglected. Once the compartment was filled with hissing light, I collapsed back into an armchair and took another drink. Now the agonies of withdrawal had faded, I was just left with all my other aches and pains. I considered letting my hair down and using a glass, which was when Batrix decided to walk in, unannounced.

"Don't you knock?" I muttered, surprised by my timid and quavering voice.

For a long time she didn't speak. The hissing of the gaslights seemed deafening. Eventually, she said, "I was not informed you were a Spook..."

Spook. Most people still found it hard to refer to the wizards directly. I was surprised that Batrix used a synonym. Nearly all heteromorphs feared their creators; most actively disliked them. Batrix clearly hated them. From the moment she spotted the bottle of luminous blue liquid, loathing had been all over her rigid, unforgiving face. I wouldn't have imagined her feeling the need to hide behind safe terms.

"Did you think an expert on the Chrysomancers simply picked it all up from a book?" I asked, glad to hear my voice sounding stronger. "Anyway," I took a deep breath, "to what do I owe the pleasure of your company?"

She seemed to be considering her answer. "Your opinion is required."

We were keeping it nice and neutral. "And what makes you think that?" I took another swig of *chavet,* giving her time to think of some particularly pedantic answer.

"Professor Alva has found evidence of tampering."

"You wouldn't like to save time and tell me what, I suppose?"

"It would be better if you looked for yourself, Scilli." The blue lenses glittered like two tiny icebergs. "You were brought on this journey for your expertise, after all." Her tone left me in absolutely no doubt what she thought of my level of expertise.

"So how long have you been a woman this time?" It wasn't a smart comment, not even clever. I was still smarting over the Spook reference. But then I'd been thinking of her as a Switcher, so maybe we were even.

She didn't betray any feelings. Maybe she thought a *chavet*-drinker wasn't worthy of her finer thoughts. "Twenty-three days, as you know full well."

Which left just five days to the full moon. I waved a hand at her long blue tunic. She was still immaculate. "Then isn't it time you dressed like one?"

It was a mean and petty remark; I couldn't think of anything cleverer and I really felt the need to say something – anything – that might crack that pinched expression. I was wasting my time, of course.

"I am a lieutenant-commander of the Internal Bureau, Scilli. What else would you have me wear?" Her blue-screened eyes looked towards my slightly worn black frockcoat, where it sprawled on the floor. "The height of fashion, perhaps? Like yourself."

"I'm a private citizen, Batrix." Even if that were true, I doubted she would recognise the term. There's nothing more public to the Bureau than a private citizen. "And a rather poor one, if you recall from my file, which you will have undoubtedly memorised down to the last full stop."

"Indeed. Then perhaps you would care to remember that I am nominally in command of this venture. I would appreciate the respect that goes with it."

I sketched a bare salute. "Whatever you say, Commander." I stood, realising somewhat belatedly that the compartment was still. The rail-train was no longer moving. Had something happened?

I made a play of smoothing my less than pristine cravat and waistcoat before scooping up my topcoat and shrugging it on. No matter how shiny the suit is getting around the cuffs and elbows, I would never meet my current employers in anything less than full dress. "Lead on, then, my delightful moon-maid."

I may have been imagining it, but I thought I saw the briefest flaw in the veneer at that remark. I filed the image away to drool over later. I might never see the like again.

We left my compartment and walked down the side corridor towards the front balcony of the stationary carriage. In spite of the huge lamp Alva had insisted was fitted to the front of his amazing locomotive-engine, more than adequate to light up the rails ahead, fifty feet or more to the front and sides, we had stopped. There had been great opposition to the *Novandik* travelling at night: few in the government had enough confidence in either it or the crew to continue travelling once the sun went down. They seemed to believe every wizard alive would attack in unity, prise the wretched machine and its carriages off the steel rails and dismantle it bolt by bolt. If that had ever been the Archimandrite's plan, he could just as easily do it during daylight hours. We'd be traversing some pretty deserted terrain before we reached Scana Carsofi. Only the professor's enraged protests at the idea had stopped the doubters getting their way. So what had changed?

All of the other compartment doors looked locked and barred. Clearly, no one else was going to be disturbed. But why should they be? They were guests; I was the hired help.

Just to prove me wrong, as we passed the third door ahead of mine, it slid open. A thin, dried-up fig of a man squinted short-sightedly out at us. A long grey moustache and what was left of his thin hair drooped. The colourful dressing-gown hanging off his shoulders dragged him further down.

"Something the matter, Commander?" he asked, in a thin and phlegmy voice. "I thought I heard noises..." His head shook with the words, as though keeping time with them. "Are we there, yet?"

"Nothing to concern you, *Gosigné* Thryme," Batrix replied briskly. "A routine check of Professor Alva's locomotive-engine."

"Then why is he with you?" The old man's attempt to nod in my direction turned into an erratic series of palsied spasms.

"She's afraid of the dark," I said. "Wants someone who'll throw a bit of light around."

He held his gaze, eyes locked with my own, despite his shakes. Then he quickly withdrew and slammed the door shut behind him.

I recognised him, of course: Pomino Thryme, the man who taught Professor Alva everything he knew. You'd never guess he was best friends with probably the world's greatest genius. But I wasn't supposed to know that.

Odd that he'd recognised me. Or was I just being too mistrustful? It's something of an occupational hazard.

Batrix was already walking away. "That man doesn't look well to me," I said, catching her up.

"I am sure I would not know, Scilli."

This, I believed totally, as much as I accepted Thryme's befuddled old man act. His body might have been frail, but the mind staring out from his rheumy eyes certainly wasn't.

The scent of a cigar washed over me. Someone must be at the carriage's open balcony end; taking in the sights, enjoying a smoke. If the Chrysomancers had chosen that moment to strike, there would be enough spectators.

Batrix slid open the carriage's end door. Senator Marab Nachollni stood framed in it, relaxed and at peace with the world, resting on the wrought iron balcony, puffing on a long, pencil-thin cigar.

If you'd never seen him before, and knew him only by reputation, his appearance would come as a shock. He was short – barely five feet – with the pallid, bookish look of a clerk, a baby clerk, barely out of knickerbockers. Even his rakish moustache and goatee failed to strike anything like a swashbuckling pose. His hair was thin and grey, further enhanced by an iron-grey morning suit. It was impossible to believe this was the fire-eating orator who had risen from obscurity to a position only slightly less powerful – and popular – than the President himself.

I had no doubt that this was exactly what Nachollni intended.

"Popular night to be out," I remarked over Batrix's shoulder. The senator's pale eyes skated over my face. His lips gave a fleeting twitch.

"I always enjoy a smoke before retiring, sir." His glance swivelled to Batrix. "Nothing serious, I hope?"

"A minor problem, Senator." I noticed the warmth which entered the heteromorph's voice as she spoke to the man. He could certainly count on her vote.

"Something magical, I fancy?"

We squeezed past him – there wasn't a great deal of room on the platform, certainly not enough room for three – and Batrix placed a foot on the first step before answering. "Perhaps. *Gosigné* Scilli will assure us one way or another."

"To be sure. Well, the government's invested a great deal of money in this venture, Commander. I trust it'll be nothing too expensive."

I faced him, trying his smile out for size. It felt too big, so I tossed it back. "I'll try to not bankrupt you, Senator." I hopped down the steps towards the ground, leaving him to his thin cigar.

I stepped down onto night-dark, marshy ground: swampland. The first few days travel would be heading south of Scan Leroth, paralleling the coast most of the way. It's marshy ground, mostly reclaimed from the delta of the River Paleroth, but easier to run any kind of road over than the sheer mountain range to the west, the Kekathi Barrier, which ran for hundreds of miles to the north and south of the city. Old stories tell of the Kekathi holding up the sky, and the highest peaks are often topped by clouds. There are narrow trails through a few passes, but they're treacherous and frequently slick with rain. Even mules think twice about crossing them. The uplands beyond the mountains spread across thousands of square miles, flat and ideal for a rail-road, but unless Alva's locomotive-engine also had the power of flight – and I don't think even the professor could manage that – taking the long way round was the only option. This meant following the mountain range south-west and crossing into the Estates of Cotechatl, where the peaks shrink and blend into the somewhat friendlier and easier to traverse Drésdiracci Mountains. There, the track could begin the ascent to the uplands and all the flat land a rail-road could want.

For now, we were stuck with the Riccobanni Territories: the wettest place in the entire Republic. All that rain coming off the Kekathi Barrier has to go somewhere. Not even the Chrysomancers had found much use for this land, except for losing bodies in. It was the perfect spot for a touch of sabotage.

The engine's huge lamp was lit. I could see a group of figures standing at the front of the train, silhouetted in the glow scattered by the damp air. Alva was easy to spot: a short, fat man with a mass of beard, obvious even at that distance. The others – four in all – were either soldiery or train crew; maybe even both. It was quite a party, not much celebrating, though.

Alva spotted Batrix and me from several yards away, and he turned to us, fat arms waving at the iron, steel and brass cube towering above him. That sounds more impressive than it is: most things could tower over the professor.

"There!" he was shouting. Alva shouted a lot, and glowered. He would have made a great actor. "Proof! Proof! The damned spell-singers have shown their hand even sooner than I anticipated."

Spooks. Spell-singers. Ever since the Philosophic Party finally won the war, and Gawn Thinos got himself elected President, no one seemed to want to call the Chrysomancers by name. Perhaps we're all trying to pretend they don't exist, denying the past. They'd been our absolute rulers for more centuries than the present government cared to acknowledge. Old habits die hard.

But then, those who upset our ancient rulers used to die even harder. Or so it's said, especially by Philosophic politicians. No one's ever come back to confirm it, and the Chrysomancers aren't likely to admit it. They just try to act all enigmatic and guileless, but they aren't fooling anyone.

Bastards. I hate them even more than Batrix does, and with more reason – I am one. Or would have been, if the end of the war hadn't saved me from final, total indoctrination.

Saved? Is that the word? Defeated is a better one. The destruction of everything the wizards held dear had left me, and hundreds of other novices, alone and worthless. All we had from our years in the various, destroyed seminaries throughout the new republic was *chavet*-dependency: the wizards' best and simplest means of keeping their young recruits reliant on them. And now *chavet* is illegal, proscribed, almost impossible to get hold of, unless you have contacts.

Sometimes I wonder how many of my contemporaries are still alive, or sane, and how soon it will be before I join them.

The four others gathered by the machine favoured both Batrix and me with the briefest of looks. Obviously neither of us were too high up in their concerns at that moment. Three of them were crew – the pilot, the pilot-assistant, and the train captain – each with a feeble yellow oil-lamp. The fourth was another guest: a foreigner. Couldn't anyone sleep?

He was a tall, dark-suited man with a thick beard and thinning hair, by the name of Scendik Boz. His claim to fame was a clutch of fiction books, published in his native Pyndria. I didn't know how that brought him to this side of the ocean or entitled him to be a guest on Alva's maiden run. I couldn't see the connection. But the look he offered Batrix suggested Pyndrians had similar views on heteromorphs to most Chrysomancers.

"So, what exactly is the problem?" I asked Alva. As noisy as a dog with three tongues, the professor was about as free with solid information as Batrix. He waved his arms at his engine again.

"There! There! Don't you see?"

I turned to look at the great mass of machinery, not certain what I was looking at. A single axle and two huge driving wheels provided the engine's locomotion, over ten feet in diameter and partly enclosed under the *Novandik*'s boxy shape. Each was turned by a forged steel rod, set in motion by large cylinders – positioned near the front and slung under the locomotive-engine's body. For easy access, I supposed. One of the crew – the pilot-assistant – raised his lamp to cast its thin glow across the massive driving wheel. It didn't help.

"The driving-rod!" Alva barked in exasperation. He tapped a cherubic finger against the steel. "See! A crack! A crack!"

I peered closer. Just about visible was a short, hair's breadth crack in the rod. It wasn't very obvious, and maybe in the daylight it would have been clearer. But in the day, we'd be moving, and who would notice then?

"And that's it, is it?" I asked, wondering at all the concern.

"It?" Alva was incandescent. "Within a few days the whole rod will fail!"

Batrix asked: "Do you have no spares, Professor?" I was glad to see someone had decided to be a little less hysterical.

"Of course," he replied, no more mollified. "We are carrying at least two of every vital part. But do you not see? The spell-singers—"

"You're suggesting the Chrysomancers did this?" I asked, just to be sure.

"Who else?"

"You mean, they sat down together and pooled their vast resources, all to put a tiny crack in that chunk of metal?"

Alva's headlong emotional charge faltered. He glared at me, but at least he seemed to be listening this time. "You have another suggestion?"

"It couldn't have happening during forging?" I suggested gingerly, waiting for the explosion that might follow. I wasn't disappointed.

"During forging! I'll have you know, sir, that all of the steel in this engine was forged at the finest manufactory in the Republic! Under my personal supervision! Every part has been hand-checked—"

I held up my hands in a vain attempt to hold off his wrath. Out of the corner of an eye, I could see Batrix's smug expression. Poor old Scilli, it said. Doesn't know a thing.

"I'm sorry, Professor – but it just seems an awful lot of trouble for so powerful a group to go to. Especially for such little effect."

The writer, Boz, caressed his beard and beamed at me languidly. It wasn't a response I took to. "I understand you are something of an expert on the Chrysomancy Party, *Gosigné* Scilli." He spoke Ramini like a native, not even a trace of an accent. A scholarly type, then. He'd have lasted about two minutes back in the good old days. That thought cheered me.

I matched him smirk for smirk. For someone who hadn't even nodded a greeting so far, he suddenly knew a hell of a lot about me. Or was he fishing? Had Batrix been talking? No – I'd sooner believe Alva had damaged his own locomotive-engine. Some things are just too unlikely to contemplate. "Everyone in Ramini older than ten years is something of an expert on the Chrysomancers, sir. But I wouldn't expect a foreigner to understand that."

"On the contrary, *Gosigné* Scilli, the people of Pyndria know about oppression only too well." Still smiling, he turned back to look at the almost invisible damage. Quite unprofessionally, I instantly promoted *Gosigné* Scendik Boz of Pyndria to the head of my hate-list. I could always revise it later when I was feeling less nettled, or when my body wasn't aching quite so much.

"So, *Gosigné* Scilli!" Alva decided it was time for him to get back into the conversation. "You are here to advise. What is your suggestion? What must we do, sir?"

"Do? I'm going back to my compartment to finish my liaison with sleep. You can do what you like. But I'd recommend waiting until sun-up before you start repairs. Some funny things haunt these swamps in the dark." I grinned, hoping he could see it clearly in the scattered light. "The Chrysomancers put them there."

Perhaps I shouldn't have mentioned the wizards. Before Alva could risk apoplexy with another temper-fit, a tiny worm of pale, unpleasant-looking light grew across the piston-rod, just where the crack was. Or rather, where it had been. Now it was a ragged gash in the steel, still glowing faintly red around the edges as the heat dissipated into the cool air.

Alva was positively exultant. You would never have guessed several hundred *dinari's* worth of machine-part had just been rendered useless. "I told you!" he crowed. "I told you! The spell-singers! They did it!" He almost laughed. "How they must fear me!"

I didn't contradict him. It would have served no purpose. But the Chrysomancers hadn't done this from their home in the north. It was too precise, too accurate, which meant that, apart from my good self – and I didn't count – there was obviously a wizard on board.

Quite a powerful one.

Chapter Four

Morning didn't so much break as sullenly take night apart and throw the bits away. The blackness turned into a sort of murky greyness, signifying that the sun had come up. I don't know which of the two conditions I preferred: at least in the dark, the main thing to fear was imagination. Once you could see reasonably clearly, the unknown took on a whole new air of menace, and you have to face it, nose to nose.

I was sitting as far away from the frantic activity around Alva's toy as I could without getting my feet wet, which wasn't very far. I'd found a broad tree-stump, around chair height, several yards from the track-bed's high embankment. It was fairly close to the water's edge, far enough from the delights of physical labour, I hoped. Sitting where I was, I could see the entire train laid out in front of me along the top of the embankment: our home for two weeks. Somewhere behind it would be the dark smudge of the Kekathi Barrier, hugging the horizon, presently blocked by the carriages and locomotive-engine. In the grey light they all looked curiously small and defenceless. Certainly no match for a concentrated wizard attack.

The repair work seemed to be progressing well. The pilot and assistant were swearing a replacement driving-rod into place, aided by Alva's gratuitous commentary on what they were doing wrong, along with the train captain's more practical assistance with wrench and hammer. Batrix was standing by and watching, but I could see by the set of everyone's shoulders that her gaze was more aggravating than any number of Alva's insults. The writer, Boz, was also there, observing.

There were almost a dozen guards keeping watchful eyes on the surroundings. Bayonets were fixed to their long muskets, hammers cocked. They wore dark blue shakos and trousers, with grass-green tunics criss-crossed by highly polished white belts holding pouches of powder and shot. These were men of the Golanek Regiment: Sharpshooters, the President's own personal guard. Alva was getting the best protection he could afford.

There was another figure standing by the front balcony of the first carriage, leaning on a handrail. Senator Nachollni, watching the work, wanting no part of it, just like me. I don't suppose he considered manual labour worthy of his calling.

I sat and observed him watching the others, listening to the sounds of the swamps: cursing men and softly lapping water.

That's the Riccobanni Territories: miles of cold, grey water with the occasional dry island sticking up like tiny, tree-marked humps. The water is never much more than a dozen feet deep – except during the rainy season. Skeletal, half-drowned trees jut out of the waves all over, draped in skeins of moss and parasitic vines. On a warm, sunny day, it probably looks quite picturesque. Today, it was cold and miserable. I was quite prepared to believe all the stories I'd been told as a boy about the things the wizards had left in the water, just for their amusement. It's strange, the number of things tyrants are supposed to find funny; in my experience they have very little in the way of a sense of humour.

All of this made Alva's overland rail-road the more remarkable, I suppose. In the past, trade routes had to skirt the swamps, taking detours which added days to a journey. Now, Alva's system ran pretty much where it liked, straddling mountain, swamp and desert. Although, steep slopes still seemed to be a problem.

Except it wasn't totally Alva's, of course. He might have conceived the idea, mad as it had seemed – even using his own height for the track gauge – but it took the sweat of hundreds of thousands of men and heteromorphs to lay the road from the east coast to the west. It ran from Scan Leroth to Scana Carsofi and had taken over six years to construct. Few lived to see it finished. There had been too many accidents to be natural, too many fatalities. The rail-road was thought to be cursed, but the only real curse was the enmity of the Chrysomancers – despots who had first lost a war and then the government, but wouldn't take the hint and go to the hell they so richly deserved.

The heteromorphs suffered the worst. There had been so many of them – until there weren't. If they hadn't been worked to death in male form, there had been plenty of use for them once they were female. The section of rail-road which ran through the swamps had been laid on top of a great ramp of dirt and stone, well above the high-water mark. Even I didn't like to think how many Switcher bodies were buried inside it. They didn't deserve that.

Some things didn't change, even with the Philosophics in control. Most continued to look on heteromorphs as expendable, slave labour. We learnt that lesson from the wizards all too well.

I can imagine how Alva had convinced President Thinos: a system running overland between Ramini's two main ports, able to travel the three-and-a-half thousand miles in less than eighteen days. Even for a country on the edge of bankruptcy after years of civil war, such a project must have sounded too good to pass up. It would mark the end of centuries' rule by superstition and magic, herald in a new era of enlightenment and science. The New Age. *Novandik*.

Hence the attention of the Chrysomancers. It was in their interests that the venture should fail. Recreating themselves as a political party may have given them a veneer of modern respectability, but a wizard is still a wizard. If anything was to go wrong on this inaugural journey, Alva, the President and the Philosophic Party would not only lose valuable prestige, the millions of *dinari* sunk into the scheme would never be recovered. Ramini would definitely take the final plunge into bankruptcy. The wizards wouldn't have to rely on their failing power to take control once more.

No wonder the professor was seeing the Archimandrite's hand everywhere. For six hundred years, Sendivogius had been titular head of the wizards' Upper Chamber, almost from the day it was formed. A twelfth *shakrat*, it's rumoured. This was no mean feat when you consider the highest confirmed level any wizard has achieved is eighth *shakrat*. He was a born tyrant and showing no signs of mellowing with age.

Batrix was starting to look around. Maybe the sight of men doing something she couldn't feel superior about was palling. She spotted me and, much to my annoyance, strolled over.

"Enjoying the day, Scilli?" she asked, standing over me in a pose somewhere between at ease and to attention. I wondered if she could stand any other way.

"Since you ask, no," I said. "The weather's terrible and the view's worse. The company could be better, too."

Batrix shrugged. The grey light had turned her glasses the colour of slate. It made her look even more unreadable. "I am heartbroken," she said. I was beginning to rub off on her.

I looked up at her rigid figure. "Do you think you could sit down? Talking like this is giving me even more of a pain in the neck."

She found a piece of overturned trunk a few feet away and sat stiffly. After a moment, she crossed her legs. She's almost relaxed, I thought. Next, she'll be offering me a cigarette.

I glanced across at the work-gang. They seemed to have finished, so I guessed we'd be under way soon. Not much time left. "So, tell me all about Scendik Boz."

"What do you wish to know?" She gave me a look that may have been superior, may have been pitying. I chose to ignore it.

"I know he's a big celebrity writer in Pyndria, but what's he doing over here? If Alva wanted someone to cover the maiden run of his rail-train, why not get one of his own writers to do it? He owns at least one broadsheet, I believe."

Batrix uncrossed and re-crossed her legs, obviously not as relaxed as I'd thought. "*Gosigné* Boz is well known as an active Revisionist, and many of his works reflect this. Some may even have been instrumental in improving social conditions amongst the lower classes in his own country. Professor Alva is aware of *Gosigné* Boz's growing reputation throughout certain quarters of the Republic, and since the author was already on a lecture tour of Ramini, he saw a chance to couple his genius with that of a spokesman against social injustice. Besides, no broadsheet hack could hope to equal the prose of a professional novelist."

Quite a speech. I could see Batrix was convinced.

"Novelist, eh? Nice word. Suggests change. But he's still a foreigner."

"You really are quite a bigot, Scilli."

"I get the feeling you don't like me," I said, which was faintly hypocritical, all things considered. I'm a sensitive man, easily hurt.

"I do not know you well enough to say."

"But you don't trust me."

"Is there any reason I should?" A fair question, under the circumstances. At that moment, I didn't trust anyone who wasn't named Wilonek Scilli and sitting on a rotting tree-stump.

"You know well enough not everyone at the Madrasaté Seminary – *any* seminary – was there by choice," I said, trying to keep the bitterness out of my voice. Even now, the memory of that place makes me angry and fearful. "The holy brothers just took who they wanted when numbers dropped." Something they did frequently: Madrasaté wasn't a healthy place to stay.

I shook off the gloomy thoughts. It wouldn't do to have Batrix think I had depths. "Would it surprise you to know that your liberal-minded novelist seems to hate heteromorphs. At least, he does if the looks he gives you whenever you're close are anything to go by."

There was no reaction at all. I used to wonder if Switchers had anything like pride or self-awareness, as we understand it. Perhaps it had been beaten out of them over the centuries, or carefully hidden. I suppose pride in a slave-race isn't much of a survival trait. Was Lieutenant-Commander Batrix any different? Could she be?

"I am sure you are aware of Pyndria's history," she was saying. "Until almost two hundred years ago, they were a major world-power, the head of an Empire which left its mark on almost every part of the world. Our own Republic grew from, and is strongly based on, the Pyndrian Empire model. But when their Empire finally collapsed, the inevitable decadence was exhibited as a spiritual malaise amongst the population, and a total withdrawal by its magical leaders. Well before the worldwide decline of magical influence, the Thaumaturges of Pyndria degenerated into a powerless cult of eccentrics. They became despised rather than feared. In recent years, it has become the fashion among Pyndrian society to loathe all aspects of magic. *Gosigné* Boz sees me as a product of magic. I doubt his upbringing will let him regard me as anything other than an object of scorn."

Interesting. Quite a bit of that was new to me. But then, I've never been particularly bright when it came to foreign history.

Just as well he's a Liberal, I thought. What would he do if he was some old-fashioned Reactionary? "Is that all?" I added.

Batrix shifted her head to one side. "All?"

"I mean, doesn't the Internal Bureau have anything else on this wonderful, right-minded, magic-hating avatar of goodness?"

"Do you think I would tell you Bureau secrets, Scilli?"

I shrugged. Fair enough. If she wasn't going to tell me everything she knew, I wasn't going to share either.

A mournful wail echoed across the swamp. It was the engine, announcing we were ready to go. Batrix stood up, ramrod straight. I got to my feet more slowly: my back still ached.

"I would like to speak with you further, in my compartment," she said. "If you have no objection?" Her request sounded like an order.

"Make it my own, and I'll agree," I said. "I've something I need to do there." Like take some *chavet*. I could feel the onset of withdrawal already. "What about?"

She didn't reply, and for a moment I thought she was simply doing her best not to hear me. Until I realised she was staring at something over my shoulder. From her expression, she wasn't admiring the clouds.

I turned quickly – but not too quickly. If something behind me was just curious, I wasn't going to scare it into an attack.

It was big. Bigger than Alva's locomotive-engine, including half the carriages. From a flat, mud-coloured head, scores of pale wriggling tendrils were reaching towards the water. Some actually brushed the surface. Then, a mouth like a small cave, lined with razor-edged stalactites and stalagmites, drowned me in breath that stank more than a hundred rotting corpses. Both head and spined torso were dotted with large yellow blisters which I had a horrible feeling were looking at me. Without thinking, I began to count them.

My right hand dived for the pocket inside my frockcoat. As I pulled out my Alva repeater pistol, I was aware of Batrix making a similar move behind me. I cocked the hammer on the weapon, conscious of the futility of the gesture. I was pointing a pistol that might misfire – or worse, backfire – at a creature the size of a house. Even if it worked, five little lead shells wouldn't even attract the thing's attention.

What's more, why hadn't anyone up at the *Novandik* seen it? One sniff of a thing like this, and I would have expected Alva to start frothing, and the Sharpshooters to begin showing off their marksmanship. But there was no reaction.

The thing swayed ponderously for a few seconds more, churning up stale mud below the heavy ripples it was creating. Its head tendrils quivered, and the pus-coloured eye-blobs stared blindly down. Then it sank back into the swamp, belching one last carrion breath at me as it vanished. I watched the waves throwing themselves against the patch of ground at my feet, the fading ripples, the widening cloud of mud and thought, of course, the water's too shallow for something that size.

I turned around, slipping my repeater back in its inside pocket. Batrix did the same with her pistol, the same model as my own, I noticed. It took a moment longer for one vital fact to filter into my slow, early morning brain.

She'd been pointing it at me.

What had she been expecting when I put my hand inside my coat? A yarrow wand? Did she think I was going to wave a magical stick and conjure the thing away? Or more likely, that I was going to order pus-eyes to destroy Alva's train with one blast of its awful breath? Well, at least some of our cards were showing. Now I really knew how much

Batrix trusted me – roughly as much as I trusted all but one other person on this journey.

The whistle was shrieking, calling the children in from play. Batrix turned her back on me and marched silently towards the train. Fine. If she didn't want to mention what had just occurred, neither did I. But I didn't think I'd be sleeping too well that night, or any of the nights left before we reached Scana Carsofi.

Chapter Five

Back in my compartment, I collapsed onto the sofa. I could feel the stomach cramp warning of the withdrawal attack growing stronger. I hadn't noticed it until then, it must have been all the fun I had been having.

The *chavet* was standing on the table to my left, along with a clean glass. The stewards had been busy. I poured a glassful and took a sip. The cramps eased. I felt alive again.

"So, my dear Bureau operative, what can I tell you?" I asked, feeling my old, cocky self once more. "My name is Wilonek Scilli. I'm less than thirty years old, but probably older than twenty-five. I have my own teeth, and after a brief, but fruitless education at the Madrasaté Seminary, all I graduated with is an addiction to this." I tapped the *chavet* bottle. "Have I missed anything?"

Batrix had followed me into my compartment, silent, judgemental. She sat down facing me, staring back at me through her screening lenses. "I believe you have missed out nearly everything."

I gave her my best shocked look. "What else could there be?"

She raised a finger. "One, you could tell me who you are. *Really* are. Two, your purpose on this journey."

"If I didn't know better, I'd say you were being perverse, Batrix. You know who I am. And you know I'm here at Professor Alva's insistence as an advisor on magic."

"Indeed." A sceptical eyebrow quirked above her glasses. "An advisor who allegedly never qualified, never even reached the lowly position of first *shakrat*. One who does not own his own abaston crystal, and, thus, would have very little chance of either detecting magic or counteracting it."

"You know as well as I do that anyone who reaches first *shakrat* will almost certainly be fully indoctrinated, totally under the wizards' control. Can you think of any wizards who work for the government?"

She stayed silent. I'd have been very surprised if she had known of any; they're supposed to be most secret.

"And before you ask – no, I didn't detect whatever spell destroyed the *Novandik*'s driving-rod. As you so thoughtfully pointed out, without my own crystal, how could I?"

Batrix shifted in her seat. "Very well, we will let that pass for now."

"Very good of you—"

"But I would still like to know why you are really here, on this journey. This entire inaugural trip has been months in the planning. I was involved at every stage. It was all settled. The professor would make the journey with a few travelling companions: *Gosigné* Boz, as a witness, a corps of Sharpshooters – the gift of President Thinos – for protection, and myself as a government representative. Then, with little more than a week to go, he suddenly decides to invite Doctor Tork, Senator Nachollni, and his old mentor, Thryme. The guards are given a different officer: Major Rengalet – a commander of dragoons, not foot. And then there is you. Why, Scilli?"

I shrugged. "Vagaries of genius, perhaps? Maybe Alva wanted a bigger audience for his triumph."

"That is what I have been trying to tell myself. After all, with one exception, each man is distinguished in his own way. You could make a case for their inclusion."

I certainly hoped she could, since I was the one who drew up the guest list. Everyone except Boz, anyway. "Except you don't believe it."

"You do not reach the rank of lieutenant-commander within the Bureau by taking on trust such a peculiar series of events."

"Meaning Bureau politics leaves you unable to trust anyone," I said. "I can accept that. But explain to me what you find so difficult. Let's take Alva's guests. This Thryme – the professor's mentor, you said – who's he, for a start?"

"A clock-maker."

"A clock-maker?" I repeated like some idiot echo in a vaudeville act.

Batrix nodded.

"Not a profession you come across often. But *who* is he, not what?"

"Professor Alva's oldest friend. Thryme helped him in the past, when Alva was just a young man with ideas but no backing. The professor was initially his apprentice. Thryme had both money and influence in the right quarters, despite his esoteric calling. The professor has often said that if Thryme had not had faith in him all those years ago, he would never have become the success he is."

"And this is by way of a kind of thank you."

"It could be seen that way. Thryme was supposedly deeply involved in the design of this train's locomotion. Despite Alva's bombast, he seems genuinely indebted to the older man."

How touching, and maybe even true. "I can't think of any reason why he shouldn't be along. If they're so close."

"Quite."

"Well, then." I drained my glass and refilled it. As much as I loathed the stuff, I could no more give up drinking it than I could water. I wondered if sometime I should ask Alva where he manages to get a supply of proscribed drink. "You said the Sharpshooters had a dragoon commander..."

"Major Trescu Rengalet of the Eighteenth Villavinté Dragoons."

I allowed myself a brief frown. "Isn't he some sort of hero?"

"As a young subaltern, he led a decisive charge at the Battle of Ombarno. It turned the tide, allowing General Skanocj's forces to take the field."

"Ah, *that* Major Rengalet. Whose singular military victory more than justifies his inclusion on this trip." I took another drink, hating every exquisite sip of the stuff.

"You begin to see my point?" Batrix asked. "Do you not find it odd that a major of dragoons has been placed in command of an infantry company? Especially an élite like the Sharpshooters."

"When has the military mind ever made sense?" I said airily. "During the war, most of the battles we won were in spite of the brass, not because of them. Now, what about this Tork? I feel like I should know him, too."

"You should. Doctor Bronex Tork is President Thinos' personal physician."

"So, what's wrong with that, Batrix? We can't arrive at Scana Carsofi suffering with head colds! I'm sure the President can do without Tork for a couple of weeks."

"We do not need a physician, Scilli. Especially one of Doctor Tork's standing."

"If you say so, Commander. Then what about our distinguished representative of the government: Senator Marab Nachollni, Scourge of the Chrysomancers, upholder of the dignity of free government and emancipator of the heteromorphs?"

Batrix sighed. "Yes, yes. You make your point, laboured, as it is. There is no obvious reason why Senator Nachollni should not also accompany us. But ... I think it is just the way everything was changed. So suddenly, so completely. I do not like uncertainties, Scilli."

"Who does?"

Both of us fell silent. I, with my own thoughts; Batrix with hers as she continued to stare at me through those blue glasses. Eventually, she spoke.

"The attack on the machine's driving rod, and that creature which rose from the swamp. There is a connection."

"Is there? Apart from the obvious – the Chrysomancers doing their best to rattle us, in which they seem to be succeeding admirably – I can't think of one."

"There is one on board, is there not, Scilli?"

"One what?"

"Now you are the one being perverse. A Spook, Scilli. An agent of the wizards."

"If you say so—"

"Do not be patronising, Scilli! You said yourself that the Chrysomancers could not attack from so far away—"

"I think I actually said something about it being a lot of trouble to little effect—"

"Whilst it appears we were the only ones to see that creature," she swept on, ignoring me. "You are here as the expert, Scilli. Explain."

I sighed. "All right, Batrix. Yes, in my opinion, only a wizard on the spot could have caused such accurate damage. That thing in the water was obviously some kind of projection, keeping an eye – or eyes – on us. You noticed it sank back into water that was much too shallow to contain it." I couldn't know whether Batrix had noticed or not, but it seemed reasonable to credit her with the observation. "The strange pus-coloured globes on its body, did you notice how many there were?"

She shook her head.

"I counted twenty-six. Which, by an odd coincidence, happens to be the exact same number of wizards in the Chrysomantic Council – both Upper and Lower Chambers."

"You think that was actually the Council, watching us?"

"I would have said no, except for the obvious glamour around it. We were too close to be affected – probably within the active field itself. If they were simply trying to remind us that they were around, keeping their eyes open, why the glamour? No – Sendivogius and his friends were taking a covert peek."

"Checking on how much damage their agent had done?"

I shrugged. This was no time to be making wild guesses.

"Then who is it, Scilli?"

"How should I know?" I snapped. "Do you think whoever it is would have taken me on one side and said, 'From one wizard to another, I'm here on a wrecking mission for our bosses'."

"Then you suspect..."

"I don't suspect anyone, Batrix! You're the Bureau agent. Suspicion's your job."

She went quiet again. I wondered what she was thinking in those silent moments, how her heteromorph brain worked.

"Then it could be anyone," she said at last.

"I suppose..."

"Even you."

I laughed. I had wondered how long it would take for her to reach that thought. "Even me. A little obvious though, don't you think?"

"The best way to hide something is to make it so obvious no one thinks anything of it."

"I was right. You don't trust me."

Batrix said nothing. I paused to collect my thoughts. "You've not covered everyone, Commander."

She looked at me quizzically.

"There's yourself, Batrix. A heteromorph. In the ten years since the war, you've become a lieutenant-commander of the Internal Bureau. No mean feat, even for a human. At this rate, you'll probably be the first heteromorph senator. And who knows, maybe, one day, even the President."

She didn't even have the grace to blush. When I'm being expansive enough to throw lavish compliments at young women, I normally expect them to flutter their fans, look at their feet, colour up, giggle – all of those annoying affectations. Not simply gaze coolly back at me. "I admit to ambitions, Scilli, but... No, not the Presidency. That honour must fall to another."

Which we both knew would likely never happen. Once the wizards had been defeated and ruthlessly legislated against, all the heteromorphs left alive had been freed. But the production of more was outlawed. There was barely one hundred left in all. And as much as the creatures resemble men and women, they were never designed to conceive. Totally unnecessary, of course. Assuming the Chrysomancy Party doesn't ever get back into power and put things back the way they were, and also assuming some Spooks aren't illegally brewing heteromorphs up somewhere for private use, Batrix and her other Shifters will be the last. In a century or less, every single one of them will be dead.

"Maybe so, but that doesn't free you from the possibility of suspicion," I continued.

She looked a little taken aback. Shocked, perhaps. Outraged? Maybe even alarmed. What's in a look, after all? For someone of Batrix's practise, nothing they don't want to be there. "I trust you are joking!"

"Why? Because you're a heteromorph? A creature spontaneously fashioned out of the elements, like a maggot from a corpse. You think that gives you a unique right to hate the wizards? You're a wizard's creation! How do I know what some Spook created you for?"

"You are insane, Scilli!" she hissed.

I wanted to offer a bland smile, but I could barely summon the enthusiasm. I suddenly felt tired. Maybe it was lack of sleep the night before; maybe it was the strain of mostly living a lie. I wanted to be off that train, under an open, sun-filled blue sky, a hundred thousand miles from anywhere.

"You could make a case for anyone on this train being your guilty party," I said. "Even amongst the crew. Have you full details on each of them? Or maybe Alva himself is your spy, have you thought of that?"

Batrix leaped out of her chair. "Professor Alva was insistent that you joined us on his maiden journey," she said, so calmly I knew she must have been close to exploding. "And I will bow to his will – for now. But I believe you to be unbalanced – perhaps even deranged, no doubt an effect of your unfortunate addiction. Nothing you have said has convinced me that you are in any way suitable for the work which so obviously needs to be done. I wish you good day, sir."

With that melodramatic exit speech, Batrix stalked from my compartment. I began to chuckle, pleased with myself for forcing such a reaction. As I reached for the *chavet* again, I felt the numbing cold sweep across my back, stiffening my neck.

I turned my head. There, to my left, apparently floating before the compartment wall, was the translucent image of an oversized, mournful face.

It lingered for a heartbeat before winking out, long enough for me to hear the one, echoing word.

"Tonight."

Chapter Six

Batrix managed to avoid me for the rest of the day. As far as she was concerned, I was tried and convicted – of lunatic incompetence, if nothing else.

I spent the daylight hours staring out of my single window, the apparently endless swamps of Riccobanni moving past steadily. The weather showed no signs of improvement, and nothing else came up to give us the once over. But for all that, I knew we were being observed.

I tried to focus my mind, and ignore the siren call of *chavet*. It wasn't easy, but I'd already drunk all of the bottles Alva had seen fit to leave me, and I was feeling ashamed enough not to go grovelling to him and beg for more. But by late afternoon, I knew simple shame wasn't going to stop me falling at his feet. And naturally, the longer I left it, the harder it got to think clearly, and the more I could justify such a humiliating action.

But one thing exercised my mind even more than craving *chavet*: and that was the brief, unexpected contact from Sanej, my controller, the man everyone else knew as Yosec: the Sebite pilot of the *Novandik*.

For him to have broken silence, I knew it had to be important. Even such a fleeting contact would have blazed like a beacon fire in the abaston of any wizard who might be watching.

As night fell, it seemed to me that the eternal swamps were slowly dwindling – giving way to increasingly larger, dry areas. If that was true, and *chavet* lack wasn't just fooling with my eyes, then we would soon be crossing the border into Cotechatl. It couldn't come too soon. The Estates of Cotechatl were still a very green part of the country – they were in the east, anyway, before we started the climb up to the plains and into the Drésdiracci Mountains. Here it was a damned sight drier than the Riccobanni Territories. Temperamentally, I've always preferred the warmer, drier lands of Ramini's central plains. I couldn't wait until we'd passed through Cotechatl, crested the mountains, and were dropping towards the deserts of the Atchinor Territories. But there was also a stop to look forward to before then: a daylight one, in the town of Jaqatlan, where there would be bands, dancing girls – a whole festival – just to welcome our intrepid band of travellers. Nothing could possibly go wrong. I wondered if that was why Sanej wanted to see me. Had he learned something?

Darkness drew in. The train came to a halt. After the previous night's excitement, even Alva's overconfidence had given way to caution and he had conceded to overnight stops so that a guard could be placed on the locomotive-engine. No one asked my opinion, but I thought it was all wasted effort – the wizards would attack whenever they fancied, if they fancied, and each delay lengthened the trip. But it did make my next task a little easier – although not by much.

I waited over an hour, listening to my fellow passengers readying themselves for bed. Gradually, the train grew quiet. The only sounds were of Doctor Tork in the next compartment, snoring, and the gravelly tramp of guards outside patrolling the length of the train.

It was time to move.

I buttoned up my shabby, slightly too small frockcoat. Uncomfortable as it was, I didn't want the noise of loose coat tails brushing against corridor sides giving me away. Carefully sliding my compartment door open, I stepped out into the corridor. Looking up and down the length of the carriage, I could see no traces of light. Either everyone was sound asleep or had blinds drawn. Whichever, they wouldn't see my furtive shape tiptoeing past their doors.

I padded towards the front of the carriage, mentally cursing every tiny squeak the flooring made. Each footstep sounded like a felled tree to my over-strained ears. I started to believe Alva had deliberately instructed the builders to leave the floorboards springy – just in case.

I made it onto the balcony end. There were no guards on either this platform or the one at the end of Alva's private carriage, which was facing me. I was able to peer out along the length of the train on either side: back pressed tight against the carriage to present the smallest silhouette possible.

There were soldiers covering both sides: four each side, working in relay. There was no way I could just step down and stroll up to the locomotive-engine without being seen.

I clambered over the balcony rail and dropped between the tracks, hidden between the carriages. Peering under Alva's carriage, between the huge but elegant trucks, it was obvious I could not crawl along the rails. The underside was hung with numerous boxes and tanks of all sizes. I hadn't a clue what any of them were for, although I could take a wild guess: water cisterns for the great man's bath – he must have a bath, while the rest of us made do with a bowl – septic tanks, and gas cylinders for his lights and heating. There wasn't enough room under the carriage for an Atarqi circus midget, leave alone an average-sized man. That route was out.

This left the carriage roof, which raised another small problem. I might be able to face down a slobbering swamp-thing, armed only with an unreliable pistol, but I cannot tolerate heights. The thought of crawling along a roof – even a flat one – over fifteen feet above the ground, was enough to turn my palms slick with sweat.

There was a steel ladder leading to the roof; for maintenance, I guessed. Assuming I could get up and stay there without getting a case of the yips or anyone noticing, I'd be fairly invisible in my dark clothing. For the first time that trip, I was thankful the sky remained overcast: no moon, no stars. The only light source was the huge lamp at the front of the *Novandik* – and that wasn't going to be casting too much illumination back across the rail-carriages; certainly not on the roofs.

Unbuttoning my coat – it was too tight for my likely panicky breathing – I dragged myself up the ladder and crawled out along the roof. It had a quite alarming slope to its sides, but the central raised ventilation strip looked as though it would give me something to hang onto. I'd be like a tree-sloth clinging desperately onto its branch.

I began to edge forward, inching along on my belly, trying to be silent. If my suit had looked worn before, it was anyone's guess what it would be like by the end of the evening. I kept my eyes locked forward, ignoring my stiffening neck. At least it took my mind off my sore back. And I was damned if I'd let myself look down.

I was almost a quarter of the way along the carriage roof when the cramps hit. Withdrawal. Perfect timing. I fought the urge to curl into a pathetic, whimpering ball, my fingers locked around the bars of a ventilator grill with the surety of blind panic. If I lost my grip, with my whole body juddering like some ancient tribal drum, I'd rattle myself straight off the roof – making enough noise to wake even the deepest sleeper. I wanted to moan, to scream. A soldier chose that moment to stroll past the carriage. Through eyes that dearly didn't want to be reminded of how high up I was, I could see the forward-sloping top of his shako and the point of a bayonet. Vertigo and nausea fought for control of my body.

The guard paused, the visible part of his cap turning back and forth. Had he heard me? The shako dipped out of view for an instant, and then reappeared. A moment later I smelled tobacco smoke. He was smoking on duty. Normally I wouldn't care, but did he have to break the rules so close to where I was about to start whimpering?

After a while, he moved away. I let out the breath I realised I'd been holding in. Now they couldn't cause me any particular trouble, the cramps died away, too. I was just left with a distant, empty ache that promised they'd be back. Getting to Sanej was more urgent than ever.

Whatever he had to tell me, I hoped to hell it was worth it.

I clamped my eyes shut until the vertigo subsided, wedging my face against the ventilators. When I opened my eyes again I didn't want there to be any chance they could so much as catch a glimpse of anything below the roof.

I restarted my slug-like progress. Somehow, I reached the front of the carriage without further incident. All I had to do now was climb down, crawl along the cylindrical water waggon and reach the locomotive-engine without being noticed. Easy, especially with my eyes mostly shut and a chance the shakes would hit any moment, unannounced.

I almost fell trying to come down the ladder. The combination of nerves and cramps had left my feet and fingers numb. I could barely feel the rungs. I have never been so relieved to step off a ladder. Then I realised the waggon had another ladder – shorter, admittedly. It wasn't my night.

After taking a rest to let my heart and breathing get back to something like normal, and peering cautiously out to see if any guards had been alerted, I swung myself over the coupling-joint, climbing up and over onto the mobile cistern. Why couldn't Alva have designed a flat tank instead of a cylindrical one. I slithered along the apex, arms and legs splayed across the curved surface, feeling about as inconspicuous as a black bear in the snow.

There was a face peering dolefully out through an arched window in the rear of the *Novandik's* box shape. I was reaching for my pistol before I realised it was Sanej, grinning out at me, or coming as close to a grin as that face would let him. Not for the first time, I wished he'd change it.

A door swung open, and I discovered a hitherto unsuspected agility, sliding down off the water waggon and into the *Novandik's* cabin in one silent, clumsy plummet.

"You nearly gave me a heart attack!" I complained. Sanej continued to grimace.

"I saw the monkey act along the carriage roof," he said. "Very impressive. Especially the part where you did that strange, on-the-belly tarantella. Pity your audience wasn't a little more appreciative."

"Sanej!" I hissed through teeth I was clenching against another onslaught of cramps. "*Chavet*! Now!"

His mournful face grew longer. He turned and rummaged around among the odd levers and switches that were part of the *Novandik's* incomprehensible workings. He dragged out a familiar bottle and pressed it into my fingers. I found it difficult to keep hold. He opened the bottle for me and raised it to my lips. A generous slug of the hated stuff blazed down my throat.

The effect was almost instantaneous. The cramps eased, my vision cleared, and I was aware of how cold and sweat-drenched I was. I nodded my thanks. Sanej let me hold the bottle and I took another swallow.

"I hate them," I said. Sanej nodded. He knew who I meant, and why. They'd left us both needing the same crutch.

He sat down in a tiny iron seat positioned on the right of his cabin. I presumed it was from there that he drove this steel monster. He was watching me, trying to pretend he wasn't. Something like a relaxed expression slowly filled his sour, familiar face.

If I live long enough to be asked to nominate the best agent who ever worked for President Thinos' government, I'd have to say Sanej Yosec – the best, and the most dangerous. He had that one quality which all the wizards could never match, not if they selectively bred heteromorphs for a million years: dedication. Chrysomancers can only buy their loyalty or terrify it into people. That kind of loyalty will fail in the end because there'll always be someone who can pay more or be more terrifying. Yosec believed in the Philosophic cause, with a passion matched only by one other thing: his hatred for Chrysomancers.

Taking that into consideration, it makes his life achievement all the more incredible. For thirty years, he had been an instructor at the Madrasaté Seminary – surrounded by the wizards' youngest and brightest. Except he wasn't calling himself Sanej then. It was there he'd recruited me.

Seeing him look all comfortable and familiar in his seat, I had to ask: "So, what's the urgency? I didn't think you'd contact me until Jaqatlan."

He reached up and took the *chavet* away from me, taking a drink himself. Placing the bottle on the floor he reached inside his greasy overalls. He produced a small lump of milky stone, shot through with golden veins. It began to glow, softly, like the moon behind thin, misty clouds. Traceries of light flickered up and down the veins, pulsing like a heartbeat. My innards clenched, and this time it wasn't withdrawal symptoms. Sanej's personal – and very proscribed – abaston stone had detected another crystal, very close by.

"Alva's using abaston power?" I murmured. We'd half-suspected, but the pompous fool had managed to avoid every attempt at scrutiny, up until now.

Sanej shrugged and placed his fragment of crystal back in his clothes. "Sort of. You can see for yourself from the proximity reaction, the stone he's using is almost exhausted. There's not enough chrysomantic energy left to pull up my socks – never mind move this locomotive-engine and four carriages."

"Then what is he doing?"

"P'r'aps yer sh'd arsk 'im?"

"That has to be the worst Sebite accent I've ever heard. It wouldn't fool anyone."

Sanej wasn't trying to be funny. He knew, as did I, what it would mean if a man, supported by the Philosophics, was dabbling in Chrysomancy. Especially a man as esteemed as Professor Alva.

"Do I need to?" I asked. Sanej wouldn't have spent all this time under the locomotive-engine's cover without prying. It was a good bet he'd already found out more than Alva wanted known.

He pointed at a flush-mounted plate, set in the back of the boiler. Almost at floor level, there was an obtrusive, over-large lever growing out of it. "Give that a swing," he said.

I stooped and grabbed at the metal. It didn't come free easily, but a couple of hard tugs set it moving. The panel swung open.

Inside was a complex of pipes and vanes, all leading off to the depths of the boiler, as far as I could tell. Surrounded by that network was a small, milk-and-gold fragment, no more than half an inch in diameter. It was held in place by two vertical steel tubes, pinning it at the top and bottom. It was abaston stone right enough. But even in its virginal youth it would barely have had enough power to move the *Novandik*, let along the entire train.

"I discovered that the first night we were out," Sanej began. "Once Law's back was turned—"

"Where is he now, by the way?" In the maze of worry and withdrawal, I'd quite forgotten the pilot-assistant.

"Sleeping, like I told him to. Don't interrupt. Alva gave us both the strictest instructions to open that panel only in a case of direst emergency."

"So, you looked anyway."

"Of course. I couldn't understand how the *Novandik* worked. It's a steam engine, but where's the fuel? All we carry is spare water. Our passengers might not have a clue about modern machinery, but my education is quite broad and inclusive. I have to know as much as a real pilot, after all."

I said nothing. I remember Sanej once taking an hour to figure out how to use a new Alva patented tin-opener.

"And that tall fancy exhaust pipe sticking up through the roof up front? It's a fake. Riveted to solid metal, with a small tube that squirts out a little exhaust steam. Just enough to make it look convincing. I checked that my first night, too." He nodded towards the fragment in its steel nest. "My guess is he's using it to heat the water, somehow. Ingenious ... if he's not a wizard himself."

"You don't think he's the one?" I asked. "Sabotaging his own machine?"

He considered it. "A complex plan if he is. Create this wondrous thing, pin all the new government's hopes to it, then destroy it, along with their credibility. Plenty to go wrong there."

I knew of crazier ideas. "Whereas you only involve yourself in foolproof schemes, of course."

Sanej shrugged, digging a well-chewed clay pipe out of his jacket. He inspected the bowl, tamped down the contents, and lit it with a grimy match. Once the thing was going to his satisfaction – blowing great, filthy-smelling clouds over me – he sat back again.

"I don't think Alva's your man, Wil. In fact, in my inestimable opinion, I'd say he might be in some danger."

I'd known Sanej for many years; he never made uneducated guesses. "You think they'd be desperate enough to actually kill him? This close to the next election?"

He puffed out another noxious cloud. "Some of the wizards *are* pretty desperate, Wil. Their political sense could well desert them if they think Alva's actually going to make it to the coast. That will pretty well put him, and this new groundswell of science, up on a pedestal. The Philosophics will be able to live off it for decades."

"People on pedestals make easy targets, Sanej," I said.

Sanej took out his pipe and spat. "There's a difference between being raised up and waving your arms about daring people to shoot."

I sighed. "So, Alva's a target, not a suspect. Anyone else I should strike off my list whilst I'm here?"

"Commander Batrix."

I couldn't resist a laugh. "I never really considered her. A heteromorph as a Chrysomancer agent would just harden people's attitudes further, against them both."

"As long as you can see that." He stuck the pipe back between his teeth. "I know how you feel about Switchers."

"I don't feel anything about Switchers. They're not the sort of thing to inspire many feelings."

Sanej favoured me with a very old-fashioned look, then he took out his pipe and inspected the bowl. He frowned, as though he wasn't at all happy with what he saw down there. "You've got to trust someone, Wil. I'd start with the heteromorph."

"You know I respect your judgement, Sanej," I said to the top of his head. "But Batrix?"

He looked up from the pipe. "I'll stake my life that it's genuine. The President's staff have vetted it, remember."

"And no one's ever evaded a full security check before, of course." I took note of his use of the impersonal pronoun. Sanej had spent so much of his life with wizards – acting like one, eating with them, teaching them – that at times he almost fooled me. Old habits, I suppose. Even he found it hard to think of heteromorphs as anything other than genderless creations.

He was smiling to himself, my remark triggering off fond memories. "Just take my word, Wil. Do what you're told, for once."

He bent down and rummaged through a shapeless burlap sack by his feet. When he straightened up, he was holding a sheaf of papers. He waved them at me. "Anyway, this is the real reason I called you."

I took the bundle and scanned the neat, precise writing I recognised as Sanej's own. There were six sheets in all; each one a short, concise biography: little gems of impropriety.

I tapped the top sheet. "Batrix won't like this, she practically worships the man."

Sanej shook his head. "Don't underestimate Batrix. That's just the official, party line it's quoting. There's a first-class brain operating under that off-hand face. You'd do well to cultivate it."

I sighed and folded the papers up. Slipping them inside my coat, I asked: "How are you keeping in contact?"

"They contact me. Irregular intervals, a couple of seconds at a time. That's why it's taken so long to transcribe all that."

There was a risk, of course. Crystal-to-crystal contact from the outside could be screened to a large extent, but never entirely. There'd still be enough leakage for an alert observer to pick up, assuming they were watching at the right time. But the overall odds had been reckoned to be in our favour. Sanej had taken a far greater risk in contacting me.

"How's Major Rengalet taking to commanding a bunch of infantrymen?" Sanej asked.

I'd only spotted the war hero on a couple of brief occasions. Neither time had he looked particularly happy. "Like a duck to molasses. He looks like he's either about to explode with indignation or rant at an innocent Sharpshooter for some imagined violation. I believe he thinks this posting is some form of punishment."

"Is he hitting the bottle yet?"

"Not obviously. He must bathe in that awful Ghalean perfume: it's impossible to smell anything else. And he's practiced enough to disguise it."

Sanej tapped the front of his teeth with the pipe stem. "As agreed, Senator Nachollni was asked to assess the *Novandik's* military potential..."

I could still visualise the ghastly scenario that had been created, aimed specifically at the senator's particular strain of patriotism. The President's vision of a fleet of rail-trains, heavily-armoured, bristling with scaled-up versions of Alva's patented repeater gun – carrying troops to trouble spots in a fraction of the time it would take to march them. "And he swallowed it?"

"Apparently."

Yes, 'apparently' was very much the watchword. Reasons can be dreamed up, but who can tell if they're believed? "What about Tork?"

Sanej shrugged. "Difficult to say. He's vain enough to believe this journey really needs a man of his calibre. The President asked him personally." He slipped into a faultless imitation of Thinos' drawl. "*Professor Alva is not a healthy man, Bronex. We can't afford to let anything happen to him. I want the best there is on that train. It's that important to me.*"

I snorted. "This train isn't big enough for all this self-importance!"

"Maybe. But I, for one, would rather have Tork around than some army barber and his butcher's knife if I take a bullet in the arm."

I appreciated the point. I just wondered if Tork saw it that way.

"Batrix is suspicious," I said.

Sanej removed his pipe, spat and slipped the stem back between his lips. "I told you it had a first-class brain."

"Doesn't make my job any easier; she suspects I'm up to something, and a liar and mentally unstable, to boot."

"An excellent judge of character, then. Take it into your confidence, like I suggested."

I rubbed the back of my neck. "O ye banned gods, but we live in mendacious times!"

"I wouldn't let your girlfriend hear you talking like that."

"Very funny."

"Trust is a luxury these days, Wil, I know that. In the present political climate, even President Thinos can't afford it. He's stood for two terms of office, and the next elections are less than eighteen months away. Presently, members of his own party are likely to be as big a threat as the Chrysomancers. Now things are settling, everyone wants to be President of Ramini."

"You think they'd know better. They're all grown men."

"Such cynicism in one so young," Sanej handed me the half-finished bottle of *chavet*. "Hadn't you better be going?"

"Everyone gets tired of my company so quickly." I stood up. "Maybe I should get another position."

"Who'd want you?" Sanej stood, too, putting out his hand. "Take care, boy," he murmured, in a tone I hadn't heard before. "This is a deep one, and I don't know if you're ready for it..."

I pushed the *chavet* bottle into a pocket and took his hand in both of mine. "Just keep pulling those levers, old man. Maybe you can get me something like real employment once we reach the coast."

Chapter Seven

I made it back to my compartment with a lot less drama. Maybe I was getting used to hanging off roofs. There was a distinct lightness in the sky by the time I was easing my door open, and I guessed dawn wasn't too far away. I took one last swig of *chavet* before corking what remained and locking it away in one of the compartment's highly polished sets of drawers. I would have to ration the stuff from now on, painful though the thought was. Alva wasn't going to keep handing it over day after day, much as he wanted my services. But I'd managed to survive lean times before without totally losing my mind; I could do it again.

After that thought, I had dropped onto the velvet sofa, as far as I could remember, drifting into sleep almost immediately. The next thing I know, I am leaping halfway to my feet, my heart battering its way up my throat, in time to the hammering on my compartment door. Someone was shouting my name. After my heartbeat quieted, I recognised Batrix at her most imperious.

"I'm coming!" I replied through a mouth which felt like the inside of an old glove. That's what comes of dozing off after drinking *chavet*. It probably rots teeth, as well.

I slipped the catch on the door, and it immediately rolled back, not quite slamming. But judging by Batrix's expression, she'd done her best. She stalked into the compartment, followed by three uniformed men with very no-nonsense expressions on their faces. Two were Sharpshooters in blue and green, muskets unshouldered and looking very large in the confined space, the third was frilled up in the tastelessly ornate blue and orange uniform of a dragoon, wrapped around the almost vertical figure of Major Trescu Rengalet. He wore his otherwise unremarkable brown hair in the tight braids fashionable among cavalrymen, and his face was half hidden under an enormous handlebar moustache. That, and a network of burst veins decorating his cheeks and nose, made him look many years older than his true age. He was clutching a polished cavalry sabre, and most of the time the point seemed to be aimed in my direction.

"Gentlemen," I said. "Please, come in. And Batrix, good morning to you, too. I'd offer you breakfast, but I've given the servants the day off—"

"Be quiet, Scilli!" snapped Batrix, her tone a slap in the face. Yesterday, she'd been furious with me, this time she was … I didn't know exactly what. This was more like good old-fashioned, white-hot righteous anger – like some mythical, wrath-consumed Patriarch. She turned to one of the Sharpshooters. "He has a pistol. In his coat, most likely."

None too gently the soldier went through my pockets while the other kept me covered. He found my repeater and handed it to Batrix. She looked it over closely.

"What's happened, Batrix?" I began, suddenly feeling very cold. Maybe it was a premonition. "What have—?"

"*Gosigné* Wilonek Scilli," Rengalet began in a clipped, military voice. "I arrest you, in the name of President Thinos and the Ramini Republic, for the wilful murder of Yosec, pilot of the locomotive-engine *Novandik*."

Sanej! I tried to say something, my mouth and brain wanted to come up with something to drown the words. I took a step forward.

Batrix pushed me back onto the sofa. My resistance was no more than that of a ragdoll.

Sanej?

"Until such times as an appropriate court of law may be convened, you will consider yourself confined to these quarters," Rengalet was saying, obviously unaware of how pointless his speech was. Sanej wasn't dead! The train was moving! Who else would be piloting it?

"You need not make a statement now, but be cautioned that anythin' you do say will be recorded and used as evidence at such a hearin'. Do you understand?"

"He's not dead!" I finally managed to squeeze out through a shrinking throat. "You're wrong!"

"You are being ridiculous, Scilli!" said Batrix coldly. "Do you understand the charges which Major Rengalet has presented to you?"

"I understand the charges well enough!" I snapped back. "It's what's behind them I'm have trouble with!"

It hit me suddenly, mercilessly: this was no trick, no sick joke by one of the passengers. Sanej was dead. My oldest friend had been murdered, and with biting irony, I was being given the blame.

"Do you deny the accusation, then?"

"Of course I do!" I tried to leap out of the sofa in anger, but the casually aimed muskets of the two Sharpshooters kept me seated. All the same, it was a close-run thing. "Why the hell would I want to kill the pilot?"

"A question that has already occurred to me," said Batrix. "No doubt your motive will be uncovered at the trial."

"If any of us live that long." Trial? At the present rate, it seemed to me we'd be lucky to get to the next Estates. "And just what makes you think I'm the killer, Commander?" It had taken me too long to think of that question, much too long. Although I didn't need any *chavet*, I still felt a long drink would go down well.

"You were seen entering and leaving the *Novandik* during the night."

"Really? And just who was up and about and being so observant?"

Batrix remained silent. Neither Rengalet nor the two guards were very forthcoming, either.

"I doesn't occur to you that this anonymous informant might be the actual killer, I suppose?" I said.

"Why should they kill Yosec and then implicate you?"

"You said it yourself: I went to see him."

"You do not deny it?"

"Of course not."

"Why did you feel it necessary to sneak around under cover of darkness?"

Ah. Now there she had me. I wasn't about to say anything, not in front of Rengalet and his guards. Sanej had assured me I could trust Batrix... But a Batrix in her present mood?

"Can I talk to you? Alone?" I asked her. It was desperate. I didn't for one moment expect her to say yes, so she surprised me by nodding.

"Now look here!" Rengalet started to protest. Batrix turned her full glare on him. Her blue lenses seemed to glow.

"Major, I have full authority here. The train is in motion. You and your men will be outside the door. What can he do? Where can he go?"

"He could assault you! Kill you with some low wizard trick! And I ain't handin' over a potential hostage simply on your whim!"

"No whim, Major." She turned back to face me. "Besides," she added more quietly, "I do not believe he would be so obvious."

"Thanks for the vote of confidence," I said, with as much venom as I could summon up under the circumstances.

The major paused uncertainly for another moment, then led his two men out of the compartment with poor grace. I stayed quiet until the door was tightly shut, waiting for another half a minute. Not that I have a morbid insecurity, you understand.

"Well, Scilli," Batrix prompted eventually, obviously growing tired of my silence. "What do you have to say?"

"I didn't kill Sanej," I said, simply.

She all but sneered in my face. "Please, Scilli – do not try my patience! You admit to being out of the train at night, evading the guards, and visiting the pilot. Protestations of innocence are a little late, are they not?"

"Of all the people on this train, the last person I'd want to kill is Sanej."

She opened her mouth to snap some retort, then closed it. "You called him Sanej." Pulling up the armchair, she sat down facing me, keeping my own pistol aimed in my direction. I got the idea. "Would you care to tell me why?"

This was it: the point of no return. I took a deep breath and closed my eyes. When I let it out and opened my eyes again, Batrix was still there, sitting in judgement.

"Sanej and I are – were – partners. Have been for many years."

Batrix allowed an eyebrow to raise itself. "Partners? In what, might I ask? Perhaps the partners had a little falling out?"

She wasn't going to make this easy. "You're not going to like this, Commander, but believe me, it's not meant as any kind of reflection on your ability." I paused, but there was no change in the expression on her face. "Captain Sanej is a government agent ... was an agent. Their best. His rank, of course, was nominal." She didn't erupt with outrage at the idea. I have to give her credit: I would have.

"To give you some idea, for most of his life he was an inside man at the Madrasaté Seminary. That's where we met."

She slowly crossed her legs. There was still nothing going on behind her face, and her eyes were well screened by her spectacles. "Inventive, Scilli – I will give you that. But if Yosec – or Sanej, if you prefer – was a government agent, what was he doing piloting the *Novandik*?"

"Someone had to maintain contact with the outside. Sanej was an expert undercover man. Put him in a room with one other person, and you'd never see him."

"And what are you?"

I rubbed at my eyes. It didn't help. "Sanej has used me in the past. His stalking horse, I suppose. He knows – knew – I always need the money. I normally just have to hang around, listening and watching. After all, who ever actually sees someone like me? I'm not even worth the attention you'd give to a servant."

"Then you claim Yosec – Sanej – was a government agent, and you are some kind of information gatherer."

I nodded, wanting that drink more than ever.

"Why did you go to see him last night?"

"We were to keep apart as much as possible, only make contact if the situation seemed to warrant it." I didn't want to add that he'd sent for me – any more hints of wizardry and she'd have me shot before the trial.

"And I assume you thought this ... theory of yours, that there is a wizard on board, was warrant enough?" I had the feeling I'd piqued her interest – but I was pretty sure she still didn't believe me.

"And he is your killer."

"He?"

I grunted something that may have sounded almost like a laugh. "Sanej said I could trust you. I never knew him to be wrong."

Batrix leaned back a little. "This still fails to prove your innocence. If you were this wizard yourself, and you killed Yosec because you recognised him as an agent – or perhaps he recognised you – this mixture of half-truths would be just the story I would expect you to tell me."

She had me there. "It comes back to you not being able to trust anyone on this trial run, Batrix. The last time I tried to tell you that, you flew out of here in a blind fury."

"Let us pretend I have had time to reconsider your argument."

So far so good. "Then, assuming I'm not the killer, and neither are you, that leaves Alva, Scendik, Rengalet or one of his men, Nachollni, Tork, Krordec the train-captain, or Law, the assistant pilot. Who's your money on?"

"This is all wild speculation, Scilli."

I pulled out some papers from inside my coat. Not all of them. I'd already spread the bundle throughout all my pockets, in case just such a moment occurred. Trust Batrix, Sanej had said, but he didn't say trust her with everything.

"Sanej gave me these last night," I said, holding them out. "Maybe they're the reason he was murdered."

She took them with her free hand and scanned through them, her face betraying nothing. Eventually, she dropped the papers into her lap and looked back at me.

"Might I enquire how he was able to obtain this information? I believe you said he was in contact with the outside?"

"He'd been an instructor at the Seminary for many years," I said carefully. "He'd acquired many skills—"

"You mean he was a wizard."

"Something like that, yes."

"And he was working for the Bureau? A wizard?"

"Do I have to—?" I sprang to my feet as it hit me. Too late again! I was getting slow. The *chavet* must already have been rotting my brain.

"Has anyone searched the body?" I snapped at Batrix. I was looming over her, and I could see she was deciding whether to call for Rengalet or shoot me then claim it was self-defence.

"Of course. Doctor Tork was called the moment—"

"Did he find Sanej's abaston stone? His crystal?"

"No, I..." Her voice trailed off as the same belated thought struck her. Sanej was a wizard, and all wizards carry their own crystals about them. If a search hadn't revealed it – and I'd never known him to hide it particularly well – that meant his murderer must have taken it.

"With two crystals..." Batrix began.

I nodded. "He'll be a hundred times more dangerous." Not even the Archimandrite carries more than one crystal at a time: the dangers of resonant amplification are too great. "Once he's retuned it with his own abaston crystal..."

"He will destroy himself!"

"I don't think that matters." Another thought hit me and I began to feel really sick. "There's another crystal on this train," I said. Batrix's face hardened. I shook my head. "Not me! I don't know how to use the damned things! The locomotive-engine – there's one in the boiler! Sanej reckoned the water's somehow turned to steam using abaston power!"

It was Batrix's turn to come out of the chair. "Alva is using proscribed methods to power the *Novandik*?"

I must admit to a fleeting glow of satisfaction at her burst of outrage.

"I shall be having words with Professor Alva shortly," Batrix murmured. The way she said it made me glad I wasn't Alva.

"Meanwhile, there's the question of my innocence or guilt," I said, wondering exactly where I now stood. Between my words and Sanej's papers, a good deal of Batrix's cosy worldview was teetering on collapse.

She paused mid-rant, eyeing me coldly behind her masking lenses. "Your case has been neither proved nor disproved. Whilst I am prepared to admit that what you say makes a degree of sense – especially in tandem with these papers – it is still a long road to demonstrating your innocence. For the moment, if you will give me your parole, I am prepared to allow you the freedom of the train. You can hardly go very far, after all. And I suspect, after the events of the last two evenings, the overnight stops will be curtailed."

"You have it, Commander. I'll even sign a paper, if you want."

"That will not be necessary. But I will be watching you, Scilli. Depend on it."

"Please do, but before you convict me, can I ask just one thing?"

"And that is?"

"I want to see the body."

She shook her head. "I am sorry, but that is quite impossible."

"Please, Batrix ... Commander. Do you want me to beg? Go down on my knees?"

There was a long pause. Eventually, Batrix turned with a sigh. "Very well. We will escort you there."

She opened the door. Rengalet's face appeared in the gap almost immediately. The two of them had a brief, heated exchange, during which time the major glowered at me several times. Eventually, he seemed to agree – Batrix probably pulled rank on him – and he stepped away.

"Outside, Scilli," Batrix called. I stepped into the corridor before anyone had a change of heart. A Sharpshooter positioned himself in front of me, a second, close behind. Rengalet was next in line, his sword sheathed. He was now aiming an elaborately decorated repeater pistol at my back. It looked as though it cost more than Batrix's and my own combined. The commander herself fell in last, my pistol held ready.

I was marched quickly back down the train, through the kitchen carriage and across to the Sharpshooters' own barracks waggon. It was as grim and dark as I'd imagined, half of it given over to a press of tightly stacked bunks. Several off-duty guards snapped to attention at our arrival. Out of the corner of my eye, I saw Rengalet absently wave them down again. The rest of the carriage was open space, with a few crates serving as tables. Gear and munitions were racked neatly against a wall.

A draped form lay in a near corner. I didn't need any guesses.

I knelt beside the shape and pulled back the cover: a thin, soldier's blanket. Sanej looked peaceful enough lying there. Whoever had laid him out had done a good job.

"Hardly appropriate spot for a corpse, I know," Rengalet said from behind me. "But it'll do 'til we reach Jaqatlan. Ain't a man here who's afraid of a body."

"Can I have a moment alone with him?" I asked.

The major snorted in disbelief. "Can't be done, sir. Can't have you fiddlin' with evidence."

"I will watch him, Major," came Batrix's voice.

"Not exactly alone," I said.

"That or nothing, Scilli."

"This is confounded irregular, Commander!" Rengalet complained.

"That may be, Major. But we are all armed, and he is almost literally surrounded by your men. I will ensure he does not tamper with the body."

Rengalet huffed and puffed some more, but eventually I heard him back away. I turned around and looked up at Batrix: looming over me barely two feet away.

"Thanks," I said, surprised at her show of compassion, if that's what it was.

"Be quick," she muttered. Compassionate or not, she was as rigid as ever.

I examined Sanej as carefully as speed and discretion allowed. His neck was broken from a strong blow to the nape, judging by the amount of skin damage. There was very little bruising, though. There were also signs of heavy bleeding from a broad scalp wound. I checked his hands. Nothing you wouldn't expect to see from a man who worked with machinery.

Laying him back down carefully, I draped the blanket back over his face. We'd both known this moment would come for one of us, sooner or later. That didn't make it any easier.

"Are you done?" asked Batrix. I wanted to stay there, kneeling by the body of the only person I've ever been able to call a friend. But that was impossible. Sanej would understand. He'd probably make some off-colour joke about it. I murmured an inadequate goodbye and got to my feet.

"I was little more than a baby when I was snatched from my home," I said quietly. "I have no idea where that was, who my parents were, if I have any brothers or sisters or even if they were left alive. Ever since then, Sanej was the only person to show me any kindness, even back in the Seminary. When I find out who killed him, I'm going to repay the compliment." I turned and looked Batrix in the eyes. "Take me back, Commander."

They marched me to my compartment without further comment. I was too numb for any more clever remarks.

Batrix slid my door open but halted me with a hand before I could go through. "I am familiar with this desire for revenge, although I have never experienced it. If your story is true, I can appreciate your feelings. But I have to tell you one thing: I will not tolerate summary justice. When the guilty party is revealed – whoever they may be –

they will be arrested and turned over to the Bureau at Scana Carsofi. Is that clear?"

"There's something else I'd like you to do," I said, in lieu of an answer.

"You never cease to amaze me, Scilli." She almost sounded amused. "For a suspected man, you have a remarkable talent for making demands."

"This is a request, Batrix." I took a breath. "You've seen those files. I think you'll be wanting to have a little talk with all of our eminent guests."

Her head tilted fractionally. "And where will I be wanting this meeting?"

"Alva's private carriage, I would imagine. After all, didn't you want to ask him a couple of questions as well?"

"And I suppose I will be wanting to invite you too, Scilli?"

"More than anyone."

She stared at me, though I suspect it wasn't me she was seeing. "I will have you sent for."

Her hand dropped away, and I wandered back into my upholstered cell. For a few moments longer, I was aware of Rengalet's hostile glare, then I heard him marching rigidly away. The guards stayed.

It was nice to be trusted.

Chapter Eight

I wasn't left alone for long. Several minutes after Batrix had left, there was a soft knock on my door. I expected it to open immediately, but after a pause, the knock came again: diffident, almost timid.

I stood, wary. "Come in," I called, wondering who was being so unusually respectful.

The door slid open. It was Senator Nachollni, looking as bland as ever.

"Something I can do for you, Senator?" I asked.

"You've been busy, sir," he said, failing to answer the question. "Killing the pilot. Most inconsiderate."

"I must try and cultivate notoriety more often. I've never had so many visitors. Was it you who claimed to have seen me last night?"

"You deny it? Interesting. No, it wasn't I, sir. I find travel an effective antidote to wakefulness. The moment my head touches the pillow, I'm perfectly asleep." He stepped into my compartment, taking a humidor from his coat and tapping free a long, thin cigar. Even with such a show of self-assurance, the clerk-out-of-his-depth look didn't waver. Without waiting to be asked, he sat and lit the cigar. Naturally, he didn't offer me one.

"Come in, Senator," I said. "Sit down." I flopped back onto the sofa. Before long there would be a permanent impression of my backside in the velvet.

"*Did* you do it, Scilli?" he asked, taking absolutely no notice of my tone.

"If I deny it, will you believe me?"

He shrugged. "I don't know. Major Rengalet and that heteromorph seem pretty convinced of your guilt. But that may well be their prejudices showing through. Rengalet, particularly, believes that a penurious, ex-student of Madrasaté would be capable of anything."

"And you have no such prejudices?"

"Nothing that matters." He shifted in the chair and drew on his cigar. "For instance, I'm not prepared to accept the guilt of a man simply because of an accident of upbringing. I know how the brothers of the seminaries recruited their pupils. And I know that until the final induction, most students remain their own men."

"Up to a point," I commented, thinking of the *chavet* addiction thrust on us all.

"Quite so. But what I'm trying to say, Scilli, in my awkward fashion, is that a man should be held innocent until his guilt is proven. As far as I'm aware, neither proof nor reason has been offered to explain why you should so wantonly murder the pilot."

"Hadn't you heard? I'm a wizard spy, smuggled aboard to wreck the train."

Nachollni laughed. It was a boy's laugh: light and exuberant. "Forgive me, sir, but I think if the Spooks had wanted to place a saboteur on board, they would have picked someone a little less..." he waved a pale hand at my clothes "...unprepossessing."

"The cut of a man's suit is a pretty thin way of assessing his character," I said, not in the least hurt. He was a smart man, above petty prejudices, and he wanted me to know that.

He shrugged again. "I know. Appearances aren't the best measure of a man. In my line of work, masks are compulsory."

They were in mine, too. Literally. I batted at the line of smoke that was gradually clotting the air between us, fighting back the urge to cough. "Forgive me for being blunt, Senator, but why exactly are you here? If Commander Batrix catches us talking, all clandestine, she'll start imagining we're allies of some kind."

Nachollni laughed carelessly. "Heteromorphs. Don't you find them a suspicious breed?"

"Can you blame them?"

He waved his cigar. "I simply thought to offer my support. Let you know that I will stand by you, no matter what Rengalet or the commander may trump up."

"My thanks. But isn't it a little late? I could have used a senator's support ten years ago. We all could."

His face hardened a little, and he had the good grace to redden. "I understand your bitterness, Scilli. The failure of this government to address the rehabilitation of all those released from the wizards' various seminaries is nothing more than a national disgrace! I've spoken to the President on that very matter, more than once; and believe me, he is all too aware of the problem. But, for the moment, our hands are tied. So many facets of the Chrysomancers' days of rule have been made illegal: abaston power, *chavet*, so many things..."

It was all I could do not to laugh when I thought of what was being used to power the *Novandik*. "Governments create laws. Governments can unmake them."

He spread his hands. "If only it were that simple. But half of the problem is not knowing what *chavet* actually is. Over-zealous citizens destroyed much of the wizards' records, after their surrender at Jaqatlan. We have some of our most gifted apothecaries working on it now, but no one anticipates a substitute – never mind a cure – in the foreseeable future."

"Meanwhile, hundreds die every year – if not every month." I knew all about the supposed destruction of the Chrysomancers' libraries and archives, and I'm convinced it's a lie. I don't think a fraction of the official figure was actually lost. Even a controlled army of incendiaries couldn't eradicate so many records in so short a time, least of all a leaderless rabble. The wizards were too meticulous; there were too many copies.

But far be it from me to contradict the famous Senator Nachollni.

"However, you, I understand, are provided for?" he said.

"If by that you mean, am I being supplied with enough *chavet*, then yes, Senator."

"Good, good. Now the war is over—"

"The war never ended, Senator," I interrupted. "The Spooks never really surrendered. They just changed the rules of engagement."

"I expect you're correct, Scilli." His tone was suddenly distant.

"You never served in the war—" I began.

"If you mean I never rode into battle, sir, that's true!" he blazed back at me, as though that was a tired, familiar accusation which never failed to anger him. Something like life rose up behind his bland, grey exterior. "Constant illness as a boy left me unfit for the rigors of military life!" He held up a pale hand, as though to illustrate the point. "Instead, I poured all of my energies into my brain. I took up the sword of rhetoric. Maybe I never distinguished myself on the field of honour, but I flatter myself that I more than made up for it in the political arena!"

"Sorry if I offended you, Senator. No offence was meant. I know a sickly childhood left you physically weak. I understand you almost died once, from infantile cough."

The colour was fading from his cheeks, though his breathing sounded laboured. He sank back into greyness. "No offence taken, sir.

I sometimes over-react. Accusations of cowardice were all too common during the war. Even now, the memory pains me."

"And you've been siding with the underdog ever since?"

He frowned. "I wouldn't have classed you as an underdog, sir. Underprivileged, maybe. Disadvantaged. But you seem to lack that air of loss which characterises the average underdog."

"I was thinking of the heteromorphs."

Nachollni began to laugh, but finished up coughing instead. Now his face was almost as white as his beard and moustache. "Someone had to help them, sir," he wheezed eventually. "And unlike the case of your sorry contemporaries, it was easily done. A piece of paper, a signature – and all heteromorphs are free creatures..."

"Making you a hero to the people, and a virtual god amongst the Switchers."

He glowered at me, angry again. For a sick man, he had a fiery temper. "I will tolerate many things, sir – but not blasphemy! Nor that foul idiom."

"Don't tell me, tell the heteromorphs," I said lightly. "Considering their origins, I imagine they can believe in just about anything if they want."

"Belief is dangerous, Scilli. Belief gave us Chrysomancy, and a thousand other kinds of magic across the world. Such belief – such talk – is to be discouraged."

"You can't legislate against superstition, Senator. It's been with us from the time of our earliest ancestors. It'll still be here in another hundred centuries."

"Superstition will evaporate, Scilli. We live in an age of reason, of science. With a little positive encouragement, such primitive beliefs will go."

"You sound just like one of my old teachers."

I could feel the look he gave me clear down to my boot-tips. "I can see there is no further point in my staying here," he said, rising to his feet. Cigar smoke swirled into a blue corkscrew around him. "You are a bitter man, *Gosigné* Scilli. I can appreciate that. However, please don't let that bitterness shield you from the outstretched hand when it is offered. I meant what I said: I am here to help you."

"Thanks, Senator. I appreciate it." I didn't get up; I watched him as he slid open the door and left. A quick – almost hurried – departure, I thought, making sure he wasn't still around when Batrix came back for me, perhaps?

I templed my hands together and stared at my fingertips. Now why had Nachollni come to see me? Really? Was he genuinely offering a friendly hand? Or trying to pump me, figure out for himself if I was Sanej's killer? And why? If so, his approach was strange – and I flattered myself that I'd gotten more out of him than he had from me.

The blasphemy act rang hollow, too. Nachollni was certainly not known for his vehement support of the Suppression of Worship Act. It was a law nobody took seriously anyway, designed as it was to prevent the re-emergence of sorcery, not prevent anyone's belief in gods of any kind. A deliberate over-reaction? A test to see how I'd respond? I wondered if I'd passed or failed.

There was only one thing I was certain of. Maybe it was instinct, or some kind of extra sense. Maybe all those lessons beaten into me at the Seminary had taught me something after all. But somewhere in that conversation, for whatever reason, Senator Nachollni was lying.

Chapter Nine

I was still thinking it over when Batrix sent for me. The two Sharpshooters standing guard outside my compartment came in unannounced, gestured for me to stand, and led me out without a word. It was a pleasure to witness such talent for intimidation.

By the time I was ushered into Alva's private carriage, everyone else had already arrived and was seated. Since no one had seen fit to leave a chair vacant, I had to stand, leaning against the walnut panelling by the door. At least I had a good view.

The carriage interior wasn't that impressive: only four of my compartments would fit into it. The plush furniture, panels and ruched blinds over all the windows probably couldn't have bought more than two senators. Alva was sitting in the widest, fattest chair in the carriage, almost directly in the centre. A cigar smaller than a man's arm was jammed between his lips.

Scendik Boz was sitting to his left, in a bizarre red-and-green suit with a strange green flower in his buttonhole. He was eyeing me with what I assumed was meant to be irony. Pyndrians like to think they're good at that. It probably masks a national sense of inferiority. After all, as a nation, they had once ruled more of the world than had any cadre of wizards. No longer. That had to sting.

On Alva's right was Pomino Thryme. His lamentably unfashionable clothes were as jaded as my own. I thought Alva could have shown his appreciation a little more and bought the old man another suit. I judged it would have gone down better than a free ride.

Major Rengalet had positioned himself nearest the drinks cabinet, nudging it with his left arm. He didn't have a drink handy, but he had the look of a man who dearly wished he had. I sympathised. He was staring glassily at the gas-lamps running along the roof. I glanced up at them but couldn't fathom their appeal.

To Rengalet's right was another venerable gentleman, but this time age didn't seem to be weighing so mightily on his shoulders. Despite almost total baldness and a face so deeply lined he looked old enough to be the Archimandrite's older brother, he sat in his chair with a rigidity that would have done the major proud. His suit was jet black, his white shirt almost solid with starch, and his head appeared to be wedged in place by a high cravat. A small pair of pince-nez dangled from his thin fingers – but judging from the steely once-over he was giving me, the inestimable Doctor Bronex Tork carried them only because he thought physicians were expected to.

Senator Nachollni was the closest to me, no more than ten feet from my end of the carriage, sitting with his back to a window on the opposite side. The expression on his clerk's face was unreadable.

Batrix had positioned herself at the focus of this crude amphitheatre, sitting perfectly at ease with her hands folded across her legs. She was no longer holding my pistol and I wondered where she'd stashed it.

My guards took up position either side of the door we had just come through. I noted two more at the carriage's far end, flanking the door to Alva's sleeping quarters.

I looked around at the assembled dignitaries, favouring them with my best smile, and said: "Let the trial begin."

All of their expressions shifted subtly; I'd spoken their thoughts aloud. The only one whose face didn't change was Batrix, what I could see of it since she was mostly in profile.

"This isn't a trial, man!" puffed Alva around his huge cigar. Clouds of smoke were already thickening above his head. If this business wasn't concluded soon, we were going to finish it shouting through a fog. "We're all here at the behest of Batrix."

"Though to what purpose presently eludes me," added Boz. He crossed his legs and began to beat time with the polished toe of his left boot.

"Now we are all present, I shall begin," said Batrix, unperturbed. "Professor Alva: who is presently driving this train?"

"The pilot-assistant." More clouds were released into the thickening atmosphere. "Law, I think his name is."

"And you are confident in his ability to continue?"

Alva nodded, which was a relief to those of us who need to breathe.

"Very well." Batrix shifted. "Doctor Tork, will you be good enough to tell us exactly how Pilot Yosec died."

Tork's gimlet eyes switched from dissecting me and focused on Batrix. "His neck was broken. I would guess he had been struck a mortal blow by a heavy object."

That was condensing it. From the nature of the wounds, I imagined his murderer had crept up from behind, no doubt whilst Sanej's attention was on the engine's few controls. The first blow had missed, grazing Sanej's skull, dazing him. It had taken a second attempt to crush his neck. Sloppy work, from one who I guessed had to be a trained killer.

"From something like a repeating pistol?" Batrix asked.

Tork thought a moment. "Perhaps."

"Was there evidence of a struggle?" Batrix asked.

Tork shook his head. "I could find nothing to suggest that."

Bravo, Doctor. Sanej's hands had been unmarked. If he'd had the chance, he would have used those hands on his killer.

"In your opinion, did the deceased know his killer?"

"I am a physician, heteromorph, not a wizard." Tork spoke without obvious irony. "All I am prepared to say is the wounds are consistent with an ambush."

"Are we supposed to believe that the pilot knew Scilli?" said Boz, his voice lazy.

"You're forgetting," I said. "I didn't do it."

"You were seen!" Rengalet managed to sound both contemptuous and affronted. I put it down to army training.

"So, you keep saying. I don't suppose the night-owl who was awake and watching us innocent bystanders would care to stand up?" I was curious, though not in the least hopeful. Our murderer wasn't going to make life that simple.

For a moment, there was the silence I expected; then Pomino Thryme raised his frail, shaking head. "It was I," he murmured in a voice as tired as his clothes. "I don't sleep well these days."

"I know how you feel," I said, hoping my surprise didn't show in my voice. "I have to take great long walks every night before I can even think about putting my head down." Thryme didn't look strong enough to swat a drowsy housefly, leave alone beat Sanej to death. But I knew perfectly well that where magic is concerned, you can't take appearances seriously. I haven't looked like me for years.

"Your continued levity in the face of this issue's seriousness does you no credit, sir," Tork snapped. If he had any idea how hard I was finding it to keep up the façade...

"Thank you, Doctor," said Batrix in a way they must teach civil servants at school. Somehow, they can both soothe you and make you feel a complete fool. "One last thing. When you examined the body, did you find anything unusual amongst the effects?"

Tork frowned. "In what way unusual?"

"Items you might not expect a person of such lowly station to possess."

"Stolen items?" asked Boz with studied disinterest. His toe was still marking time rapidly. I think he was storing all this away in his writer's brain, hoping to find a use for it someday. "Indiscretions, perhaps?"

Batrix ignored him. "Well, Doctor?"

Tork shook his head. "From what I could tell, Yosec owned nothing other than the clothes he wore."

That answered that. No abaston stone. The murderer must have taken it, which just left two more questions: why? And did he know Sanej was a wizard before he killing him?

"This whole affair seems to be twistin' and turnin' like some ten-copper doxy!" complained Rengalet. He was only half looking at Batrix, the rest of his attention was still concentrated on the liquor bottles on his left. There was a familiar craving just beginning to nag at my concentration. "One moment we've got a simple case of murder, probably committed by that *chavet*-eating, failed wizard, to delay Professor Alva's triumph – then you're worryin' about what the confounded stiff had in its pockets! Do you enjoy complicatin' matters?"

I got the impression Batrix wanted to look at me for support. Perhaps it was the way she twitched her head, maybe it was just wishful thinking. Whichever, she paused an awfully long time before speaking.

"Major, it would appear that Yosec was more than a simple pilot." She sighed, either at what she was about to say, or at the thought her employers had been less than forthcoming with her. "He was an agent of the Internal Bureau, placed here even without my knowledge."

Nearly everyone sat up a little straighter at that.

"It seems Yosec was not his true name, and he was also a wizard."

That got their interest. Suddenly everyone was leaning forward, talking at once. Batrix sat mutely in the chair, staring at her knees, waiting for the hubbub to die down.

Boz was the first to make himself heard. "You mean the Ramini government – the Philosophic Party – is employing Spooks for its own secret operations?" He was almost ecstatic. He pulled a small leather notebook and gold propelling pencil out of an inside pocket and began to scribble. "What a wonderful, improbable story this will make some day!" He finished writing and put pad and pencil away. "Except, of course," he added wistfully, "no one will believe a word of it."

I noticed Alva was the first to stop gabbling in alarm. He was flushed, with a distracted look settling over his fat face. It appeared that the good professor was feeling not a little surprised that his government felt him – and his invention – important enough to protect with two agents. And one of them covert, to boot. Well, I could be generous. Let him think that if it made him feel better.

Senator Nachollni was shaking his head. "I find this very hard to believe."

"Worried you're not party to everything the President does, Senator?" I asked. He gave me an angry look that was out of its depth on his face. "But then, you'd hardly admit you knew in advance, would you. Not at this stage."

"You're offensive, sir," he said stiffly. "Rather high-handed for a recognised drug addict." His understanding nature had vanished quickly.

"And you're a politician. I hurt only myself. How many have your actions – or inactions – harmed?"

Nachollni's answering expression made him look like a sulky office boy.

"Would you mind telling us how the *Novandik* is powered, Professor Alva?" Batrix's calm voice rose above the angry undercurrent filling the plush carriage. You had to admire the way she could change tack abruptly. Another civil service trick, perhaps?

"Steam, as I'm sure you already know," replied Alva, puffing out more clouds of his own. He wriggled fleshly in his chair, preparing to give us all a lecture on his genius. "Steam, formed under pressure from heated water, has a great deal of propulsive energy contained within it. Harness that energy through valves, cylinders and pistons, and you can move the most massive object."

"I am sure we are all aware of the theory, Professor," remarked Batrix dryly. Pretty much all of Ramini was by now. He'd expounded on it enough times through lecture tours and news-sheet interviews. "What I specifically wish to know is, by what is the water heated?"

Alva may have hesitated for a moment. "In the boiler—"

"Not where, Professor, what. The *Novandik* carries several thousand gallons of water in its attendant tank, but no obvious fuel. Every man here will agree that to raise water to boiling point requires fuel of some kind. What exactly is the fuel of the *Novandik*, Professor Alva?"

It had gone quiet; the attention of the entire lounge was on Alva. He was sweating visibly, but with his over-stuffed bulk that wasn't so unusual. What was uncharacteristic, however, was his difficulty finding words. His mouth flapped minutely, but nothing managed to pass through his lips. The most expressive parts of him were his rapidly paling cheeks and darting eyes.

"Well, Professor?" Batrix urged, her voice gentle and cajoling. "Surely you have no new method beyond the understanding of mere laymen?" I could swear she was enjoying this. Obviously, Sanej had been right. There was more steel to Batrix than just a complaisant party manqué.

Finally, Alva came to some decision. He straightened himself, tugged at his ballooning waistcoat and removed his cigar. "It seems evident to me that you are already fully aware of the method, Commander," he said, as grandiosely as he could under the circumstances. "But for the benefit of everyone else here, the water is heated using an abaston stone."

Chapter Ten

The silence following his announcement was overwhelming. Clearly, while learning your pilot is a spell-singer who also happens to be a government agent is something of a shock, discovering your country's greatest engineer is using illegal methods to power his inventions is just a little short of world-shattering. No one seemed to be breathing. The self-renewing cloud of smoke around Alva began to thin out.

"You mean this whole thing is some kind of wizard's joke?" Nachollni managed to rasp out, his entire frame quivering with outrage.

"I trust we were not invited on this journey simply to be made fools of!" Although Boz's voice was alive with disgust, he looked neither shocked nor surprised.

"Gentleman, gentlemen!" Alva was making placating gestures with the palms of his hands. "Please, please – let me explain!"

Surprisingly, he got the attention he wanted.

"As you know, the Chrysomancers of Ramini have long used abaston crystals as their source of power. For years, I have been fascinated by this. Do the crystals provide the occult power themselves? Or are they merely a focus for the magician's will?"

"Dabblin' with spell-singer baubles!" Rengalet spat. "You ain't no better than Scilli, here!"

"Which makes me no worse than the Republic's finest brain, Major," I said. "Thanks for the compliment."

"I meant it as no compliment, sir!"

"If you would be so kind!" Batrix was glaring at us both. I was happy to fall silent: baiting the military has always been too easy. Rengalet shut up, too, but more from some personal concept of good manners than Batrix's intimidating look.

"I performed various experiments on a fragment of crystal I had ... acquired," Alva continued, having the grace to stumble over his words. It was a good act; I don't think anyone fell for it. "I discovered that the crystalline matrix itself contains enormous potential energy, which the magicians have been able to tap into. But more than that, I found the crystals could be made to release that energy source as heat, or light. They are a power source a thousand times greater than wood, or oil. Even a piece that is useless to the Spooks, drained and valueless to them, can be made to release its last stores of power and energy!"

He held up his left little finger, indicating the nail. "A fragment of abaston crystal, no larger than this, can release enough energy to heat up and hold at boiling point some five hundred gallons of water, for a period of several days! The spell-singers abused this power – used it to enslave, buttress their primitive ways. But we can employ it scientifically, lighting and heating the homes of the world, power an entire fleet of locomotive-engines. Who can imagine what may come of it?"

The carriage was silent again, everyone digesting his words. I wondered if the President had known about the power source all along. I could imagine Alva selling it to him as the way forward – a scientific breakthrough using the tools of superstition – swords into ploughshares: the sort of punchy phrase politicians like to use in lieu of actual conversation. And I had to admit, it was a smart concept.

Although, I imagined the Archimandrite would have apoplexy when he learned his precious stones were being used to boil a giant kettle.

"Did you have any intention of ever revealing this secret to us, Professor?" Batrix asked.

"It was no secret in certain quarters," he replied, confirming my suspicions. "But I saw no reason why I should publish all of my methods. I have enemies, you know. Rivals."

"Quite so." Batrix shifted her gaze to the frail clock-maker. "*Gosigné* Thryme, I believe you, alone in this carriage, have known the professor all of his life."

"For most of it, yes." His head continued to shake a little, as though denying his own words. "He was apprenticed to me as a young boy."

"You taught him clock-making."

"All of the arts. The movement; various kinds of clock mechanism: sand, water. We weren't allowed to make mechanical clocks once, you know. For years, the Archimandrite banned all clockwork..."

Except for the huge, gold-and-silver monstrosity which covers one of the walls of his villa at Dak Talini. Few know about it, but I've actually seen it. I also knew it had been Pomino Thryme who built the clock, some forty years earlier. Politicians don't have a monopoly on hypocrisy; despots have always been far more practised at it.

"Did he show any of his genius then?" Batrix was asking.

Thryme nodded; or tried to. His palsied shakes turned the nods into peculiar, circular movements. "Tissa has always been able to see beyond everyone else's imaginations. He was making innovative suggestions for movements even before his three-year indenture period was out. The man who grew from the boy knew more about clocks than I had gleaned in a lifetime!"

"And that made you proud, I imagine?"

"Of course—"

"Yet after working together for ten years, you threw him out. Why was that, *Gosigné* Thryme?"

The old man fell silent, at a loss for words. His headshakes grew ever more violent as he looked desperately at Alva. The professor paid him one glance, then looked away. Evidently, his old pupil wasn't in any mood to help.

"Was it because that even back then, Entissodamo Alva showed a certain ... disrespect for the law? For accepted behaviour? Did he not believe that any rule, any law, which stood between him and his goal, was unworthy of being obeyed?" Considering how little time she'd spent glancing through Sanej's notes, Batrix seemed to have retained a frightening amount of information. Was that how a simple heteromorph had made it so far up the Bureau ladder? A memory like that would be very useful in the ceaseless battle of internal politics.

"Yes!" Thryme's vague, old man expression had vanished under the anger now filling out his sad face. He was suddenly alive again. So much for being Alva's oldest and dearest friend. A more cynical man than me might have thought Thryme hated his erstwhile pupil.

"He would not be told! Even before the wizards' power was broken, and the President elected, Tissa dreamed of combining their damned sorcery with our growing understanding of natural science!"

"Shut up, you old fool!" Alva snarled at him, thrusting his face to within an inch of Thryme's. "No one wants to hear your jealous ravings!"

"Speak for yourself, Professor," I said. "I'm fascinated."

"I told him endlessly that he was endangering us both," Thryme forged on. He didn't even seem to be aware of Alva's raging face, so close to his own. "The wizards used to guard their secrets jealously. If they had learned of his bastardised experiments, I shudder to think of what they would have done!"

"But they did nothing, old man!" Alva shouted, spittle dotting Thryme 's face. "Even then, they feared me!"

"And then, when President Thinos took power, and all magical practises were declared illegal, Tissa persisted!"

"Do you think the President didn't know?" Alva turned away, spreading his arms to include us all. "Do any of you believe a project as large as this rail-road across the Republic, the construction of the *Novandik*, could be done without the head of the country not demanding to know exactly what I had planned at every stage?"

"That's a hell of an accusation, sir!" Senator Nachollni protested, leaning forward. "To claim the President would approve, no matter how tacitly, the use of methods specifically proscribed in the new Constitution!"

"But probably true," I added. "The manufactories who built the *Novandik* would be curious how the machine was supposed to work. Only a presidential order could kill that curiosity, backed by military persuasion if necessary. Make every worker who wanted to stay out of gaol, with all of their parts intact, conveniently deaf, dumb and blind."

"Aren't we straying from the point?" Boz said. "I thought we were here to look into the murder of the pilot, not badger old men into fits of anger."

"And how did you arrive at that assumption, *Gosigné* Boz," Batrix said. "I merely called you all here. I made no mention of a reason."

The writer shrugged. "But a fair assumption, surely?"

"Assumptions are a dangerous luxury, sir, and frequently wrong. There are too few pertinent facts here for us to construct anything other than wild guesses." She paused for moment, collecting her thoughts or being melodramatic. "*Gosigné* Boz, have you ever heard of the *Plytath a'Pyndr*?"

Boz's dancing toe jerked to an abrupt halt, otherwise he was relaxed charm personified. "Of course. A very old Pyndrian society. It dates back centuries. Little more than a drinking-club, really."

"Of which you are a member."

"You are very well-informed, Commander." His calm expression may have faltered a little. "Yes, I was honoured to be asked to join five years ago. Just after the success of my first book."

"A drinking-club, you say." Batrix steepled her forefingers and tapped the end of her nose with them. "A drinking-club that happens to include not only the First Lord of the Pyndrian parliament, but nearly all the members of both governing and opposition parties, several heads of policing organisations, plus military and naval chiefs. What intriguing revelries you must have."

"They probably get roarin' drunk and think maudlin thoughts of the golden days of their dead empire," laughed Rengalet. "The past is just about all Pyndria has now."

"Nothing is permanent, Major!" Boz threw back at him, his relaxed composure almost completely eroded. "Fortune runs in cycles, as the Ramini Republic will discover one day!"

"A threat, sir?"

"An observation, Major." Boz took a deep breath, absorbing a new calm from it. "Ramini may be the bright new heart of the world at present, but one day – when you and I are dust – the Republic will be brought as low as Pyndria."

"And meanwhile, *Plytath a'Pyndr* seeks to reverse the fortunes of your country, perhaps?" Batrix suggested quietly.

He laughed. "How? How may such a small body of men even dream of an undertaking of such magnitude? Your imagination does you credit, Commander, but I think it grows overheated."

The good Doctor Tork decided to join in the fun. "I am not so sure. I spent some years in Pyndria, studying Anatomy at Lunbywan

University. *Plytath a'Pyndr* was a popular subject amongst the students. It was regarded as everything from a club for morbidly regressive fools to a secret police force. Although it was presented as nothing more than *Gosigné* Boz says, the Spooks certainly hated *Plytath a'Pyndr*. Anyone under their jurisdiction who could be proven a member was executed."

"Obviously didn't like drinking-clubs," I said. "Bit of an extreme hangover cure though, don't you think?"

"You are all being way too dramatic," Boz insisted.

"Didn't the President make some allusion to foreign anarchists in his Address to the Republic last year?" Tork asked thoughtfully.

If Thinos had, I certainly didn't remember it. But distrust and xenophobia were taking a controlling hand in that carriage. Uncertainty, and a degree of fear, had gripped them all for too long, now they wanted some answers. Even if they had to create them out of nothing.

"It strikes me that Bronex Tork is not a particularly Ramini name," Boz countered, his tone childishly peevish.

"My parents were from Atarqé!" Tork replied, his own voice waspish. "I admit it with pride. I am from immigrant stock! Our family name was originally Tor'Eq. Since every family in the Republic can trace its origins to similar immigrants, I trust you are not seeking to make capital out of it. I have served the President faithfully all of my life: first as a true patriot of the Republic, and later as his personal physician. If you wish to find anarchist elements on this train, I suggest you look no further than the crew: they are all Sebites!"

Just about all menial workers are imported foreign labour: the government had to find someone to do all the dirty work once heteromorph culturing was declared illegal. Importing underpaid workers was how the Republic began, several centuries ago. Only back then they called them colonists. It was a simple choice: fill out the newly discovered continent with the disaffected or pioneering souls of the rest of the world, or become prison-grounds for the then burgeoning Pyndrian Empire. Needless to say, hundreds of thousands of misguided fools flocked to the new lands under the wholly unjustified belief that the wizards overseeing them were, somehow, going to be less despotic than the ones back home. Quite the reverse. None of which justified Doctor Tork's obviously biased comment. But Atarqé and Sebitslaya have never been happy neighbours.

"I, myself, come from a proud Balgysan family which settled here three generations ago," said Major Rengalet. He didn't sound proud, just provoked. Maybe he thought someone was going to start casting slurs at Balgys next. "I have always believed the Republic's strength lay in its diversity."

Well, he would say that. It was virtually word for word what President Thinos had said in his acceptance speech ten years ago. I didn't swallow it any more now than I had the first time I'd heard it. Ramini's diversity has enabled the ruling parties to shift blame onto whoever and wherever they liked countless times down the centuries. It has left deeply ingrained racial images that haven't faded with the Philosophics' rise to power. To the President's credit, he hasn't stooped that low. But then he hasn't had a crisis requiring a scapegoat yet, and up until now there has always been the Spooks.

All through the bad-tempered recriminations, Batrix sat like a blonde-and-blue statue. She waited until Rengalet had finished and then cleared her throat loudly. "Gentlemen, we are not here to apportion blame to anyone or anybody."

"Then why are we here?" demanded Nachollni. "So far, all you have done is reel out various ogres from our pasts. The pilot has been murdered; we have a suspect. What purpose does all this baring of unpleasantness serve?" Just as well I wasn't relying on his outstretched hand for help.

Batrix smiled sweetly at him. "Senator, you have long been recognised as the man who, almost single-handedly, rescued heteromorphs from the yoke of slavery. For that, you have my most grateful thanks, and the thanks of every surviving heteromorph."

"Very gracious, Commander," the senator acknowledged with a faint bob of his head. "But isn't this another blind alley?"

Batrix ploughed on, ignoring him. I thought I knew why: even one as hardened to political duplicity as Batrix would still be hurt to find their faith has been so misplaced.

"You are feted throughout Ramini – no, the entire world – as the man who defined freedom when, two years before the first free elections the Republic has ever known, you stood up and defended the rights of heteromorphs as living, thinking creatures. It was a pivotal speech, coming at a point when both the political and physical battles against the wizards were beginning to favour the Philosophic Party. And courageous, considering how much power the Chrysomancers still wielded."

Nachollni waved a deprecating hand, but his clerk's features were uncertain.

"And yet, on the very morning before that speech, you were breakfasting with Gawn Thinos, at that point still an idealistic leader of a powerless faction, and said – I believe this is an accurate quote – 'If I could ensure the defeat of the wizards without freeing a single one of those vile Switchers, I would do so.' Am I correct, Senator?"

"Where did you learn that?" Nachollni's face was now whiter than Doctor Tork's shirt-collar. I could barely hear his strangled whisper.

"Is it true, Senator?" Batrix persisted.

"And what if it is?" The senator lurched to his feet, almost slamming his shoulders against the carriage side. His face was ugly with emotion. "What possible bearing can it have on the death of a pilot? A human pilot!"

"I do not know, Senator," said Batrix, rigidly calm. "Perhaps you would care to tell me?"

"Do you see what this magic-spawned thing is doing?" Nachollni turned to face his fellow passengers. "It's attempting to turn us against each other: create distrust, discord." He spun about, arm jabbing towards me. It was an impressive act. "It would not surprise me if it was in league with him! They're both the work of the spell-singers!"

"What a heartening sight."

Nachollni sputtered to a halt at the sound of the new voice. Everyone in the carriage turned in the direction from which the words had come, all except me. I already knew what was there, or rather, who.

It was the Archimandrite: standing in the corner to my left, the rigid body of a Sharpshooter guard toppling slowly away from his still faintly glowing staff. Much too slowly to be natural, and too stiff to be still alive.

Sendivogius was dressed in his most dramatic style: violently coloured robes with huge dragon-wing collar that made him look like some particularly poisonous sea creature. He was carrying a tall, gold-leafed staff, topped with an abaston crystal bigger than a man's fist. The costume he prefers when he wishes to impress, and, I admit, I was impressed. Not by his garish dress, but rather that he was prepared to waste the huge amount of energy necessary to project all the way from Dak Talini. How many Chrysomancers were draining their crystals just for this show? He was either very confident or needed to appear so.

"My apologies for my tardy arrival." He gazed around like some benevolent uncle, his favourite pose. "I assume my lack of an invitation was an oversight. I'll ignore such ill-manners this once." The guard's body finally hit the carpeted floor with barely a sound.

The Archimandrite glanced down briefly and stepped over the corpse. "Please, continue with your fascinating discussion. Don't let me interrupt."

"What are you doing here?" gasped Alva. He had come to his feet, his face a good many shades paler now. The fact that he wasn't bellowing in his usual manner showed how much Sendivogius' interruption had alarmed him.

"Why, I've come to join you in your fascinating experience. Your 'Voyage Into the Unknown Lands of the Future!' Was that not how one of your sycophantic news-sheets described it?"

"Get out of here, wizard!" Rengalet was also coming to his feet. "Guards!"

"Don't!" I shouted. "They'll just shoot each other – or us. They can't harm him. It's merely a projection." While he was quite capable of hurting as, as demonstrated by the dead Sharpshooter. The Archimandrite enjoyed stacking the odds in his favour.

"Perceptive." Sendivogius glanced at me. I could tell he was trying to remember if we'd met before, if he could recall my face. He wouldn't, of course: I'd never worn this one before. After a moment, he dismissed all thought of me and took two steps into the carriage.

Rengalet leapt.

Side-stepping the major's reckless attack, Sendivogius raised his staff. The crystal pulsed once. Rengalet flew across the lounge, smashing into the far door. His body flopped to the carpet like a mound of washing.

"Foolish, foolish," the Archimandrite murmured.

"If you've killed him...!" Nachollni yelled, in full righteous flight.

"He will live. But it would have been just as simple to destroy him. Remember that." Even before Sendivogius finished speaking, Rengalet awoke, lacerating the air with non-stop oaths. The Sharpshooters who had been on guard were tending him. Sendivogius bowed slightly, as though acknowledging the major's continued existence as a tribute to his own control.

"Now, Professor Alva," he continued. "An impressive creation, sir. My compliments. You realise, of course, that I cannot let you complete your journey."

"You cannot stop me, sir!" Alva replied with more confidence than I felt. "If you interfere with the *Novandik*, the Chrysomancers will be exposed. It will be a declaration of another war, one which you know you cannot win."

The Archimandrite laughed. "My dear sir, I have no intention of being so obvious. Of course, we could not hope to best your unimaginative President and his pedestrian government in a war. None of us here are fools. We all know how powerless the Chrysomancy Party is at present. But that will change. In the meantime, you – and all the wonders of your blasphemous science and engineering, which have so enthralled the weak minds of the populace – must be demonstrated to be nothing other than dreams. The nebulous promises of fraudsters."

"Ah – we're all going to disappear in a tragic accident. Is that it?" Even though I was just within his arm's reach, the Archimandrite refused to acknowledge me further. It didn't matter. We both knew I was right. "Fall into the Riccobanni Swamps, perhaps? No – too late for that. We'll be out of them in an hour or so. Crushed in a landslide, then? Die of thirst out in the desert regions of Atchinor? Please, a clue is all I'm asking for..." Or be ambushed by the winged thing that's probably been pacing us ever since we left Scan Leroth, I didn't add.

"Could you silence your dog, Professor?" Sendivogius said calmly. "His yapping grows tiresome."

"Which can only mean he is correct, sir." Alva glanced thoughtfully at me before returning his attention to the Archimandrite. "Your war is to be with us, on the *Novandik*? A cowardly ambush that will reveal nothing of your hand?"

"The government will still know who was responsible," Nachollni added.

The Archimandrite shrugged, smiling amiably. "They will suspect, Senator, to the point of virtually knowing, perhaps. But that is still a long way from proof."

"Bastard!" Nachollni launched himself at Sendivogius, before any of us could move. Anyone except the Archimandrite, that is. Evading the senator's clumsy lunge, the wizard stretched out a hand. I couldn't be sure he even touched Nachollni, the movement was so swift, but in less than a second there was a vivid flash which left me temporarily blinded, and a scream. Then something crashed into my legs. I fell clumsily, landing on a gasping senator. He was still alive, but I didn't like the wheezing sounds coming out of him. What had he been thinking? He wasn't a fit man, and he'd seen what happened to Rengalet. Trying to prove something?

"You really must learn to curb this impetuosity," I could hear the Archimandrite say. "Patience is strength."

I kept blinking my eyes to clear the purple blot that had replaced the lounge. I'm sure there were tears – floods of them. Eventually, I could make out smudged silhouettes. Everyone seemed to be frozen in a tableau, the Archimandrite threatening all with his staff. Everyone was standing, but cowed. Only one figure seemed to be still seated, which had to be Batrix. Nachollni, struggling out from underneath me, was the only one left with any sense of movement.

"But, as I see I've outstayed my welcome," the Chrysomancer was saying, "I will take my leave." I found it difficult to hear him above the senator's laboured breathing.

Maybe it was my still-blurred vision, but an instant later, it looked to me as though the Archimandrite was no longer there. No fancy pyrotechnics, no claps of thunder. Which probably meant he regarded Alva and our party too highly for such parlour tricks. It also showed he meant business.

A guard began to help Nachollni to his feet. No one thought to give me so much as a kind word. Maybe they thought I'd already had a soft enough landing.

Nachollni and Rengalet were laid out carefully on the carpet, and Doctor Tork started to examine them. As nobody seemed to be thinking about me anymore, I groped my way back to my compartment. Business was concluded for the day.

Chapter Eleven

I didn't quite make it back. Halfway down the corridor of the passenger carriage a familiar bluff voice hailed me: Alva.

I stopped and turned. He came rolling towards me, still carrying his enormous cigar. Thankfully, it had gone out. He halted less than two feet away, blocking the corridor.

"How did Lieutenant-Commander Batrix find out about the abaston stone?" he demanded, his beard jutting in outrage.

"I don't know," I replied with a shrug. "Ask her."

"I did, sir; I did. She wouldn't tell me."

"Then you're out of luck."

As I turned to go, two podgy hands held my arm tightly. Alva's grip was a lot steelier than his size and condition would indicate.

"This Yosec," he persisted. "Was he really a government agent?"

"Why do you keep asking me, Professor?"

"Because it was made very clear to me that you – along with the senator, Doctor Tork and Major Rengalet – were to be added to my guest list, at very short notice, sir, very short notice. And at not an inconsiderable degree of inconvenience. I do not like inconvenience."

"Well, I appreciate your position, Professor," I said, disentangling his fingers, not appreciating it one bit. "But I don't know any more than you."

"You'll forgive me if I don't believe you, sir," he growled. He began patting his pockets. "Do you have a match?"

"Then believe me when I tell you I don't smoke," I said, relieved he wasn't able to light up in the corridor.

He frowned: first at his cold cigar, then at me. "You tell me that Yosec was a government agent—"

"*I* said no such thing."

"Whilst you yourself were placed here at the insistence of people at the highest level. Do you expect me to believe both of you were not, in some way, working together?"

I put on my innocent expression. "Commander Batrix knew nothing about the pilot, Professor, and she's the government representative on this venture. If the Bureau didn't bother telling her, what makes you think they'd inform someone like me?"

"And yet it's claimed you killed him!"

This was getting tedious. "No, I didn't kill him. *Gosigné* Thryme saw me walking down this corridor, and I admit to being up, unable to sleep. But no one claims to have seen me getting into the *Novandik's* cabin, leave alone clubbing the pilot to death. Not even a guard. Are you suggesting a Sharpshooter would miss something so obvious?"

Alva's complexion turned ashen again. It occurred to me he really ought to consult Doctor Tork. If someone didn't succeed in killing our eminent professor before we reached Scana Carsofi, he'd finish the job himself.

"I refuse to believe it was one of us, sir! That is, I think, your implication? Why not one of the stewards, or – or one of the guards?"

I shrugged again. "Anything is possible. But what you need to uncover, is a reason. Why should anyone want to murder a simple pilot?"

Alva made no comment. He pulled out a large handkerchief and swabbed at his face.

"Either because they were aware he wasn't just a simple pilot – which means they knew more than anyone on this journey had a right to know – or because they were frightened into believing *he* was the one who knew more than they should."

Alva lowered his handkerchief. He didn't look any less sweaty. "What do you mean, sir?" he muttered. "What do you mean?"

"The pilot of your locomotive-engine would be able to discover many things, Professor. Such as the power source..." I let that thought dangle.

His beard twitched as the muscles below it clenched. "Are you suggesting...?"

"You said it yourself: you have enemies. You also claimed Law could pilot the *Novandik* perfectly well. If you thought your big secret was about to be revealed, or stolen, I think you're the kind of man who wouldn't shrink from murder to protect yourself. Not after years of habitually ignoring any law which you considered inconvenient..."

I thought he was going to strike me. The hand clutching the handkerchief grew very white. For a moment we both stood there, a silent tableau, awaiting some climax. Then he strode rigidly away, too angry to even curse.

Back in my compartment, I unfolded the sofa into the narrow bed and threw myself onto it, rubbing my eyes. I didn't believe anything of what I'd said – even Alva wouldn't go so far just to protect a known secret. Even if it was only to a select few. But I had to keep everyone off-balance, until one of them stumbled.

A sharp cramp knotted my stomach, taking me by surprise. Withdrawal didn't normally come on so suddenly.

I propped myself up and scanned the compartment, before remembering the *chavet* was all gone. Even the drop Sanej had bequeathed me was drunk. This was a serious situation. If the withdrawal agonies were allowed to build, it wouldn't be long before I was a hopeless, unreasoning pile of self-pity. Death was perfectly possible. I'd seen it happen, once, as an object lesson back at the Seminary. It's a miserable way to go. Worse than any other death I can think of.

I stood, willing away the cramps for just a few more minutes. Alva had agreed to supply me with all the *chavet* I needed, but that was before our scene in the corridor. I didn't think that he'd be quite so kindly disposed towards me just now.

There was a knock from outside. I muttered something encouraging and the door slid open. Batrix was standing in the corridor, holding a very familiarly shaped bottle. I didn't dare hope...

She came in, shut the door carefully behind her, and handed me the *chavet*. Somehow, she managed to convey the feeling she was doing something underhand behind her own back and didn't want to know about it.

"You shouldn't have," I said, managing to stifle the urge to uncork the bottle and drink straight from it.

"I know." She seated herself in the armchair. Brushing an imagined piece of lint from her trousers, she looked at me evenly.

"How are Rengalet and Nachollni?" I asked.

"Well enough. The major was up and swearing quite imaginatively within a minute. The senator is still weak, but Doctor Tork is sure no permanent damage has been done."

"Serves them right," I muttered. I wasn't feeling particularly sympathetic.

"Did you gain anything from that piece of theatre?" Batrix asked.

"Theatre, Commander?" I gave the *chavet* one final, lingering glance, and put it down on the compartment floor, out of sight. Time enough for that when my heteromorph conscience wasn't about. "You expressed concerns over the extra guests on this trip. I thought you'd like the opportunity to examine them."

"On the contrary, you simply allowed me to tell everyone in Alva's lounge exactly how much we know about them. Air a few unpleasant details. If one of those is a wizard, and a murderer, I have effectively declared war on them. We have put them on their guard."

"The moment that connecting rod was melted they announced their presence. That's when war was declared. This is our way of acknowledging the fact and increasing the pressure. We're saying, 'We know you're there, and what's more, we know all this, too.' Certainly, they'll be on their guard, but they already were. This way we tighten up the anxiety a little."

"How?"

"Because our man will be thinking that if we're prepared to admit we know this much, how much more are we keeping to ourselves? It's a game, Commander. A nasty little game."

"And how much are you keeping to yourself, Scilli?"

"What makes you think there's anything more to know?"

Batrix sighed heavily. I don't think she liked this devious approach. A direct attack was more her style. "Do you have any suspects?"

I laughed, somewhat bitterly. "As far as I can tell, every one of them is a suspect. My only problem is that not one of them has a reason to murder Sanej."

"That you know of."

"That I know of." I dropped back onto the bed. "Very well, Wilonek Scilli, bold investigator, will correlate and compare. What have we got?" I stuck a thumb in the air. "One: Professor Alva. Driven, obsessed with his own success and sense of destiny. Not above ignoring the law when it suits him. Somehow, somewhere, he's being supplied with abaston crystals. Conclusion?"

"He has contacts with active Spook enclaves, if not with the Chrysomancy Party itself," Batrix replied.

"Very good. We'll make a detective of you yet." I added a finger to the thumb. "Two: the author, Boz. Member of *Plytath a'Pyndr*: the innocuous gentleman's drinking-club. Took great pains to assure us how harmless it was. But it isn't harmless, is it?"

"According to Bureau sources, *Plytath a'Pyndr* is to all intents a fundamentalist group which looks back to some mythical Golden Age, before the Spooks. When everything was peaceful and light and magic, as practised by Pyndrian Thaumaturges, had yet to be corrupted by what they see as more decadent wizards."

I couldn't tell whether Batrix was being consciously ironic. "And, of course, they want to return to this Golden Age of enlightened magic, which means getting rid of the nasty, corrupt wizards..."

"Correct."

"Along with science and technology, which are equally decadent. Am I correct?"

"You are well-informed."

"I read widely." I raised another finger. "Three: old man Thryme. For someone who is widely accepted as Alva's closest friend, he has a pretty jaundiced opinion of the man's achievements. Jealous, perhaps?"

"Undoubtedly. Thryme was an acknowledged star in his own firmament before Alva eclipsed him. He surely feels belittled by his own pupil."

"Very poetic, Batrix. Never let them say you have no soul. Well, unless the old man's a better actor than I give him credit for, he's not likely to be a wizard sympathiser."

"But he may hate Alva just enough to sabotage his greatest triumph."

"Exactly! We're devious creatures, us humans, don't you think?"

"I have always known that, Scilli," Batrix replied. I didn't bother looking, but it sounded as though she was smiling.

"Very well. Four: Doctor Tork. Putting our Pyndrian writer's racial bias to one side, Tork is from Atarqé. The last I heard, wizards still had that country firmly in their bony little grip."

"Correct. The native religion pretty well ensures Spooks are revered as gods. It will be many years before modern, enlightened thinking makes any headway there."

"If ever." Modern, enlightened thinking? And this from a creature grown in a vat as some bearded dolt mumbled spells over it? What strange times we live in. "Which means he could be just as big a fundamentalist as Boz."

"But he does practise modern medicine. Something no traditional Atarq would do."

"Never heard of a cover, Batrix? Remember Sanej: all those years working as a tutor to up-and-coming wizards?"

I heard her sigh. "I work as a simple Bureau representative, Scilli. No one talks about the..." she paused, as though in distaste "...other departments. People like Yosec might just as well not exist."

I straightened my last finger. "Five, then: dear Senator Nachollni. The man who became the saviour of the heteromorphs simply because he couldn't think of any other way. Delightful man."

"Being a glib politician does not make him a suspect." Her voice had lost all of its growing warmth. She certainly hated the good senator. Not that he didn't deserve it.

"Agreed. But do you know he came to see me shortly before you sent for me, offering me his support. He claimed you and Rengalet had already decided my guilt. Odd how fast that support vanished when he saw how the wind was blowing through the lounge. I haven't been able to work out what he really wanted."

There was no obvious reaction to my honesty. Maybe she couldn't think any less of Nachollni at that moment. "And that is no reason, either."

"I know. Worrying, isn't it?" I sat upright. "Him and Rengalet are the only two who don't seem to have any reason to either be saboteurs or working for the Spooks."

Batrix was looking at me, her head on one side. "And this worries you?"

"Of course. First rule: never trust a man who doesn't have at least one hidden motive. Sanej taught me that."

"You are twisted, Scilli."

"And here's me thinking you liked me for my big blue eyes."

Batrix fell silent, standing up with detached slowness. "It occurs to me that you already knew everything that was said at the meeting." She was facing the door, speaking soft and thoughtfully. "There was no need for it. At least, not as far as you were concerned." She turned to face me; her expression was as unreadable as it had ever been. "You had me arrange it merely for my own benefit."

"Not entirely."

"Thank you, Scilli. It was a valuable lesson." The ice was back, along with the iron-laced spine and frigid stare. Damn!

"I'm sorry, Batrix, but—"

She held up a silencing hand. "No, you were quite right. I needed to learn that no one aboard can be trusted. Perhaps I have learnt it too well."

She was about to leave when the entire compartment gave a shudder. It felt as though the whole carriage was about to collapse. Batrix stumbled, falling over the armchair.

I heard shouts, what sounded like explosions. The *Novandik's* shrill whistle cut the air. There was another shudder which almost threw me off the bed.

Moments later, we weren't moving. The entire train had slammed to a halt.

Batrix climbed back to her feet, attempting to regain some semblance of dignity. She smoothed at her tunic. "What was that?"

"Let's find out," I was already sliding the door open. "I suspect the Archimandrite has made his first move."

Chapter Twelve

Batrix and I leapt to the ground from our carriage's end platform. I almost landed on Pomino Thryme, who was pacing anxiously at the bottom of the steps, muttering incoherently. I couldn't be bothered to listen too closely. I was far more concerned with whatever had brought the rail-train to such a devastating halt.

We were out of the swamps, mostly, and the weather had improved. Thin pale clouds still covered the sky, but there was a promise of blue. I wasn't sure if there was also something else hiding behind those grey wisps: something big and many winged. The ground was still pretty level and wet, but short, spindly needles of stone rising from the damp earth announced the approach of more rocky terrain. The Kekathi Barrier was to the north now, a sullen bruise along the horizon. Once we left Jaqatlan, the haul up through the Drésdiracci Mountains would be the first serious test of the *Novandik's* abilities.

If it was still working.

As far as I could tell, the locomotive-engine was undamaged, although it looked curiously dead. There wasn't a trace of movement or steam that I could see. All four carriages had jumped the rails, leaning at crazy angles. At least none of them had fallen. I could see Rengalet and a group of his men already assessing the damage. I supposed if anyone could get the carriages re-railed, it would be the major and his band of Sharpshooters. You have to hand some things to the military.

Alva was already up by the *Novandik*, close to panic, if his rapid, pointless arm-movements were anything to go by. A couple of Sharpshooters were also with him, and even as I reached the locomotive-engine, two more eased the moaning shape of Law, the pilot-assistant, out of the circular cabin. He was clutching his right hand, his entire body racked with irregular spasms.

"What happened?" I called to Alva.

He flapped his short arms like a headless, overfed bird. No help there.

I glanced around. Doctor Tork and Boz were both coming rapidly towards us. "Tork!" I shouted, pointing at the injured Law where he'd been lain on the ground. "See to him. Quick!"

"Taking command now, are we, Scilli?" said Boz, his tone cryptic.

"Unless you want the job." I grabbed the handrails and hauled myself up into the locomotive-engine's interior as quickly as I could. I don't know how Law and Sanej managed it with such grace.

Inside it was all wrong. I should have felt the heat radiating off all that steaming water inside the machine's boiler. Instead, it was cold, near freezing. My teeth were chattering with seconds.

I stuck my head out of a window. Below, Tork was looking at Law's injured hand. I hadn't noticed before how unnaturally white it was.

"How is he, Doctor?" I called.

Tork barely glanced up, as though unwilling to take his eyes off the patient. "He'll live. Might lose his fingers, though. Perhaps the entire hand."

"Severe frostbite?" I asked.

This time he did look at me. The surprise on his face wasn't all reserved for my medical acumen, I'm sure. "Yes. But how does a man get frost-bitten standing next to a hot boiler?"

"Easily, when the boiler's about as hot as a glacier." I looked about, saw Alva. "Professor! Would you join me up here, please?"

A few seconds later, he appeared gasping, red-faced, at the top of the ladder. He floundered inside, followed by Batrix. She obviously had no intention of missing anything which might be relevant.

"What is it?" panted Alva, pulling out his handkerchief. He mopped his dripping brow.

"Stand here if you're too hot." I stepped back from the waves of cold coming off the metal.

He moved closer, the heated irritation on his face giving way to perplexity. "Impossible!" he breathed. "Impossible!"

"Not at all. Where does the abaston crystal go?" I could hardly admit that I already knew.

He stiffened immediately. Guilt? Or a reluctance to give away trade secrets? After a few moments, he bent – with some effort – and went to pull on the lever at floor level.

"Don't!" I yelled.

Startled, he almost collapsed back onto his rotund fundament. "You damn' fool—" he began to bluster.

"Do you want to lose your fingers, like Law?" I asked.

After a moment of prodigious scowling, he bundled his handkerchief around the lever, and pulled. The panel swung open, and Alva started to reach inside.

"Out of the way." I shouldered him aside. I'd worry about ruffling his feathers another time. I dropped to one knee and took a glance inside the panel. Alva huffed himself upright, no doubt aiming a battery of visual daggers at my unprotected back. I leaned in closer, my breath condensing in white, ghostly clouds.

I pulled back and looked up at Batrix. "Do you still have my pistol?"

"Why?"

I pointed at the open panel. "I need to get the crystal out and would rather not sacrifice a couple of fingers in the process."

She glanced at me, then the open compartment, weighing up possibilities. Eventually she dipped a hand inside a tunic pocket and removed my repeater. Movements cautious and stiff, she handed it over.

Using the gun's barrel, I levered the milky crystal fragment off its perch. It dropped and rolled across the cab floor.

"Don't touch," I said to Alva and Batrix. "Just hold your hand close. You can feel it."

Alva crouched awkwardly, aiming the flat of his hand towards the fragment. "*Tzénobog!*" he gasped, recoiling.

I noticed that Batrix managed to ignore Alva's unfortunate profanity. If anyone on board would be a rigid enforcer of the Suppression of Worship Act, I'd have wagered on the commander.

The professor came clumsily to his feet again, looking at me in surprise and concern. Batrix reached out her own hand. The faintest of frowns creased her brow, the only outward display she was prepared to make.

"What is it?" Alva said to me, almost pleading for an answer. "What?"

"You said yourself that an abaston's crystal structure can be tapped to release the energy contained as heat," I said. I was guessing wildly. I'm no expert, no matter what anyone thought, but it felt right. "Whoever did this must have somehow put your heating stone into reverse. Instead of boiling the water, it sucked all of the heat out of it."

"Ice?" Batrix didn't exactly sound incredulous, but it was a good imitation.

"She'll be damaged!" Alva cried. I guessed he meant the *Novandik*. "The expanding ice will have ruptured pipes. Maybe even cracked some of the forged moving parts!"

"Only if it's solid in there." Another thought hit me. "Did the crew know where the crystal was located?" Sanej had found out through professional nosiness, but would he have mentioned it to Law? It bothered me how the pilot-assistant had become so badly injured, so quickly.

"Not exactly. But both Law and Yosec had instructions that, should anything begin to go wrong with the heating, they were to release that lever." He gestured at the handle on the open panel. "Such an action stops the abaston stone's heating process."

Well, that explained it. Following instructions, as the *Novandik* began to lurch to a halt, Law had grabbed the lever. It wasn't all that hard to imagine just how cold the metal must have been. The abaston fragment would have been draining heat from everything around it, not just water.

"How does that stop it?" Batrix was demanding. Her literal mind wasn't going to let anything drop.

Alva balled his hands into fists. For a moment, I didn't think he was going to answer. "The process is purely mechanical," he replied eventually, and very testily. "A pressure of a few hundred pounds across the stone causes it to generate tremendous heat. A steel rod is forced down on the stone when the panel is shut, and the lever thrown. A simple interlock system. Pull back the lever, and the rod withdraws. It was a safety device initially, to ensure the stone could not be heated without the panel in place."

"Then Law must have loosened the lever just enough to release the pressure." Whoever had attacked the stone had effectively reversed the effects of compression. To cause such a fundamental change in a crystal not even attuned to them meant our spy was a very high-level wizard indeed. Fourth or fifth *shakrat*, at least. "I think he saved all our lives."

I could see Alva considering this very carefully. After a few moments, he backed out of the interior and lumbered his way down the ladder. I could hear him bawling at Doctor Tork, bullying him into doing everything he could for the unfortunate pilot-assistant. I didn't quite catch the good doctor's reply. Whatever it was, it only made the professor yell louder. At least Law was going to be well looked after.

"What do you propose to do now?" Batrix asked me. I wished she hadn't. I could see only one course of action, and it wasn't one I relished.

"I'm going to have to attune this crystal fragment to myself," I said. Was my brave, manly voice trembling, just a little? "And then reverse the effects of whatever glamour has been placed over it."

"I see." She paused a moment, taking a deep breath. "Have you ever attuned an abaston crystal?"

"No. School was cancelled before my class got that far." I know my flippancy annoyed her, but it was all I had.

"But you know what to do? The principle involved, I mean."

"The theory, yes. That was whipped into us ceaselessly." I slipped my pistol back into a coat pocket – Batrix saw but said nothing – all the while looking nervously at the fragment which was lying on the cabin floor. I could see ice forming around it, congealing out of the air.

"I know the first thing I have to do is touch it."

Chapter Thirteen

I had quite an audience for my attempted tuning: Alva, Boz, Nachollni, Rengalet, Thryme, Tork. Even Law was fascinated. It probably took his mind off the pain.

As I lay the crystal fragment by the trackside – wrapped in my frockcoat since it still showed no signs of warming up – I wondered how many in my audience wanted me to fail. Fatally, at that. There'd be at least one.

Most of the Sharpshooters were on sentry duty. Rengalet had decided it wasn't worth the effort trying to re-rail the carriages if our motive power was never to pull again. Besides, we weren't entirely out of the swamps yet, there was still the odd stagnant puddle nestling in rocky hollows or where the dirt was oversaturated. No one wanted to be caught by surprise if any relatives of the many-eyed thing Batrix and I had seen yesterday morning took it into their heads to come calling.

"Will this take long?" Rengalet asked. He already sounded bored, or he wanted to be somewhere else, somewhere with a good cellar. I just stared at him, not trusting myself to speak.

"What happens if you cannot attune the stone?" Alva called.

"Well," I said, peeling back the layers of coat and looking at the deceptively fragile and harmless fragment currently coated in a thick rime. "Those of you who're still in one piece will be stranded." It worked. They all but one took several shuffling steps away from me.

As usual, Batrix stayed exactly where she was. Was she as sceptical with everyone as she was with me, I wondered. Or was I just the lucky one?

"Is there anything I can do to assist?" she asked.

"Yes." I dropped onto my knees in front of the crystal, looking like a man at prayer. "If I do something wrong, you can pass this on to my next of kin." I rolled the deep-frozen chip of stone to the ground and tossed her the frockcoat. Batrix didn't bother to ask if I actually knew of any kin.

I leaned forward, not at all sure what I was supposed to be seeing. As I did so, a sudden, cruel shudder cramped my neck. I pulled myself upright, raising a hand. Sure enough, it was shaking. The withdrawal that had been threatening since the 'trial' was flexing its muscles. Now, of all times.

"Perhaps there is something you can do after all," I said to Batrix. I kept my voice low, not wanting everyone to hear. Even I have my pride.

"And that is?" she asked, just as softly.

I held up my shaking hand, trying not to appear too pathetic. She looked at me blankly for a moment; then the aloof hardness that pinched her eyes told me she'd understood. I could take her contempt. I just needed *chavet*.

She left quietly, taking my coat with her. I amused myself in her absence by looking at the abaston fragment from all angles, admiring the way the layer of ice was growing fractionally thicker with each passing moment, and wondering just how I was going to touch the crystal surface without losing my fingertips.

I knew that physical touch was just a part of the ritual. The real contact was on a much more spiritual plane. But spirituality has never played much of a part in my life. Even back in the Seminary I was always the one thinking about dinner when I should have been meditating. I have the scars to prove it.

"Here." Batrix's voice interrupted my thoughts. The *chavet* bottle from my compartment was dangling in front of my face. Concealed, I noticed with a stray pang of gratitude, by my coat. I took it quickly.

"You're an angel, Commander. A heavenly moon-maid." I uncorked the bottle and took a deep drink. The shivers disappeared almost immediately.

"Take it steadily, Scilli," she said, stepping back a little.

I slipped the bottle between my legs, safely out of sight. "Just wait until someone forces an addiction on you," I muttered.

I leaned forward, confident I wouldn't need any more *chavet* for several minutes. None of the ice had melted; the crystal wasn't warming up. I wished then that *chavet* had some kind of sedative effect, like alcohol, instead of just being addictive. At least then I could down the entire bottle, get recklessly drunk, and not feel the skin of my fingers being burned off by the cold.

"Do you intend to outstare the crystal, Scilli?" came Rengalet's distant taunting voice. "Or will we be seein' some kind of action before long?"

"If this fails, you'll have more action than you'll know what to do with!" I muttered to myself. There was nothing for it.

I licked my lips: my entire mouth was very dry. I reached out a hand. This time the trembling had nothing to do with *chavet* withdrawal. What was it Sanej and the other tutors had always said?

Focus through your fingers. Your hand is nothing more than a manifestation of your will. The physical touch is just an outward symbol of the real contact. One day, you will not need it...

It was fine for them. I bet they'd never tried attuning a crystal that was happily draining every degree of heat out of anything within range.

So, this was what ten years' selective memory loss came to: everything that I'd learnt at Madrasaté, everything that was driven into me with the slash of a cane, an entire childhood that I'd successfully buried up until then. I was going to need to dive back into those dirty waters and trawl up memories of a past life that may well damage me more than any amount of *chavet* withdrawal.

Who said you can't escape your past? If it had been Boz in one of his interminable social tracts, I was going to murder him. I hate smug, self-satisfied philosophy.

I tried to settle down, block out all external distractions. If Rengalet had made another remark at that moment, he would have beaten Boz to whatever reward the afterlife held for him. After what seemed endless days of sweaty effort – during which I was convinced I could never do it again, I had sworn I never would after all, never even try – I slipped into a trance. Although 'fell' might be a more accurate word for it. I was only aware of myself and the crystal fragment before me, which was pulsing, like some psychic beacon, dragging at me.

Slowly, terrified I was going to lose concentration and snap back into the real world, I tried to distil all of my awareness into an intense ball, force it down my arm and into the fingers hovering close to the crystal. It was a bizarre sensation. I was aware that I was not in my body, while at the same time I could feel myself contract into a bright pinprick of identity, a mote drifting around my organs.

I travelled through my heart and past my lungs – none of which seemed to be moving – down the entwined passages of arteries and veins, skimming the translucent blue-white sheaths of nerves and tendons. I felt myself being forced past dense bundles of pale red muscle, and finally into my hard, bony fingers. There I paused, taking a symbolic deep breath. I was going to need to move those fingers across the gap insulating their frail flesh from the crystal's deadly cold, move the arm of an organism that I no longer filled, make the leap through both warm flesh and frigid crystalline skins, and push away what would, by then, be disembodied hands before they became too damaged.

Easy. I was tough. I'd survived Madrasaté, where many had been crushed. I got out of bed every morning and could look myself in my borrowed eyes...

Feeling as though I was an ant pulling an elephant, I moved the arm, infinitesimally slowly, ponderous. I knew I could never force it back before the crystal had destroyed most of my hand with its awful cold. It neared the fragment. I felt the contact in my soul rather than a physical touch. I leapt across. For an instant the minute spark that was me froze, then it was seared by raging heat. I felt as if I'd plunged from the most remote depths of the void surrounding the world into the heart of the Sun. There seemed to be no way I could survive.

And yet, I clearly had. I was inside the crystal fragment, drifting along the blazing lattice. No, it wasn't the structure. What I saw – if 'saw' is the word for it – was that very power which Alva was tapping for his *Novandik,* and which the Chrysomancers had used for centuries. It mimicked the crystalline matrix, flowing over it like blood across a skeleton.

Well, I thought, now I'm here, what should I do next? I was just a speck, adrift inside a crystalline universe, and about as powerless. I had no idea how I was supposed to proceed. When I'd suggested the idea to Batrix, I was hoping there'd be some kind of clue if I made it this far – a sign saying *Open Here*. Instead, I was stuck in a bright cavern, with not so much as the remotest idea of how to get out again.

While I was thinking all that, quietly panicking, I hadn't noticed the gentle, insistent tugging sensation from all angles. It took this odd sense of being thinned out to grab my attention. And even then, it was several, subjective moments before it was obvious what was happening. The power lattice was hauling on my particle of consciousness, dragging at it from all directions. I was gradually being stretched across the crystal matrix, eased out like dough. Panicking even more, I tried to squeeze myself back into a concentrated point, but the crystal pull was too strong. No matter how slow or gentle, it was inexorable. It was going to tear me apart.

Yet again, I was wrong. The crystal knew better than I. Maybe this was how the first Chrysomancers learned how to attune themselves. Rather than tearing me apart, the power lattice was combining with my speck of consciousness, spreading me over the matrix like a second oily layer. For a few exquisite moments, both the crystal and I were one. Its power was the blood warming my body, the abaston crystal was my flesh. With no more effort than twitching an eyebrow, I could juggle buildings as though they were empty boxes. If I flexed muscles of pure force, I could move the world...

Then, the sensation was gone. Feeling more wretched than during any *chavet* withdrawal, I collapsed in on myself again, falling down through a crystal universe that was rapidly growing dimmer. In moments, it was totally black, but I couldn't stop the endless falling.

Chapter Fourteen

Someone was calling me. Their voice was sharp and clear, like a wineglass being tapped.

How did they get in here? I wondered. A Spook? Had the murderer followed me into the crystal to make sure I wasn't coming back? It was still dark, but I didn't seem to be falling anymore.

"Scilli!" The voice sounded angry and familiar. If only I could see. "Then I suggest you open your eyes!"

What? Open my...? Since the voice seemed to have more damned sense than me, I took its advice and forced opened my eyelids.

It was still dark, the dark of sundown. Batrix was looking down at me, her expression an uncharacteristic mixture of concern and anger. Well, the concern was uncharacteristic.

I was lying flat on my back, gazing up at a purple sky, in which a few stars were already coming out to play. Feeling like I'd already made a big enough fool of myself, I dragged my sore body into a sitting position. It was a mistake. The sky suddenly decided it didn't want to be above me anymore and took a nauseating swoop towards the ground. It flattened me somewhere along the way.

"Careful, Scilli," Batrix's voice seemed very distant. "You have been unconscious for quite some time."

"How long?" I think I said. I remember forming the words and doing all the things you do when you speak, but I couldn't hear them.

"Three hours. After you touched the crystal, you collapsed, and no one could rouse you."

The crystal! I pulled myself back up again, a little more cautiously this time. I looked at my hands: there wasn't a mark on either one. The cold hadn't harmed me.

I tried looking around, but my stomach was still too crammed with nausea. Each movement threatened to roll me flat on my back again. Batrix held something in front of my wandering eyes.

I squinted, forcing my vision into focus. It was the crystal fragment. She was holding it between two fingers.

"It's not cold," I said, demonstrating my amazing powers of observation.

She cupped my right hand and placed the fragment into it, clamping my fingers tight around the crystal shard. "I think you may call yourself a wizard from now on, Scilli." There was a certain bleak irony in her voice.

"Thanks." I didn't feel so happy at the idea either. I reached out an arm and, leaning on Batrix's shoulder, pulled myself to my feet. Rocking and weak-kneed, I finally got to look around. My audience had gone; they'd probably lost interest when all I did was lie on the ground. The *Novandik's* headlamp was lit, along with the carriage lights and a few more oil-lamps hanging off well-positioned stakes. I noticed all four carriages were back on the tracks.

"Someone's been busy," I said. "Rengalet been ordering the troops around while I slept?"

Batrix looked at me. She was troubled; even in my unfocused, wool-stuffed head state I could tell. "No," she said with a fractional shake of her head. "You did it. Whilst you were unconscious."

I did? I looked at the carriages again: all neatly standing on the rails, coupled to the *Novandik's* water trailer. For all the world as if that was how they had always been and always would be.

I did that?

I opened my hand and took another look at the crystal fragment. It worried me, more than ever.

"Alva will be needing this," I said. I wondered if I was still not talking clearly, since Batrix was giving me a very strange look. Whatever, as I set off towards the waiting *Novandik*, my legs weren't co-operating fully.

Alva was waiting by his precious locomotive-engine. He looked anxious. I hoped it was for his invention and not because he saw me coming. I held out the fragment between thumb and forefinger.

"All done," I said. "You can try warming the boiler up again."

For a moment, he looked reluctant to accept the fragment, as though wary about touching me. Then he sighed loudly and took it.

"That was quite a show, sir," he grunted, turning to start up the ladder to the machine's platform. "Quite a show."

"Hope I didn't snore in my sleep." I followed him up, praying he wouldn't slip. Inside the locomotive-engine it was still chilly. Evidently, three hours wasn't near long enough for however much water the *Novandik* carried in its boiler to thaw.

Alva was fitting the sliver of abaston into its niche. Before shutting the panel, he reached up to a wheel a foot or so above it and turned it to the left until it would go no further. Then he pushed the panel firmly shut and tugged the lever home.

He came awkwardly to his feet, breath whooshing out as though he was being squeezed. I'm sure I've met sicker men, but I don't recall where.

He was muttering to himself, his voice hoarse, the words guttural. "If we turn up the pressure slowly..." He began turning the wheel to the right, one slow degree at a time, all the while staring myopically at a dial. "Heat it through gradually... It might..."

I could see what he was thinking. If the water hadn't frozen solid throughout the engine – in which case our journey was all over – turning up the crystal burner a fraction at a time would thaw out the ice gradually, lessen the chances of any secondary damage.

I felt it the very instant pressure across the crystal began the power bleed. It was as though I was the one being crushed. I could even feel the heat building up, oozing through my pores.

"If you'll excuse me," I muttered. Alva might have grunted something, but I doubt he even heard. He was too intent on his dials and wheels.

I gracelessly stumbled down the ladder, barely avoiding falling. The further away from the locomotive, the better I felt. But I was still all too aware of the crystal's fate. Obviously, there would be no avoiding it.

Batrix was waiting, a few feet away from the *Novandik*. She was watching my less than dignified exit with her head on one side, arms folded, frowning. "Feeling no better?" she asked.

"I was," I muttered. I found the bottle of *chavet* in my coat – probably slipped in there by my stern guardian angel – and took a deep drink. It made no difference: the crystal's pain didn't go away. "What they failed to mention in class was just how intimate you get to an attuned crystal."

Her eyes flickered, from me, to the locomotive-engine, and back. She didn't say anything, but I she'd obviously worked it out.

"Now, if you'll all excuse me," I said, turning a little drunkenly towards the carriages, "I'm about to die on my feet. Bed, and real sleep are called for, I think."

I took one step, and even before I'd started the second, there was a cry from beyond the circle of oil-lamps. It was one of the Sharpshooter guards, and he sounded pretty troubled, which was bad since, as a rule, very little can trouble a Sharpshooter, other than being filled with holes before they get a chance to shoot back. As yet, I hadn't heard any shooting.

"Come on." I virtually dragged Batrix after me, quite a feat considering the state I was in. We headed towards the darkness beyond the lamplight, out of which the guard was still yelling. Gradually, his words began to make sense.

"Attack! Attack! Rally on me! Attack from the south-east!"

He had damned good eyesight. Even out of the lamps' glare, in the darker night, I could barely see a thing. I prayed that my eyes only needed time to adjust and it wasn't a side effect of everything I'd been through. If Riccobanni was about the throw us a farewell party, I needed all of my senses.

A dozen or more Sharpshooters ran past me, bayonets already fitted to their muskets. I couldn't imagine what they were going to do with them. If whatever was attacking us was anything like the creature which had loomed over Batrix and I, their bullets and knives would have as much effect as raw eggs on a cliff-face.

The firing started a moment later: a rapid salvo of large calibre fire, followed by a chorus of the loudest, highest-pitched wails I have ever heard. They pierced my woolly head like a cold knife. Something was hurt – or just plain irritated – and there was more than one of it. I felt for my repeater – Batrix had left in in my coat, illegal gods bless her! – drew it free and cocked it. I don't know what I thought a pistol could do that a musket couldn't, but the act was comforting.

Then they appeared out of the night, six in all, all something like fifty feet tall: heads no more than beaks lined with hundreds of teeth, hides which glistened like oily leather in the diffuse wash of the *Novandik's* headlight, striding upright on pairs of tree-trunk legs. Several pairs of gnarled, nastily taloned upper limbs flexed, snatching at the night air, as though already pulling us apart.

Six more Sharpshooters appeared from behind us and fired another volley. It had no effect. The things just wailed in chorus again, either in pain or simple defiance.

One swooped with a swiftness that seemed impossible. A soldier was caught up in half of the thing's sets of talons. The remaining ones ground him to mince before he could even begin to scream. It was almost merciful.

I pointed my pistol and fired. Even if I'd been at closer range, I doubt the shot would have had any effect. I cocked and fired four more times. The repeater misfired twice. Yet even so, I felt I was just throwing pebbles at a moving statue.

Rengalet appeared at my shoulder. He was yelling at his men, urging them on. I grabbed his tunic and spun him to face me.

"Fall them back!" I shouted into his fierce expression. He looked at me as though I'd made some crude suggestion about him and his mother.

"Fall back?" It may have been meant as a laugh, but the noise he made was too obscene to be called that. "A soldier of the Republic don't ever retreat!" His war-boosted self-regard was enjoying the chance for a bit of justifiable bloodshed. He was probably also more than a little drunk.

"Then he's a damn' fool!" I waved my empty pistol at the steadily advancing things. "Even mortars couldn't hurt those! Where's the honour in getting us all killed just to prove a point?"

"You're a coward, Scilli! I always suspected it!"

"And you're too stupid to know any better!" I turned my back on him, facing Batrix. "See if you can get some sense into our war hero!" I yelled above all the wailing and gunfire. "I'm going to see if Alva's got his engine working yet!" Not waiting for any objection from either her or the gallant major, I forced myself into a hobbling run, back towards the lamp-lit *Novandik*.

Alva was still bent over the controls. Only the needle on the gauge seemed to have moved. The pilot-assistant, Law, had joined him on the platform, his arm heavily bandaged and in a sling. He didn't seem any more capable of movement than the professor.

"Is it working?" I said, hauling myself into the cabin. Only Law turned to acknowledge me – and only fractionally at that.

"What?" muttered Alva, his muffled voice coming from somewhere under his coat. "What?"

I tried hard to keep my patience, but the renewed sensations of being slowly crushed and feverish heat were rapidly eroding my cheerful temperament. "Is the crystal warming up!"

"Yes, yes. Of course it is!" The professor favoured me with a fractional glance, which grew to a stare when he spotted my pistol.

"Trouble?" he asked softly. I think he believed the repeater was for him.

"Certainly." I pulled out a handful of preloaded paper cartridges, which held both ball and a measure of powder, from a waistcoat pocket. I started pushing them into empty cylinder chambers, tamping each one home with a ramrod pivoting at the barrel's side. "We need to get the *Novandik* running as soon as possible and as fast as possible, before heroic Major Rengalet gets all of his men killed in the name of the Republic." Once all five chambers were loaded, I dropped the spare cartridges back into the pocket and fished a load of firing caps from another.

"We'll be ready to move in half an hour or so," Alva said testily, returning his attention to the gauge and wheel.

"Which will be twenty minutes after we're all dead!" I capped each of the repeater's five firing nipples, shoved the remaining caps away, and cocked the pistol. Looking out of a window, I could just about make out the approaching shapes of the things. "You've got around five minutes, Alva!"

"You cannot be serious, sir! What if there are sprung rivets, or split pipes? We could all be blown clear back to Scan Leroth!"

"We'll be dead anyway if you don't!" I grabbed the back of his collar and hauled him, spluttering and purple, to the window. "Make your choice: them or the *Novandik!*"

He hissed something. I think it was the name of his favourite banned god again. It always surprises me how the most erudite men can still cling to the oddest superstitions.

"Yes," he breathed. There didn't seem to be much point holding him any longer. I let go and he turned back towards the controls, muttering abstractedly. "Yes. Full pressure. The water's above freezing now. It should take the heat. As long as there is no serious frost-damage to the boiler. Yes – full pressure." As he maintained this little conversation with himself, he was turning the wheel again, and with much less delicacy. I watched the gauge as intently as he did as it crept with alarming speed towards a red line.

"What happens if the needle crosses that line?" I asked, casual as you like.

"None of us will be around to notice," mumbled Alva.

"I knew it would be something reassuring." I returned my attention to the unequal battle outside. The six things were coming closer. Nothing Rengalet or his men were doing made the slightest difference. I wondered how many Sharpshooters had been lost already, and if Batrix was still alive.

Then the commander, Rengalet, and around a dozen Sharpshooters backed slowly into the full glare of the *Novandik's* headlight. The guards and heteromorph were all firing steadily at the oncoming creatures, reloading calmly, as though this was nothing more than target practise on a firing range. I expected that from the Sharpshooters, but Batrix?

Despite all the pounds of lead slamming into the things' bodies, they weren't slowing. Except for the strange wails – which for all I knew could have been cries of derision as much as pain – they failed to react. And why should they? The things were obviously creations of some wizard with time to spare. Something as mundane as powder and shot would be useless.

And with Sanej dead, there was no one on our side capable of doing the necessary: opening up a magical hole for them to fall into, throwing up an impenetrable barrier – whatever spell a practised wizard would use. I wondered if that had been the reason for his murder.

"Alva! We don't have much time!" I shouted. "Can we move yet?"

"A moment. A moment!"

I risked a glance over my shoulder. He was still huddled over the wheel, and the needle on the dial was perilously close to the red line.

"A moment's about all we have!" Looking back to the retreating line of Sharpshooters, I could see they were down to eight, but still reloading and firing with mechanical detachment. Batrix was no less cool, emptying her repeater into the jaws of the nearest creature, then retreating carefully as she reloaded. I wondered if I would have acted so calm.

"Whenever you're ready, Alva!"

The six creatures were no more than fifty feet away now. If they stooped they might almost touch the front of the locomotive-engine with those tooth-filled beaks.

"We have steam!" Alva shouted from behind me. "Steam!"

I leaned out of a window and yelled as loud as I could. "Everyone! Back on the train!" Over the cacophony of firing, the creatures' wailing and bellowed orders, I didn't think they could hear me. I sucked air into my lungs until I thought they'd rupture.

"Get on the train!"

Batrix turned and nodded brusquely. She grabbed Rengalet's arm and waved with her pistol towards the *Novandik*. The major acknowledged with a brief salute and began ordering his men back. Pausing for one more volley, they retreated at the double, racing past the locomotive-engine, climbing untidily onto the passenger carriage's balcony end. Batrix made it onto Alva's private carriage. I saw her waving at me over the water tank.

"Now!" I bellowed. A few more strides and those things would be sitting on us. I began firing myself, adding to the fusillade that continued to pour uselessly from balconies, open windows and doorways. The things were so close I could see the impact of every shot. Each one was absorbed with the faintest of ripples. It was like shooting into mud.

My nerves were at screaming point. Move, Alva. Move! Then, I was flung backwards by a massive shudder.

My first thought was that one of the things had seized part of the train. But we were moving. Slowly, we were gaining speed. The two driving wheels were spinning, trying to find traction. I smelled something like hot flint, and guessed sand was dropping from a hopper somewhere, adding to the grip. The wheels abruptly stopped spinning, the train shuddered again, and we were moving, faster and faster. We were accelerating to the top speed of twenty miles per hour at a rate I'm sure Alva had never designed the *Novandik* for.

We sped past the six things. Somehow we didn't hit any. Or maybe we just drove through one and didn't even notice.

I looked back. They had stopped, apparently giving up. That bothered me. They'd been close enough to reach out. The *Novandik* wasn't accelerating that fast. Some of their multiple talons could have raked the *Novandik*'s roof, or the carriages, as they passed. Had it all been a diversion? If so, for what?

I clapped Alva on the back. "Well done, Professor!"

He turned around and beamed smugly up at me. He obviously didn't need my good opinion of himself. "I shall remain on the platform until we reach Jaqatlan. There may be problems yet."

"Whatever you think best, Professor." Anything to keep him happy and quiet. For myself, I needed to get back to my compartment. But since Alva wasn't about to stop and let me off, and we were going too fast for me to simply jump down, I was going to have to climb across the water waggon and hop onto the balcony end of his own carriage.

Doing this in the dark on a stationary machine was one thing, but at twenty miles an hour?

Thinking about it wasn't going to get me across. Dropping my repeater back into its pocket, I stepped through the door in the rear and out onto a narrow footplate. For a few moments I stood there, clinging onto a handrail, looking back across the water car, and the trail of carriages swaying and bobbing in the *Novandik's* wake. And I'd thought the rail-road was level.

There was no sign of the six things out of the swamps. I could still see the abandoned circle of oil-lamps retreating into the night, but nothing else. So, they were almost certainly a decoy.

Keeping my eyes straight ahead, I reached out, grabbed a handle on the water waggon, and swung myself across. So far, so good. Next, I hauled myself up onto the round top, and began to edge myself, arms and legs asprawl, towards the first carriage. Perversely, my destination seemed to be getting further away with every moment.

I stopped to look around, the side of my face resting on the water car's cold surface. Alva was leaning negligently out of a cabin window, watching my progress with vindictive relish. And not so long ago, I had been the hero of the hour. How soon they forget!

Ignoring the professor's small-minded attitude, I turned back to face the way I was meant to be going. I could see Batrix watching me from the leading carriage's balcony, leaning against a metal roof support. At least she wasn't laughing.

Like some child who's still struggling to grasp the concept of crawling, I edged myself the rest of the way, slithering along the tank's polished surface, my fingertips trying hard to sink into the metal. Somehow, I must have managed to climb down the rear end and step onto the carriage's rocking platform. I have absolutely no memory of doing it.

"Enjoying the ride, Scilli?" Batrix asked. I hung onto the balcony's wrought iron railing as though it was the love of my life.

"I'm thinking about taking up an easier job," I mumbled. "Like a Riccobanni game-warden."

Batrix snorted and swung the carriage door open. At least I wasn't going to have to crawl across the roof again. I ducked through gratefully, and into Alva's bedroom. It was almost three times the size of my compartment but had little more in the way of furniture. The difference was that in here you could turn round without breaking a leg on something, and the plush looked several times deeper.

Batrix led me through to the lounge area. It was immaculate. You'd hardly imagine that a few hours ago the Archimandrite had laid out two of our passengers without messing a hair. I shuddered. I couldn't help imagining that His Nastiness was still around, watching us all and enjoying the comedy.

Then we were out and back in my carriage. There were Sharpshooters standing in the corridor – either by order or simply too overwhelmed by the luxury to go back to their own crude barracks on wheels. We had to squeeze past; none of them seemed particularly inclined to let us through. Was it me? I wondered. Or my chosen companion?

Last compartment. My stop. Before I could say anything to Batrix, she turned about and walked away. Not even a "Sleep well".

I shrugged and slid open my compartment door. In the lamplight, I had a moment to appreciate how efficiently the place had been wrecked, before something banged off my skull with an impact that made my ears ring, and the gloom turned to total blackness.

Chapter Fifteen

I don't think I was out long. Just enough for Batrix to reach her own compartment, see the mess it also had been left in, and hurry back. She found me stretched out on the floor, already coming round.

I recall being lifted onto the chair and opening my eyes – only to have them blinded by an oil-lamp standing on a table inches away. I must have groaned, or shrieked, or something equally manly, because the lamp was slid away, to be replaced by Batrix's features, equally close. As the light from the out-of-sight oil-lamp lit her face and passed through her blue lenses, it struck me that her eyes were brown, really dark brown.

"Are you hurt?" she asked. Her severe features looked softer somehow. It must have been the lamplight.

"Yes, thank you," I replied, pulling myself up straighter in the chair. "Do you have to stand so close?"

She flinched, the harsh planes sliding back into place. "If it offends you—"

"Far from it," I muttered softly. I probed my scalp gingerly, wincing at the goose egg I found nested there.

Batrix lowered herself onto the sofa-bed. She gave me a long, intelligent look. "In four nights, it will be the full moon," she said. In another situation, I might have said her tone was bitter. "And I will become a male."

The full moon. I'd quite forgotten that little detail. The thought made me feel odd, almost lost. "Ah, yes," I murmured. "Nothing ever stays the same, does it?"

I looked away and concentrated on my surroundings, now ruined; this had been an expensive compartment the last time I'd looked. Meanwhile, a little man with a very big hammer had woken up inside my skull and was flailing it about with gusto. I rubbed at my eyes. "Someone's obviously been busy."

"My compartment is the same," Batrix said. "Which is why I was coming—"

A cry of shock, or rage, interrupted her. It sounded like the senator.

"I don't think we're alone," I observed. "What's the betting every compartment has been ransacked?"

"Whilst our attention was diverted by the attack?"

"You're learning, Commander. Obviously, I interrupted our destructive party in mid-sack." I touched my battered skull. "I don't suppose you happened to see anyone coming out of here on your way here?"

Batrix shook her head. It had been a forlorn hope, anyway. If whoever it was had slipped along a corridor full of Sharpshooters, they'd obviously taken precautions. Magical ones.

Four enraged faces appeared at the doorway: Nachollni, Tork, Thryme and Boz. "Commander—" the senator began.

"I know," I chipped in before Batrix could speak. "All your compartments have been ransacked. Welcome to the club, gentlemen."

"But what the devil for?" protested Tork. He took off his pince-nez and waved them aggressively at the ceiling.

"Well, until we find out if anything's missing, we're not likely to guess, are we?" I looked at each of the angry faces. "None of you has bothered to check yet, I suppose?"

"We've only—" began Tork.

Batrix raised a hand, shutting him off. "Then I would appreciate you looking, Doctor. In an hour we will re-assemble in Professor Alva's private carriage. I imagine that will give you all adequate time to search thoroughly. Are we agreed?"

They all nodded and vanished back into the corridor.

I glanced at Batrix. "One of us had better find Rengalet. See if whatever meagre pieces a soldier considers necessary have been disturbed. Then you should sort through your own belongings."

She stood. "I will go. I doubt he will be inclined to pay you much attention."

"Then I'm going to have a drink – the real, alcoholic sort that sends your nerves into oblivion. After which, I'll think about tidying this mess up." I began to stand, winced at the increasing throb in my brain, and thought better of it. I was getting really tired of the constant war on my person. I wondered if there was any part of me that didn't hurt. "I'll see you in an hour."

She hesitated, on the verge of saying something more. Instead she nodded curtly and left.

After a while, ignoring my throbbing brain, I decided it was time I got that drink.

⁝⁞

About the only place you could get a drink in this place – outside Alva's private supply – was in the kitchen carriage. At least I didn't have to go far: left turn out of my compartment, step through the carriage's end door, hop from balcony to balcony, and I was there.

The kitchen carriage looked identical to the passenger's one, even on the inside, if you didn't take too long a look. The same narrow corridor ran down the side, but unlike the passenger carriage the rest was divided roughly in half. One section housed the resting area for the half-dozen stewards, two chefs and couple of assistants, in conditions hardly less spartan than those enjoyed by the Sharpshooters in their wheeled barracks. The rest was occupied by the kitchen and pantry, with storage, work-surfaces, ovens and cooking ranges ingeniously arranged to squeeze as much into the small area as possible.

Sandwiched between the two – little more than a widening of the corridor, mid-carriage – was a cramped, single-tabled dining area, laughingly called 'the café'. It was intended for anyone who fancied a quick snack or hot drink between mealtimes without troubling the staff. In reality, no one ever ate outside their compartments and didn't give a damn how much they troubled the staff. The stewards used it for their own relaxation. Who could blame them?

It was also the best place to find the drink I so sorely needed. However, I wasn't the only one who knew that. Stepping into the café area, I found Major Rengalet half-slumped over the table, gin bottle in one hand, glass in the other. His tunic was dirty with mud and smoke, the braids in his hair unravelled. Behind the fierce moustache his face was too shiny, his eyes wet and distant. This was not a man filled with pride.

He barely shifted his gaze as I carefully lowered myself onto one of the two other chairs. Sudden jolts of pain were multiplying in my skull.

"Lieutenant-Commander Batrix is looking for you," I said.

"She found me," he mumbled. "No more than a few moments ago."

Time passes in an unreliable manner when the brain starts to float in drink, but I believed him. Batrix had left my compartment less than five minutes before me, and the first place she'd look would be the Sharpshooters' black box. She'd have to pass by the café.

"Did she mention all our rooms have been ransacked?"

He nodded heavily. "Our waggon was done over too – a very hasty search, looked like: guns knocked over; gear thrown about. Me own kit was the worst. Ain't seen a thing like it since trainin' camp, d'you know..."

"Nothing missing?"

"Can't hardly tell – place such a confounded mess!" He splashed some gin into his glass and gulped at it. "Ain't likely, though. Ain't like I have anythin' worth takin'."

"Nevertheless, I'm sure Batrix will be grateful if you check."

He grunted, about as noncommittal as you can get.

A steward's face appeared through a hatch at the sound of voices. I ordered a brandy – a big one – and the face vanished back through the hatch with a brisk acknowledgment.

"How drunk were you when you led the charge at Ombarno?" I asked.

His eyes jerked up to meet mine. They were harsh with anger. "What d'you mean?" he snarled.

"Come now, it's hardly a secret..." The steward appeared with my brandy. He placed the glass before me and disappeared with a bow. I waited ten seconds before resuming. "General Skanocj had mentioned your drinking several times in unofficial communiqués. It was tolerated simply because it never interfered with your duties as an officer and soldier."

Rengalet laughed bitterly. "If I hadn't been so drunk, perhaps I'd never have taken the decision I did—"

"Making yourself a hero..."

"And losing the lives of hundreds of men in the process!" His affected, military accent had disappeared, leaving a soft, north-eastern burr in its place.

"If we'd lost that battle, it would have cost thousands more."

"So they say!" He poured himself more gin and practically threw it down his throat. I took a deep pull on my own drink, and wondered how long it would take to deaden my own pain.

"And ever since, you've been so consumed with guilt that you're now only a few sips away from a hopeless, permanent drunk."

"Is that why I'm here?" he demanded, the faintest whine of self-pity in his throat. "Commanding a company of foot-sloggers!"

"Men of the Golanek Regiment, Major. The presidential élite."

"Mud-skaters, every one of 'em! No matter how good they can shoot!"

"Your drinking goes back well before Ombarno, Major. Whatever you're scared of, I don't believe it's that the people of Ramini will discover their great war hero was blind drunk on the day he turned the war."

"Think what you like..."

"Or maybe it's because your father was simply a farmer on the Kant Ordotha. I imagine your fellow officers never let you forget that."

His fury was showing no sign of abating. "My father owned nearly twenty-five percent of the Kant! He was more than some dirt-farmer!"

"I don't suppose that made much difference in the officers' mess."

"To hear them speak, you'd think their families had lived in Ramini for two thousand years, instead of coming across with nothing but rags on their feet a few hundred ago, just like everyone else!"

I drained my brandy. It may only have been my imagination, but the man with the hammer in my head seemed to be flagging. "If you don't mind me using an army phrase, Major – horseshit! The mockery of a few upper-class idiots might be painful at first, but you're a major in the Eighteenth Villavinté Dragoons. A decorated war hero many times over. Mess opinion shouldn't bother you now, unless you're less of a man than I think you are."

"Then why am I here, eh?" he spat. "Important war heroes aren't assigned nursemaid duties!"

"You drink," I continued, despite the outburst, "simply because you feel guilty. But not because of the deaths of those under you, or because of your lowly origins."

The rage vanished from his face as he took a drink from the bottle, ignoring his glass altogether. I had the feeling he already knew what I was about to say.

"You have – how can I put it? – the same attraction to other men that I, for example, would have to a beautiful woman—"

He shot to his feet. "How dare you! I ain't goin' to sit here and—" The military dialect was back.

"Sit down, Rengalet." I tried to snap the words out, but instead they barely staggered, as worn out as me. "Your military buffoon act isn't fooling anyone. Sit!"

He collapsed back in his seat as though all the air had been abruptly pulled out of him. "How...?" He took another, long pull on the gin bottle. "How did you know?"

"Surely the point, Major, is if I know, how many others do also?"

Rengalet seemed to be sagging further into his seat. "I have always been ... discreet. I was so certain it was a secret." He looked at me directly, his bleary vision sharpening. "This is leadin' somewhere, I'm sure..."

"I would have thought it was obvious, Major. I am not judgemental, understand, but your lifestyle – your 'discreet' lifestyle – is still subject to the severest penalties in the military, I believe."

"Punishable by hangin', Scilli, as you know full well..."

"Indeed. And information such as I have – in the wrong hands – could be used very profitably, as some would see it."

"Blackmail, is it?" He almost sounded relieved. "Can't say I'm surprised, Scilli. You look the type..."

"Not I, Major!" I managed to sound even more offended than he had. "But others might."

He frowned ponderously. The gin wasn't helping him think clearly. "Now you've lost me," he muttered.

"The Spooks, Major. Or are you going to pretend you're not being blackmailed by some Chrysomancer?"

This time, he didn't leap indignantly to his feet, but the look in his drink-glazed eyes was agony. More than his pride had been hurt: this time I'd impaled his very honour.

"You think – you believe! – that I could be blackmailed into betrayin' me own country!" It came out in a pained whisper.

"Everyone has a price, Rengalet. Someone who takes refuge in a bottle just because of guilt over their sexual alignment might easily be bought."

He drew himself up in his chair. Despite his ragged tunic, dishevelled hair and drink-stained face, he managed to project a soiled dignity.

"I am what I am, sir," he said, softly but firmly. "I make no apology for it. But yes, fear of discovery, of exposure – yes, damn you, even guilt! – drove me to drink years ago. I am no less a man for all that. At times, I despise myself and my vile lusts; and at such times I will take more than is good for me. It is for myself that I hide, Scilli. My own pride and dignity – such as it is – that I pretend. But for Ramini, for President Thinos, I will face anythin': ridicule, sanction, contempt, death – even from a rope for my perceived crimes! If you'd asked for money to buy your silence, I would have paid it and damned your eyes. But I will not put me own selfish needs before those of me country!"

The hell of it was, I damned near believed him. Drunks can often wax articulate, but that was one of the most impassioned speeches I'd ever heard from someone with a whole bottle of gin inside them. "Well, Major. Sorry if I offended you."

He stood – a trifle unsteadily – and bowed. "I wouldn't expect a creature such as you to understand honour or dignity, Scilli. But I will accept your apologies, nevertheless." He made an attempt to neaten the frogging on his soiled tunic. "And now, per your suggestion, I'll go and see if me kit ain't all there, d'you know. Good day t'ye, sir."

He jerked another bow and strode back to his men in the barracks carriage, his pride and tainted dignity an almost visible mantle about him. There are times when I can almost envy people like him.

The man in my head was definitely losing his enthusiasm. I shouted for the steward. Another brandy should put him well and truly to sleep before I had to meet up with Batrix again.

Chapter Sixteen

Outside the carriage, a festival was in full, noisy swing. Meanwhile, I was looking in the vanity mirror above my compartment's washbasin, thinking how drawn the dark, swarthy features staring back at me were. It certainly wasn't the face of a man about to join in the celebrations; more like one about to shake hands with his executioner. Not my original, of course, and I still hadn't grown used to it. Not enough time. Had there been that much grey in the thick, black hair before I had boarded the rail-train? I honestly couldn't remember.

But I wouldn't have to endure it for much longer. If we ever reached Scana Carsofi, these particular features would be consigned to history.

Sanej had always refused to submit to face changing. The process didn't alarm him – though it did hurt like hell occasionally. He'd always maintained that after living with the same features for so long, it would feel like a form of betrayal. Like cheating on the wife he'd never had.

I sighed. Brushing at my suit, knowing full well it made no difference, I glanced briefly out of the window. Everywhere was gaiety: smiling faces and celebration. I felt like shooting somebody. I wasn't all that concerned who.

Before I could punch the stranger in the mirror, I walked out into the corridor.

After an hour, everyone had reported to Batrix faithfully. Not one of them could find anything missing. The only one whose accommodation hadn't been ransacked was Alva himself. Although the professor's carriage was normally locked, in all the excitement he'd forgotten, which explained how Batrix and I had walked through so easily. I should have thought something of it at the time. Thryme tried a half-hearted attempt to make something out of that detail, but no one rose to it. Whoever had been sneaking around would be certain to ensure their own compartment was just as messy as everyone else's.

Added together, I was left with three conclusions: our phantom room-wrecker assumed Alva's carriage was locked so didn't try; they were making some pointless attempt to put Alva in the frame; or they knew perfectly well the professor didn't have whatever it was they were searching for.

It appeared no one else had it, either. Or if they had, and it was now gone and they were keeping tight-lipped about it.

Once Batrix had dismissed everybody, I'd given up thinking about it and gone to bed for twelve hours, most of which were spent asleep, no doubt aided by the two brandies. When I woke up, we had crossed the border into Cotechatl and the whole train had drawn to a halt in the pretty border-town of Jaqatlan, the festival already in full-throated commotion.

With nine dead already, I didn't feel much like celebrating.

I stepped out onto the balcony platform with trepidation. I hate parties, and this one was certainly one of the biggest I'd ever seen. It was hot, too. Although the sun still hadn't managed to boil away any of the thin clouds, there was a damp, warm breeze oozing up from the south, all the way from the coast. Despite the ocean being over a hundred miles away, the air was spiced with brine.

A seething crowd of locals surged around the train like multi-coloured porridge. Everyone was dressed in the local costume: a gaudy mixture of coloured silks and lace – for both men and women – that owed precious little to the peasant dress it was supposed to represent. How many peasants can afford more than one change of clothes, let alone ones as bright and rich as these?

There were no buildings in sight, but a few market stalls had been set up on the edge of the crowd. They were doing a roaring trade in local wine and stuffed cornmeal pancakes. The smell was surprisingly enticing.

I could see the blue shakos of Sharpshooters dotted among the heaving mass, so a few of them were out enjoying themselves. No doubt the rest of the guests and crew were swallowed up in there somewhere. All, I thought, except Batrix. Try as I might, I couldn't imagine her throwing her rigid dignity to one side and joining the throng. She was probably stuck in a corner somewhere, a pained expression on her face, untouched drink in her hand. If I could find her, we could be miserable in tandem.

I stepped down off the platform and was engulfed by the crowd. I was overpowered by the combined aromas of sweat, overpowering perfumes, alcohol, and oddly enough, sugar. It was terrifying. I was glad Rengalet had left most of his men on board, mounting a heavy guard of both the *Novandik* and its train. In a mass like this, anyone could sneak on board.

If it came to that, anyone could slip a knife through some unfortunate's ribs. I renewed my mental rosary of curses to heap on Alva's fat head. He had insisted on accepting the mayor of Jaqatlan's invitation, despite everyone's strongest objections: Rengalet, Batrix, Nachollni, my own, not that anyone listens to me. I imagine he wanted to bask in the adulation of a bunch of provincials who didn't know any better.

I spotted Alva, leaning through one of the *Novandik's* windows, addressing the crowd. He must have been standing on a box. His beard was split by a huge grin as he shouted down to the admiring court. His face was flushed and shiny, quite aglow with self-regard. And there was Batrix, standing between locomotive-engine and water waggon, almost out of sight of the crowd, but with the professor in easy view. Arms folded, her face was a blank picture of studied indifference, just as I'd thought. Only the drink was missing.

I considered joining her, but I heard movement behind me and turned, warily. It was Pomino Thryme, shuffling uncertainly through the carriage door onto the balcony end. He halted, eyes widening in alarm at the sight of the crowd. I understood perfectly. In that mêlée, a man as frail as he appeared would last about as long as a peach in a mangle. I sat down on the lowest carriage step.

"They call this a festival," I remarked. "I've seen friendlier battles."

Thryme gazed vaguely down at me for a moment, his rheumy eyes trying to focus, despite the palsied shake of his head. "They're an excitable people," he wheezed eventually. "They want to celebrate the arrival of a wonder. It's not every day that the greatest inventor in the world passes through in his most fantastic creation." His voice was too thin for me to be sure, especially over the background noise, but it sounded to me like he was being heavily sarcastic.

"I don't see you joining in much."

"I'm too old for such things."

"Then I must have been old for a long, long time." A cold shudder clenched my body, unannounced. *Chavet* withdrawal already? But I'd only just...

Except I hadn't just anything. *Chavet* addiction is no respecter of sleep. As far as my body was concerned, over half a day had gone by. Sleeping or awake, it didn't matter.

There was a hip flask in my pocket which I'd filled with decanted *chavet*. It was so much easier than having to dash back to my compartment when the need arose. I started to reach for it, then dropped my hand. It could wait. The chills weren't anything like bad enough yet.

I looked across the quivering mat of heads into the distance. I could see undulating hills, the start of our climb up into the Drésdiracci Mountains. "How far away is Jaqatlan?" I asked.

Thryme looked uncertainly about before motioning over his shoulder. "Five miles south. When the rails were laid, Tissa was more interested in the best route than how near the towns were."

"Unfortunate if you want to get on board," I commented. So much for servicing the needs of the country. "Anyone with goods to send to Scan Leroth or Scana Carsofi faces one hell of a walk."

"That will change," the old man said with peculiar confidence. "Towns can expand; new spur rails can be run off the main road. This is not the only rail-road Tissa plans, *Gosigné* Scilli. If this one line can prove itself successful, he hopes to persuade President Thinos to let him build dozens of new roads, criss-crossing the Republic, covering hundreds of thousands of miles."

An alarming thought: dozens of *Novandiks* steaming back and forth across the country, each with an abaston stone heating the boiler. I could see the wizards going into a new trade, robbing rail-trains for their crystals.

Another shiver crept up my spine, and my teeth clattered. I wouldn't be able to hold off for long.

There was a bout of cheering from the crowd. I looked towards the *Novandik*. The mayor of Jaqatlan had joined Alva on the locomotive-engine's platform, and the two men were standing with arms thrown about each other like long-lost brothers, waving at the crowd with free hands. It was nauseating.

The mayor was barely taller than the professor, and almost as wide. His uniform was as elaborate – and as bogus – as the traditional costumes flowing below him. He was dark-skinned and black-haired; his moustache waxed into two magnificent shiny wings which arced from his face. Not bad for a man patently touching his seventh decade. I decided he and Alva deserved each other.

"My friends!" the mayor called out, waving his free arm again at everybody present. If he thought that included me, he could think again. "I want you to join with me today in welcoming our distinguished guest, Professor Alva, and his miraculous new machine, the *Novandik!*"

There was a carefully orchestrated roar of spontaneous applause for the professor. He beamed benignly at everyone; his modesty as false as the mayor's hair-colour. I noted that none of the other passengers on the journey rated a mention. Perhaps the mayor really was as parochial as he looked. I wouldn't expect him to have heard of either Boz or Thryme, but I couldn't help wondering if he had something against Senator Nachollni or Major Rengalet. After all, Cotechatl was one of the first Territories to be made a Constitutional Estate by a grateful President, in recognition of the role played in ending the war. Hell, Jaqatlan had even hosted the Surrender!

A frigid cramp twisted my guts, followed closely by several seconds of chills. I clenched my teeth against the shakes. I was going to have to take some *chavet* pretty soon.

"Withdrawal?" Thryme wheezed. I took a deep breath and waited a few moments. Nothing more happened. I nodded.

Thryme's quavery head bobbed erratically. "I sympathise."

I wasn't feeling up to his sympathy just then. "And what would a clock-maker know about it?" I snapped.

He held up his right hand. It shook as badly as his head. Funny I hadn't noticed before. "Do you see this?"

I nodded.

"Do you know what it is?"

I nearly answered without thinking. After all, he was an old man, shakes were to be expected. But I caught myself before I spoke; he wasn't doing this just to show me his eyes and hands weren't as sharp as they'd been.

"Javier's Palsy," I said. Instantly, I could understand some of Thryme's anger at his old student. Javier's Palsy had been diagnosed three or four centuries earlier, when a seventh *shakrat* Chrysomancer, named Ilion Javier, deigned to wonder why so much of the forced labour – human and heteromorph – digging abaston stones from the earth was afflicted by the same symptoms: shakes, rheumy eyes, gastric disorders and eventual death. Although wizards aren't naturally given to medical curiosity, Javier had done some research. It took him very little time to discover it was caused by the abaston.

Crystals are pretty stable things. You can throw them around, heat them up, freeze them, and nothing much happens unless you're the wizard attuned to them. As I'd found out for myself. But during mining, it's inevitable some get chipped or broken by the heavy tools. When that happens, Javier discovered there was a release of some kind: a force or energy, perhaps related to the heat release that Alva had discovered. Although not dangerous in itself, exposure over a lengthy period – and slave workers were at it night and day until they dropped – produced the effects that were to be named after their discoverer: Javier's Palsy.

Not that the wizards stopped using humans and Switchers to dig up their ore, but at least they could give the cause of death a name.

"Alva careless with his work?"

Thryme gave me a bleak look. "He discovered that pressure released heat very quickly, and he knew perfectly well the effects of exposure to damaged crystals." There was no mistaking the bitterness in his voice now. It was clear even above the chatter of the crowds around us. "But he was driven. You've seen how he acts: blundering through and over everything and everyone in his path. It took him several years – and many destroyed stones – before he knew exactly how much pressure to apply. And how much was too much…"

"During which time you were frequently exposed," Another arctic chill drifted leisurely up my spine. I clenched my teeth to get the words out. "But why not Alva? He's not a well man, but he doesn't look like a Palsy victim."

Thryme raised both hands, twisting them together, as though he could squeeze the shaking away. "Tissa never had my dexterity." His face twisted as he said this. "His fingers were always too short, too fat. It was my job to align the crystals, perform the minute adjustments to his pressure equipment."

"Whilst he stayed safely out of range." No wonder Thryme threw him out, and why he hated him. Was that hate strong enough for him to sabotage the *Novandik*?

"Take a drink of that stuff if you need to," Thryme was saying. "At least you can alleviate your pain."

That was all he knew. Another cramp gripped me, dragging broken pieces of glass through my bowels. Enough of the noble suffering. Pulling the flask out of my coat pocket, I uncapped it and took a deep drink, relaxing as the cramps faded blissfully away.

Except they didn't. Another spasm of chills shook me violently. I bit my tongue. I doubled up, as if clutching the icy blade that was working its way deeper into my gut. The wave passed. I gulped down more *chavet*, yet that only brought on a fresh attack.

I rolled off the step, barely feeling the hard ground as I rammed against it. Trying to hold my hands steady, I poured a little out of the flask into my upturned palm. It looked like *chavet*. I took another sip. It tasted like *chavet*. The next wave of agony had me on the ground, raking at myself, groaning and snarling.

It wasn't *chavet*. Not only wasn't it soothing the pains of addiction, but each mouthful was also making the withdrawal worse, amplifying the terrible cramps ten-fold.

I had to get back to my compartment. There would be some *chavet* there, in its bottle. Real *chavet*. Its luminous blue body able to stroke away the pain. I was in agony.

I staggered upright, almost tripping over the carriage steps as I looked for the way back to my carriage. There were people everywhere, on all sides, pressing closer to the locomotive-engine to see the great professor and hear what he had to say.

I pushed forward. Dark faces stared at me in alarm, and then I heard laughter. Look at the drunk, they all seemed to say: let's have fun with the sodden fool.

I staggered forward, arms flailing. I couldn't blot out the garish sea of faces, the blazing teeth. Wet mouths and painful gouts of colour swirled around me, pulsing forward and back, forward and back. I no longer knew where I was, or in which direction my carriage and my compartment, lay.

I was going to die.

The gnawing in my guts grew more insistent. I just wanted to drop to my knees and curl up: get away from the pain. Whatever was in my flask was potent stuff. Deadly.

My eyesight was fading. I let myself go with it, riding it down to sweet, final oblivion. Peace at last.

All right, Wilonek Scilli, I heard a harsh voice, *you talk tough. You can trade bitter ironies with the best of them. Now prove how tough you really are: walk back to your carriage.*

I tried to laugh, but I groaned and stumbled some more instead.

This is the real Scilli, is it? the voice sneered. *Once life starts to get too hard, he just wants to lie down. Give up. Run away.* I didn't much care for the voice's attitude. What gave it the right?

"Sanej?" I muttered. I don't think the words got past my throat. Sanej always was a martinet from the 'cruel to be kind' school of thought.

If you do not have the stomach for it, just give in, Scilli! The Novandik *can manage perfectly well without you.*

Damn that voice! My vision swam back from wherever it had gone. I was still standing, just. The crowd of Cotechatli were still milling around me, enjoying the free show.

Another gut-wrenching cramp almost ripped me apart. I wanted to howl. Tears drowned the prancing shapes around me. Colours ran together like an abstract painting.

The pain subsided again. I blinked away tears. Over the swarming heads I recognised the cabin of the *Novandik,* and inside it something faint, remote. Something I could barely feel through the numbing pain, yet woken by my proximity.

The crystal.

The fragment of abaston, clamped away in the teeth of Alva's machine, it was attuned to me. I could feel it responding to my presence, my pain. It could save me. Perhaps.

I lunged towards the locomotive-engine, swatting at the figures rearing grotesquely on all sides. I fixed my eyes on the machine, keeping my eyes fastened on it, no matter how much it bucked and tossed. Like an unbroken horse, it tried to rear away from me, snap its reins. But I held on. Neither the *Novandik* nor my treacherous body were going to keep me away from the crystal.

My hands seized iron rails. Slowly, pain rippling through me with every step, I began to climb up towards the platform. But it was so far away. Clouds were forming around the towering peak of the roof. Mist began to roll down the sides towards me. I would be lost. Stranded in the fog, miles above everyone.

The rails vanished beneath my hands, and I fell forward. Groping through the thickening mist, I felt the metal of the platform under my fingers. On my hands and knees, my body feeling like it was stuffed with broken glass, I groped towards the panel: my crystal's prison. The mists swirled, blocking my vision. The terrible cold flayed the skin from my bones. Invisible mountain trolls disembowelled me.

Then, I had the lever in my hands. With what little strength and feeling I had left, I pulled it open, reaching for the fragment I couldn't see. It urged me closer, encouraging me: a mother to her toddling child.

The trolls were angry. I was going to escape them. They were howling out their fury, crashing great boulders together. My fingers closed around the piece of abaston. I cried out to it like a deserted lamb. It answered.

৩৩৫৫

The lack of sensation was blissful. The pain was gone so completely that I felt numb all over. I didn't want to move. I just wanted to lie motionless on the platform whilst the trolls raged all around me.

Trolls? I opened my eyes. The trolls were part of the withdrawal, surely? No, they were there. Alva and the mayor, looming over me, trying to out-shout each other.

"What is the meaning of this, sir?" Alva was managing to drown out the mayor, but it was a close-run thing. "What do you think you are doing?"

"Surviving, Professor." I dragged myself to my feet in painful stages. Every muscle ached. I felt about a hundred. But I was alive. I was going to have quite a bit of pain for the rest of the day to remind me. Again. "Proving how tough I really am."

Batrix was standing by the rear door, leaning against the frame as though she hadn't a care in the world. She was smiling. Just. I think I knew what that thin smile meant.

Voice in my head, be damned! No wonder it had sounded so familiar!

Chapter Seventeen

Four Sharpshooters were detailed to carry me back to my compartment, despite all my protestations that I was fine. I didn't get a very smooth ride. I suspect the four guards were pulled from the off-duty pool, not happy at being dragged away from the party.

After dropping me carelessly on my lowered sofa-bed, the four disappeared fast. My failed murderer could have come in and finished off what he'd started with the fake *chavet*. Everyone seemed to be exploiting every opportunity to remind me of my place on this trip.

Doctor Tork appeared at my side abruptly, as if he'd materialised there. He glared down at me as though he considered my collapse some kind of personal affront.

"So, what happened to you, Scilli?" Even before I could reply, he was pulling back my eyelids and staring hard at whatever my eyes revealed.

"Weren't you there?" I asked. "I thought I was the highlight of the day."

He half turned and opened up an impressive-looking doctor's bag. "Always ready with the funny remarks, aren't we, Scilli? What are you hiding yourself from, I wonder?"

"Me? Whatever there is, Doctor. But you didn't answer my question."

He forced my mouth open, pressing down on my tongue with a foul-tasting metal rod. He grunted. "If it's any business of yours, I was helping some of the natives in the crowd. Backward peasants are always getting carried away on occasions like this. Several women had worked themselves into hysterical fits." He took the rod out of my mouth and dropped it back into his bag.

"I trust your gentle healer's ways put them right, Tork." I could still taste whatever liquid he used to swill his instruments with. Rather belatedly, it occurred to me the rod might have been poisoned.

Tork stood up straight and gave me his most piercing look. "You don't like me, Scilli. Perfectly fair. I don't enjoy your company much, either. But it pleases my professional soul to tell you that I can find nothing wrong with you. Whatever was in that poisoned drink has left no lasting effects. And to answer your question, yes, I did set the women to rights again. They may be simple peasants, and I, Doctor Bronex Tork, but above all else they were patients and I the physician."

"Very commendable." I swung myself into a sitting position. "But your bedside manner could still do with improvement."

"If you want a bedside manner, find yourself some obsequious quack who'll charge you two hundred *dinari* to tell you exactly what you want to hear." He snapped his bag shut. "I'm interested only in the truth."

"And charging four hundred."

He stabbed his pince-nez towards me. It made me feel glad he wasn't holding a knife. "Yes, I am expensive, Scilli. But I'm also the best damned physician in the republic! Otherwise, why would Gawn Thinos employ me?"

"Maybe it's your overwhelming humility?"

"Damn me, but you're an odious creature, Scilli! How dare you presume to judge your betters! What would gutter trash like you understand?"

"Ah, what indeed." I lay back on an elbow. Tork's outburst was quite entertaining, in its way. "For example, how about I know for a fact that all Ramini students sent abroad for study were recruited by the Spooks as minor informants..."

He stopped dead. His pince-nez slowly drooped from their threatening angle. "What are you suggesting?"

"Suggesting? Nothing in particular. But you certainly know a deal more about the *Plytath a'Pyndr* than the average medical student. Despite that entertaining tale you gave us in Alva's lounge, very few Pyndrians have even heard of that particular drinking club. Fewer still talk about it."

For several seconds, Tork made no sound or movement. Then he shoved his pince-nez into his waistcoat pocket with an angry motion and snatched up his bag. "Yes, it's true, I was forced to spy for the wizards during my years in Pyndria, and I did unearth a little about the *Plytath a'Pyndr*. For some inexplicable reason the pathetic little society was of some interest to them."

"Then you know it's neither little nor pathetic."

Tork sighed irritably. "Very well – yes, yes. It does seem to have insinuated itself throughout every level of Pyndrian society and government. But surely that is Pyndria's problem, not Ramini's. What has any of it to do with me?"

I gestured vaguely with my free hand. "Maybe nothing. But it does occur to me that a man recruited as a boy might still be working for the wizards."

He threw his bag back onto the bed, barely missing my legs. "I resent your accusation, and strongly deny it!"

"Of course you do. But you admit your family originated in Atarqé, a country where wizards still have almost total control. Perhaps your loyalties aren't as clear cut as you'd have us believe?"

"You have absolutely no cause for this slanderous—"

"The *chavet* that nearly killed me was adulterated, Doctor. Something a wizard could easily do – or someone with apothecarial skills. I believe that Atarqi physicians are also apothecaries?"

"The extent of your knowledge is becoming very annoying, Scilli."

"Is that a threat, Doctor?"

"Merely an observation. Yes, in my parent's country, healers are also magical practitioners. They have no choice: it's a matter of law. But they are little more than witch doctors compared to medical practises in Ramini. I am a physician – a scientist! I have no more idea what constitutes that foul elixir of yours than I do the colour of the Archimandrite's bedroom walls! And I have no intention of subjecting myself to your foul, unsupported innuendo any longer!"

He made a grab for his bag again and slammed my door wide on his way out. In all, a very accomplished performance.

I flopped back onto my bed again, squeezing my eyes tight as a brief swirl of nausea tugged at my brain. "The drapes and bedding are blue, everything else is gold," I muttered to myself. "Even the carpet."

Shortly after that, I drifted off and slept clear through to the morning. The sounds of fun and enjoyment outside my carriage didn't bother me at all.

Chapter Eighteen

Batrix and I rushed for my carriage's rear door, slamming aside a guard who had made the unfortunate choice of standing in our way. He looked confused and affronted in equal measure. Bursting through the door, we could see the kitchen carriage, about ten feet behind the train and slowly dropping further back. A steward was standing on the end balcony, staring at us helplessly. None of the carriages had any kind of braking equipment.

We'd left Jaqatlan some two hours earlier and were already climbing steadily into the Drésdiracci Mountains' lower foothills. The incline wasn't particularly steep – that delight lay ahead of us – but it was enough to drag at anything not coupled to the second passenger carriage. Slow, stop, and eventually send into a gently accelerating ride back down towards Jaqatlan.

And somehow the kitchen and barracks carriages were no longer connected to the rest of the rail-train.

Major Rengalet was watching the widening gap with exaggerated interest. He was hanging on to our balcony rail with one hand, the other clutching an empty bottle of gin.

The rail-train came to an abrupt, juddering halt, almost toppling Rengalet from the platform. I grabbed at his tunic, hauling him back – not that he showed an inch of gratitude – then leapt for the ground.

I ran forward along the length of the train, towards the *Novandik*, cursing at every stride. Law, the pilot-assistant, was leaning through an open window. His face was screwed up with confusion.

"Wesh 'eppenin'?" Amplified by worry, his Sebite accent was thick enough to grease the locomotive's pistons.

"We've lost the last two carriages!" I yelled back, leaping for the ladder up to the platform. "Get this thing into reverse! See if you can catch them up!"

He looked horrified. "On deesh trek? She'll jum' der railsh!"

I swung inside the *Novandik*, pulling out my repeater pistol, and waved it under the terrified pilot-assistant's nose. "I didn't ask your opinion!"

It's remarkable the effect one of the professor's patented firearms has on an unarmed man, no matter how unreliable. I dread to imagine a time when the design's been perfected and everyone has access to a five-shot pistol. Without further word, Law threw a lever. Slowly, the *Novandik* began to reverse.

I pocketed my gun to show how much I approved. "Keep it steady. And be ready to brake when you're told."

He nodded vigorously. Guessing he could be trusted to carry on unsupervised, I backed out of the cabin, shinned down the ladder and hit the ground running. Even going slowly, the rail-train was travelling at more than half my normal running speed. I'd never make it to the second – now last – carriage before wearing myself down. Instead, I hopped on board Alva's private carriage. The two Sharpshooters on the platform levelled their muskets, pointing them in my general direction.

I waved impatiently at the end door. "Open it!"

Neither of them seemed inclined to do so. I think one may have been the guard I'd slammed aside earlier; he wasn't going to get caught again.

Moving even before I knew what I was doing, I grabbed one musket – wrenching it out of the guard's hands – and tossed it away. A moment later, I had the disarmed Sharpshooter by the throat – if he was the one I'd caught by surprise earlier, it just wasn't his day – while I aimed my pistol at the other's face.

"What if I say please?"

It took several agonisingly slow moments before the guard weighed up the options. Eventually, he lowered his musket and fumbled with a set of keys. I leaned out from the balcony as far as I could, using my unfortunate guard's throat as an anchor. There were no real bends in the track, and I couldn't see the rogue carriages. There was no way of knowing how far behind they'd fallen.

The carriage door swung open. I threw my guard against the other and pushed inside. Dashing through the sleeping area, I was in the lounge a moment later. Alva was there, trying to block my way through, managing to look both angry and bemused. The flesh visible through his whiskers was mottled and ugly.

"I demand to know what is happening, sir!" he barked. "I demand it!"

"We're trying to catch up to the last two carriages." I elbowed him to one side, propriety be hanged. "Someone's thoughtlessly uncoupled them."

Leaping the gap between carriages, I ran along the passenger carriage's corridor, re-joining Rengalet and Batrix on the rear platform. The major was standing watching the disconnected kitchen carriage with the indifference only found in the profoundly drunk.

The rogue carriages were no closer than they'd been when Law had braked the *Novandik*, yet no further away, either. As far as I could tell, both they and the rail-train were about matched for speed, but that wouldn't last. The longer the rogue carriages were left to roll on down the slope, the faster they'd get. Eventually they'd be running too fast for the track, and either jump the rails or come flying off at a bend. Law wasn't going to push the locomotive-engine much faster, and I could see why. The *Novandik* wasn't designed to run water waggon first, and over such hurriedly laid track, speed was inviting disaster. I don't suppose our passenger carriages would take kindly to being raced over uneven rails either.

I turned around to go back inside, but Tork, Nachollni and Boz had joined us. They were crowding each other for the best view, blocking my exit. I pointed at the senator.

"Nachollni, get back to the locomotive-engine and try to persuade Law to open the machine out more. We'll never catch them at this speed!"

He looked back at me, making no move. I clenched back the urge to throw him through the door at his back to start him on his way.

"If you'd be so kind, *Gosigné* Senator." I was unctuousness personified, it worked.

He bowed curtly and made his way down the platform steps and stood to the side of the track, waiting. Even he was fit enough to grab the *Novandik's* ladder as it steamed past him. I found myself half hoping he'd slip under the wheels.

"And meanwhile we wait?" Batrix said.

"Unless you've a better idea."

The kitchen carriage looked to have gained a little on us. If somebody didn't come up with a plan soon, two carriages, full of catering staff and off-duty soldiers, were going to provide us with a front row view of destruction. The steward was still standing on the balcony end, watching us staring helplessly back at him. I hoped he'd do something intelligent and jump off before it was too late. I didn't want to be still looking him in the eyes when both carriages sailed off down a slope.

"What's keeping Nachollni?" I muttered. Surely the senator had reached the *Novandik* by now? So why wasn't the rail-train speeding up? Every moment saw the last two carriages slipping further away.

"Use the abaston stone."

It was Batrix, standing close enough to be rubbing shoulders with me. She murmured again, too soft for anyone else to hear: "Use the stone."

"Stone?" I hissed, somewhat less circumspect.

"The one in the *Novandik's* boiler," she replied, impatient that I hadn't already thought of it. "Are you not attuned to each other?"

I almost laughed out loud. A lifetime's indoctrination in the chrysomantic arts, and I have to be reminded of that by one of my erstwhile tutors' creations. There are times when I'm convinced that there is, after all, a god, and he created us just to have something to laugh at.

I reached out, trying to feel that contact which I'd experienced only twice before. There was something, far, far away ... almost over my mental horizon. But I couldn't get any closer. It felt as though the harder I tried, the more skittish the contact became, and the further it pulled away.

I let go. "Useless," I murmured. "Either I need to be closer, or it's too busy being drained of what little power it has left by Alva's machine."

"Unfortunate." Her whisper was devoid of any emotion.

I continued looking at the lone steward gazing back from the slowly gaining kitchen carriage. His terrified expression seemed to be specifically aimed at me. I smashed my fists against the iron balcony rail. I had never felt so damned helpless!

But why wasn't the steward trying to get away? The rogue carriages weren't moving that fast!

"Jump!" I yelled. The steward shrugged; he didn't seem able to hear me. I cupped smarting hands around my mouth and shouted again, the word tearing at my throat. *"Jump!"*

This time he moved. He turned and called something back through the door behind him, and then lurched towards the balcony steps. For a moment he paused, staring at the ground that was streaming past below him.

"Do it, you idiot!" I shouted. "You're dead anyway if you don't!"

I saw him ball his fists and leap.

And be smashed straight back onto the platform.

Any other time, the expression on his face would have been comical, but it simply added to the icy pit that had dropped open in my guts. The steward was sealed in. Whoever had released the coupling pin between our carriages had first taken the precaution of making sure no one was going to escape.

No wonder none of the Sharpshooters had leapt off. I can imagine our thoughtful secret wizard, just to be on the safe side – or maybe as an extra sadistic touch – isolating each vehicle. The soldiers and staff were going to their graves sealed within their own particular carriage.

"Law!" I screamed at the sky. "Get this hell-damned piece of junk moving faster!"

He didn't hear me, of course.

The rogue carriages reached a sharp bend and began to follow it round. The rails were tracing the curve of a cliff-face, the track-bed cut into freshly exposed rock. It was less than a hundred feet down the slope to the thickly wooded level ground below, but it might as well be a thousand. Even a fifty-foot drop would be enough to smash the wooden carriages to shards. Sealed inside, no one was likely to survive.

"If they can just make it to the level," I muttered to myself. I thumped the balcony rail again, keeping rhythm with my words. I felt a hand on my shoulder. I glanced around at Batrix. She looked as haggard as I felt. She shook her head.

"You cannot help them now, Scilli. Come away."

She tried to pull me back inside the carriage, but I resisted. I wanted to watch. I needed to.

"Get everyone inside!" I ground the words out. I could barely move my jaw; my teeth were locked in a permanent snarl.

Batrix didn't move. She simply stared back at me, defiant, stubborn. Just another day when everyone knew better. Then something inside her relaxed, deflated. She turned away, shepherding Boz and Tork back inside the carriage. A moment later, I was alone at the end of the rail-train, except for Rengalet, who was too far gone to know what was happening anymore.

"Welcome to the club, Major."

Right up to the last moment I was expecting the *Novandik* to make a sudden lurch. I was hoping we'd catch up with the fleeing carriages, and somehow make a rescue. But we remained doggedly at the same speed. The rogue carriages slipped further and further away; the bends grew more frequent. With something like seventy feet to go to level ground, there were two sharp bends, one after another, twisting first to the right and then the left. The soldiers' wheeled barracks jumped the rails, dragging the kitchen carriage after it.

I shut my eyes. But I could still see that lone steward standing on the end of the carriage as it tumbled and smashed down the slope. His face wouldn't leave me.

After a few moments, I opened my eyes. The track ahead was clear. But to the left, sprayed across the slope, were the remnants of the two carriages.

The derailment had split them both open. Smashing through the trees clustered along the incline had finished them off. There were shattered timbers and twisted fingers of metal strewn across the slope. No sign of movement.

The *Novandik* began to slow. Law didn't need telling. I was off the carriage platform and stumbling down the slope before it had come to a halt.

I kicked unidentifiable planks aside. Some were dull black, some bore glossy hints of the Ramini flag. I wrenched at the pieces of iron and steel that had embedded themselves in the ground. There were plenty of bodies. All broken, none breathing.

I became frantic, desperate. I threw chunks of debris aside in a crazy search for someone – anyone –alive. I tripped over an axle hidden under a shattered pile of planking, and lay there, not sure whether I should be sobbing or gasping in pain.

Hearing footsteps crunching through the wreckage made me look around. It was Batrix. Good old faithful Batrix. She stooped, caught me under the arms, and pulled me to my feet.

"It is over, Scilli," she said quietly. "Leave it."

I felt myself beginning to laugh. It was a stark, uneasy sound. After hearing it I shut myself up. It made me nervous. I felt inside my coat pocket and pulled out a hip flask of *chavet* – the pure, unpoisoned stuff. Taking a deep swig, I noticed how much my hand was shaking. "What about burying them?"

"Leave that to the Sharpshooters." The few that are left, she didn't add.

I nodded and glanced up at the waiting train. Pale and unhealthy-looking faces were peering from windows. Death had left its mark on everyone. I began to walk up the slope, carefully picking my way through shattered pieces of carriage and tree.

Nachollni was waiting for us, his face drained of colour and glistening. I thought he was about to burst into tears.

"I'm sorry," he muttered. "But Law wouldn't make the machine go any faster. Nothing I could say—"

"Law," I muttered. I pushed the senator aside and strode straight for the *Novandik*. I could already see Law's Sebite features peering out of a window. He looked scared. He needed to.

Once I was within range, I began bawling at the pale, sweaty pilot-assistant. "Why didn't you speed up? All those men are dead now! You could have saved them!"

His hands waved through the window: a gesture of helplessness. "Der profesha! E wou'n' lemme—"

"What d'you mean!" I grabbed the ladder, ready to climb up onto the platform and start taking my anger out on the man. "Where was Alva?"

Law pointed a shaky hand toward the private carriage. "Dere! 'E kep' shoutin': 'Too fesht! Too fesht!' I wesh too shcared...!"

"What was the senator doing all this time?"

"Tryin' t'argue wich der profesha. But even der sheneta coon chenge der profesha's mind! Dey kep' arguin' – beck en' forch, beck en' forch..."

"Alva!" What the hell was he thinking? I jerked away from the ladder and stalked back towards the private carriage. No one tried to stop me going through the door this time. I kicked it open. "Alva!"

He didn't answer. Unlikely he was out getting his precious hands dirty. Hiding in shame somewhere?

"Alva!"

I tripped over something. I almost kicked it aside before recognising it. A small, podgy hand. Alva's, of course.

He was crammed into the small space between the foot of his bed and a dividing wall, crumpled and curiously tiny. It looked like a damned uncomfortable position, but since he was clearly dead, I don't suppose he cared all that much.

Chapter Nineteen

I didn't have much time. Sooner or later, someone was going to walk in and discover Alva's body. That would be bad enough, finding me still with it would be disastrous.

I dropped onto my knees by the body's side. I bent low, almost grazing the carpet with my nose. There was no obvious bruising on Alva's neck, and very little blood, eliminating him being bludgeoned to death. A fatal spell, maybe? There were plenty I knew of, and plenty of Chrysomancers capable of casting them. Or maybe he hadn't been murdered at all. Maybe Alva's death had been from natural causes.

And maybe Sanej caved in his own skull out of sheer boredom.

Straightening up, I gave his body a cursory examination. None of the exposed skin had any kind of marks, or at least nothing recent. I quickly frisked his pockets. There was nothing in any of them, none of the huge cigars he favoured, no matches, no handkerchief – even his pocket watch was missing.

I got to my feet. Either the killer was also doubling as a thief, or his employers weren't paying him enough.

Next, the sleeping area. It was untidy, suggesting someone had made a very hasty search of the place, even more so than the one I was doing. But Alva having one last, final seizure could equally have caused the mess. I couldn't afford second guessing.

Pulling out my pistol – maybe I wasn't as alone as I thought – I opened the door to the lounge and stepped through.

It was in an even bigger mess than the sleeping quarters: furniture was overturned, upholstery and drapes were ripped, the carpet was rucked and untidy. So much for natural causes. Our mystery compartment searcher had finally gotten around to Alva's private carriage, unfortunately for the professor.

Now I had a problem: what to do if someone arrived. It wouldn't be too long before they finished collecting the bodies and creating a temporary graveyard. We certainly couldn't take the bodies with us. If someone like Tork wandered in and found me in a half-wrecked compartment with Alva's corpse...

When they discover the professor, and the mess that has been made of his private carriage, it was going to have to be on my terms, in my time.

I left the carriage from the lounge end. It took only a moment to locate a couple of Sharpshooters: a sergeant and lance-corporal. They were standing alongside the train, just staring down the slope at the wreckage below, watching their comrades lining up the dead in neat rows. The lance-corporal's face was bloodless.

I dropped to the ground. Both heard me and turned in my direction, muskets coming to bear on my coat buttons. They were nervous, justifiably. Judging by their expressions, they'd be only too eager to find a scapegoat.

"Sergeant. Just the man." I started to take something out of my coat's inside pocket, freezing when his musket was raised further. I pulled back my coat to reveal that there was nothing underneath it. "I need to show you this. I'll be careful if you are." Slowly, I dipped into a pocket and withdrew a folded and sealed sheet of paper. Holding it between two fingertips, I offered it towards the sergeant.

"What is it?" He was still suspicious.

"Read it. If anything leaps off the page and tears you apart, your lance-corporal there can still shoot me down."

"Thin comfort to me." He took the sheet off me, not looking all that mollified, and broke the seal. I noticed the other Sharpshooter had taken me at my word: his musket was aimed straight for my head. If the sergeant sneezed without warning, my brains would be all over the carriage sides.

A few seconds later, the sergeant snapped to attention, grounding his musket hilt with a stamp. For a moment, the lance-corporal looked baffled, then decided it was probably best to follow his sergeant's example. Sometimes military discipline can be useful.

I held out my hand for the paper. It was returned with a sharp salute. "Now, I have a few orders for you. They are to be obeyed without question and at the double. Is that understood?"

"Sir!"

"Good. I want you to round up all of the guests on this trip..." I waved down towards the wreckage "...I imagine you'll find most of them down there. Once they're done, of course. Bring them to Professor Alva's private carriage. Then mount and maintain a guard on all sides. No one leaves or enters without my permission. Is that clear?"

"Sir!"

"It's possible Major Rengalet will try creating a fuss – if he sobers up in time – but I'm sure you know your duty, Sergeant."

"Yes, sir!" Was there more enthusiasm to that reply? Had Rengalet managed to alienate his men with his attitude and drinking? It wasn't hard to imagine.

"Thank you." I started to climb onto the balcony again when a thought struck me. "Could you make sure Lieutenant-Commander Batrix is the first to arrive? Give us five minutes before you bring in the rest."

He saluted again. "Whatever you say, sir." He snapped to attention once more, turned on a heel, and marched away. The lance-corporal fell in behind him. I got back inside Alva's carriage.

I could do nothing but wait until Batrix arrived. There was little point in trying to search further, mainly because I didn't know what I was looking for. Whatever it was, the killer still hadn't found it, that seemed pretty certain.

I passed the time by gazing out of the carriage windows. The Drésdiracci Mountains loomed in the west like a jagged wall. In the late afternoon sun their peaks glowed black and silver. The highest of all – Mount Ponosan – still bore a sugary cap of snow. Somewhere up there was the Treniccni Pass, a high-altitude gorge, some several thousand feet above the sea, often impassable during the winter. But, as with the mule trains that would soon be replaced by steel and steam, this was still the only way Alva's rail-road could reach the west coast, and Scana Carsofi.

There was a knock on the door, and I turned in time to see the sergeant ushering Batrix through. She looked tired and grey, her blonde hair was harsh and dull. Once the Sharpshooter had gone, shutting the door behind him, she remained exactly where she'd been left, staring at me.

"I have been given the impression I should be saluting you." Her voice sounded hollow and defeated.

"Are you all right? Do you need to sit down?" She looked about as healthy as Alva had last time I'd seen him breathing. It wasn't a cheering comparison.

"I am perfectly fine, *Gosigné* Scilli. The sergeant hinted that you needed to see me urgently."

Well, if she insisted. "This way." I beckoned for her to follow and walked into the sleeping area. I pointed towards Alva's body without a word. None were needed.

Batrix's grey features sagged even further. She stepped forward two steps. "Did you kill him?"

"Even if I had, I'd only deny it."

She nodded, sighing deeply.

"I'd appreciate you taking a look at the body," I said. "See if you can find anything I missed."

Batrix got down onto her knees with the stiffness of an old man. She was suffering. It was the approaching full moon, of course. The changes inherent in a heteromorph's life were heralding their arrival.

She examined the corpse with a peculiar fastidiousness, holding her body and head back as far as possible, whilst stretching her arms and hands to their maximum. Everything she touched was with just her fingertips. But for all that, I don't think she left any part of the corpse or clothing unexamined.

When Batrix had finished, she came to her feet, rubbing the palms of her hands on her trouser legs.

"Anything?" I asked.

"Nothing obvious externally, or not that I can see. There is evidence of old scarring on the tips of all ten fingers, though."

"The result of years spent playing with fire."

"Do you have any conclusions about his empty pockets?" She was still looking at the body with a weary fatalism.

"The killer was in a hurry. Maybe the train had already come to a halt when Alva discovered him. There was no time to waste searching his pockets for whatever they think is so important—"

"So, they used magic." She made it sound dirty.

"Displacement spell. Anything and everything in the professor's pockets is transported instantly to wherever the killer wants."

"Such as their own compartment?"

"Exactly."

She turned to face me. "Then we must begin a thorough search immediately." She tried to walk past, but I grabbed her arm.

"No, Commander. First, our killer's already had the chance to sift through whatever Alva was carrying and dispose of it. Second, time is exactly what we don't have."

She looked at me questioningly.

"The rest of the passengers will be along shortly." I shifted my grasp and, guiding her by the elbow, led her towards the door. "Shall we join them?"

∞

The sergeant's timing was immaculate. Within a minute, all of the remaining passengers were assembled in the lounge. With one exception, they looked irritable and tired. Major Rengalet was the odd man out, his ruddy features now pale and sheened in sweat. Despite the perpetual drunk's talent for sobering at a remarkable rate, I knew after a couple of gins, he'd be incomprehensible again.

I summoned the guard. "Where were they all?" I asked quietly.

He thought for a moment. "Except for the major, they was all in their rooms, sir."

"And where was Rengalet?"

The Sharpshooter's face pursed itself into disapproving lines. "Hanging over the rail at the end of the train, sir. He didn't look well."

"I bet. Thank you, Sergeant. Maintain a guard outside as agreed."

He snapped a salute and marched away.

"Would you be kind enough to tell us what's going on, Scilli?" Nachollni demanded loudly, once again the self-elected spokesman.

Without a word, I beckoned everyone to follow. Batrix preceded me, opening the sleeping quarters' door and holding it as I, and my band of disciples, filed in. Before everyone's eyes could fully adjust to the dimness, I pointed towards Alva's misshapen corpse.

"Now, which of you is responsible for that?" I asked.

189

It took a moment for my words, and the shape, to register. When they did, a collective groan filled the compartment. I scanned each face, trying to read individual reactions. Thryme looked resigned, perhaps even relieved. Tork glowered. Nachollni's expression was of a man witnessing the destruction of his entire world. Boz showed no reaction at all. Rengalet simply gaped stupidly. This was nothing I didn't expect. But then, I already knew my man was a consummate actor. He'd proven that time and again.

"It's all over," the senator muttered. I could almost believe he was close to tears.

"Alva, perhaps," Batrix said from the doorway. "But not the dream."

"I never thought you were the dreaming type, Commander," I said. "But, yes, Alva's gone, and we need to know how. Doctor Tork, can you perform an autopsy?"

He looked round at me, expression close to mutinous. "I am not some paltry surgeon-dentist, sir!"

I bit back an angry retort. I should not allow myself to be needled by his professional pride. "Indeed not, Doctor. But you will have instruments with you, I imagine. And you've already told us that you studied anatomy."

He sniffed, barely mollified. "Of course…"

"And the professor was – at least for the duration of this journey – your patient. There's no one here better qualified." My words echoed Sanej quoting Gawn Thinos: *I want the best there is on that train.* Well, if base flattery's good enough for the President, I can live with it.

"I'll need to fetch my bag." He started forward.

I held up a hand, not wanting him to discover he wouldn't be allowed to leave. "No need. A guard will bring it." I looked towards Batrix. "Commander, would you ask the sergeant outside to bring the doctor's bag?"

She nodded and left, allowing the door to swing shut. Even if her natural caution didn't order the sergeant to search the bag, I was confident a Sharpshooter's cultivated distrust would make him do it anyway.

"And what if he's the murderer?" Rengalet muttered thickly.

"Who? The doctor?" I gave out a bleak laugh. "And what if his is? Alva's already dead. I don't see that he can do much else. Unless you think he'll amputate the soul we're supposed not to believe in."

"You are tedious, Scilli," snapped Tork. "Rengalet I can forgive, he's barely been sober the last two days. But I think you enjoy being deliberately offensive."

"I do my best," I said, still smiling.

"Gentlemen, please." Boz righted the compartment's only chair and threw himself languidly down. "Let's not begin this tiresome mudslinging again. It only benefits our murderer." He began to pull a long cigarette from his case.

"I'd appreciate it if you didn't smoke," I said. "At least, not until the doctor's finished his examination." From the corner of my eye, I saw Tork frown. "There may be toxic fumes involved. Tobacco smoke could mask any distinctive smell."

The Pyndrian shrugged and put the cigarette away.

"Perhaps he wants to cover up a smell," Rengalet slurred. "Perhaps he knows exactly what killed the professor."

Boz pointedly ignored the major. Seeing that he wasn't about to get any response, Rengalet made his heavy way towards the door and swung it open. "I need a drink," he muttered, vanishing into the lounge.

"Perhaps we should all have one." I gestured towards the door. Nachollni, Boz and Tork stepped through eagerly enough, but Thryme seemed reluctant to leave. The sag in his shoulders – indeed, his entire body – suggested loss, but his face was unreadable. Was he torn, reluctant to leave his old friend, or did he intend to hang around and make sure Alva wasn't about to get back on his feet again?

"*Gosigné* Thryme?" I prompted. He didn't seem to hear me or pretended not to. "*Gosigné* Thryme!"

His head jerked up. He gazed around as though he'd just awakened from a nightmare. I pointed at the door through to the lounge again.

"Shall we?"

He nodded briefly and trudged past me like a man in a trance.

In the lounge, everyone had arranged themselves in a similar pattern to our first meeting a few days earlier. Rengalet was by the drinks again, but this time he'd poured himself a large gin. Boz was sitting carelessly in the centre of the parlour, smoking the cigarette I'd denied him earlier. Nachollni was floating about the carriage like a soul in limbo. Thryme had slumped himself listlessly beside the author. Batrix was already standing over by the exit, pretty much in the same place as I had last time. How times change.

This time, I took centre stage. There was no point in trying to play the feckless amateur detective any longer. The joke was wearing thin, and by now our man would have learned the truth anyway. I spoke into the silence.

"We know the professor was still alive when the two carriages were uncoupled."

Nachollni stopped his aimless wandering and interrupted. "He was alive up until the crash. That Sebite assistant and I wasted precious minutes trying to persuade him the locomotive needed to go faster!"

"Yes. Law told me about that. Curious."

There was a knock on the door. Batrix opened it. The sergeant entered, carrying Tork's bag. The doctor took it – virtually snatching it off the Sharpshooter – and treated us all to his hardest stare, before retreating to the sleeping compartment. I nodded my thanks to the guard, who left smartly.

"You were saying that something was curious," prompted Boz, blowing out a plume of smoke. "In what way?"

"Well, partly because I find it hard to believe that even Alva would put the safety of a machine over the lives of two dozen men..."

"Then you didn't know Tissa," sighed Thryme. He raised his head, but his eyes refused to focus on anyone.

"Maybe. You would know better than anyone, *Gosigné* Thryme. But my main objection is that the only time Alva was not within sight of a least one other person was immediately after the crash."

"Your point, Scilli," muttered Nachollni. He made for the drinks cabinet and poured himself a generous brandy. Rengalet clutched at the gin bottle as though he was worried the senator was likely to run off with it.

"My point should be obvious. After the crash, we all came off the train. Always assuming that the killer even had the time to upend this carriage and murder Alva, who was there on board to do it?"

"I assume from this reasoning that you believe one of us present is the culprit?" asked Boz, waving an arm at the lounge.

"Of course."

Nachollni drained his glass. "Why us? Why not one of the staff?"

I stared back at him, hard. "Granted a guard or steward could have had access to Sanej – the pilot Yosec – but you're forgetting: all of the stewards, the train captain, and most of the Sharpshooters, are lying in graves at the bottom of a slope outside. You think one of them did it?" I was shouting now, glad to be able to release some of the tension and anger I'd been supressing.

The senator flinched. "One of the surviving guards, then..."

"Prepos'rous!" Rengalet waved his glass at Nachollni, almost losing his grip on it. "I'd trus' those boys with me life!"

"I rather think you are, Major," commented Boz, his tone acid.

Nachollni poured himself another brandy. "Then you persist in this stupid claim that one of us is the murderer?"

"I know it," I said, forcing myself to calm down. Unpredictable outbursts of rage are more effective than a prolonged fury, they unnerve the opposition.

"Which, by definition, means one of us is also a wizard!"

"Obviously, Senator. How else could they be in two places at once?"

"I warned him," Thryme murmured, his voice hollow and lost. "I told him no good would come of it. You can't deal with people like that. They have no honour!"

"Who's that, Thryme?" I took a step towards him. His eyes met mine, and I hesitated.

"Sooner or later, I knew they'd come for him," he mumbled.

"Leave the poor old fool, Scilli," Nachollni snapped. "He's raving. The shock of Alva's death must have unhinged his mind."

"Tell me who, Thryme," I coaxed the clock-maker, ignoring the senator's compassionate sentiments. I edged closer, lowering my voice as I approached, trying to act conspiratorial, show him I wasn't one of them – whoever they were. "Tell me. Just me."

"They have their secrets, you see," he said, his eyes suddenly coming alive with pleading. He wanted me to understand, to sympathise. I wanted to as well, but I wished he'd give me more of a clue. "If you steal from them... And he would insist on visiting all the time. That awful place..."

I made a wild guess. "Madrasaté?"

Thryme reached out a shaky hand and tugged feebly at my lapel. "I knew he could sneak in ... he had friends there, you see... But, I told him, sooner or later they're going to spot you..."

I straightened up. A little lock in my brain sprung open with a click that must have been audible. Things made sense, suddenly, but I was still feeling a damned fool. I'd been so sure.

I was turning around and walking back to my mark in this little tableau when the door from the sleeping area opened and Tork stepped through. All eyes swivelled to him and I took the opportunity to slip my pistol out of its pocket.

I waited until Tork had found himself a seat. "Well, Doctor?"

He took a moment to remove his pince-nez and polish them. Once they were fitted back onto his predatory nose to his satisfaction, he leaned back in his chair and templed his fingers.

"Death was instantaneous, as far as I'm able to judge. Caused by massive trauma to most of the major internal organs. Yes, I don't imagine he could have lived long after that."

"For the benefit of us poor laymen, Doctor," I said. "Could you specify what you mean by massive trauma?"

He peered at me over his pince-nez. "Disruption, *Gosigné* Scilli. Heart, liver, spleen, lungs, kidneys: thoroughly distributed throughout the entire thoracic and abdominal cavities, like paste. You're the resident magical expert: explain that!"

I could, all too easily. "I'm sure you've already formed your own opinion, Doctor."

"Opinion be damned!" spat Nachollni. "It's magic! What else could it be?"

"What indeed." I raised my pistol and aimed it generally in everyone's direction. All except Batrix, that is. "Now, gentlemen, before we go any further, I'd be grateful if you'd hand over all your weapons."

Chapter Twenty

Nobody moved. For a good many seconds I'm sure no one breathed. Every face registered a spectrum of feelings: from numb confusion, to disbelief, to reluctant understanding, and finally outrage.

Tork was the first to speak, burning with indignation. "This is the limit, Scilli! Now you go too far!"

I pointed the muzzle more specifically in his direction. "Please retake your seat, Doctor."

"It may have escaped your notice, but we have just lost our supplies and a goodly number of men. This is no time for—"

"Sit, Doctor."

He glowered at me a moment longer before dropping heavily into an armchair. Nachollni's eyes swung between the two of us. He licked his lips. "What is this?" he managed to choke out.

I glanced towards Batrix. "Would you do the honours?" I waved my repeater at the outraged group. Giving me a puzzled look, she moved towards them.

Not surprisingly, they were all carrying pistols of one kind or another. Rengalet's elaborate repeater was in its holster. Nachollni had a small, twin-shot pistol tucked away in his coat. He almost looked panic-stricken when Batrix found it there. Both Tork and Thryme had identical repeaters to my own and gave them up without a word. Or at least, neither took it amiss when Batrix frisked them.

Boz handed an elegant flintlock pistol over without prompting, but when Batrix insisted on checking – for her own peace of mind – you could see him trying to writhe his skin away from her touch. Try as he might, he couldn't keep the repulsion off his face.

Once Batrix had disarmed them all, I tugged at the sash of the nearest window. The loud roar of the wheels surged in. "Throw them out."

As she tossed all five guns through the window, I levelled my own at her head. "And now your own," I said, just loud enough to be heard above the wheels.

Her head snapped round. Even through the blue lenses, I could see the shock, the betrayal. "You—" she began.

I cocked my pistol. "Please, Commander. I would hate to have to fire this."

Moving with painful slowness, she removed the gun from her tunic. It joined its fellows through the open window.

I waved her back. "If you'd be good enough to join the others..."

Like a large cat backing off prey that had the temerity to defend itself, she moved away from me. There was a seat next to Tork and she took it. And all that time, her eyes didn't flinch from my own.

I closed the window and faced my reluctant audience. "Now I have your undivided attention, I think it's time I straightened out a few details. As I'm sure even the dimmest of you must have guessed by now, I'm not just an impoverished proto-wizard dragged along on this expedition by Alva to advise on the possibility of magical assaults..."

"Jus' as well," muttered Rengalet. "You ain't done much'f a job s'far!"

I had to acknowledge this. "You already know that the pilot, Yosec, was an undercover agent by the name of Sanej and working for the Internal Bureau. And, true to the untrustworthy days in which we live, so am I."

"Hell and damnation!" swore Nachollni. "Is there anyone on board who doesn't work for the damned Bureau?"

"There's no one else that I know of," I said. "But knowing the way the Director's mind works, I wouldn't want to wager a week's salary on it."

"I thought *it* was supposed to be the only Bureau representative!" Tork jabbed a thumb towards Batrix.

"So did she," I said. "So did everyone. That was rather the point."

"Why the secrecy?" asked Boz in his familiar drawl. "Are the Spooks still so powerful?"

"You're a fine one to talk about secrecy, Boz. Has the *Plytath a'Pyndr* been so forthcoming about its real objectives? The resurrection of Pyndria as it was in its Golden Age, isn't it? Those hazy, non-existent times before the nasty wizards came along and corrupted the natural forces of earth to their own ends? Sounds to me like the *Plytath a'Pyndr* simply wants to replace one bunch of wizards with another."

"How dare—!" He moved faster than I'd seen him move since we'd met, coming out of his seat like a mortar. He didn't get far though – not with my pistol aimed squarely between his eyes.

"Sit down, *Gosigné* Boz," I asked in a voice so quiet Batrix would have been proud of me, in other circumstances. "You're making a scene, and I know how much Pyndrians hate to make a scene."

He slumped back into his chair, slowly. Everyone was moving so slowly today.

"As I think we agreed earlier, the murderer is also a wizard. Even if reason doesn't tell us that, the evidence does."

"The cause of Alva's death you mean?" said Tork.

"That, and the fact someone can creep about the rail-train without anyone – even the guards – seeing them."

"An invisibility spell!" Nachollni cried, as though he'd just made some brilliant deduction.

"Naturally. But whenever a wizard makes himself – or anyone else – invisible, the subject goes blind to the normal world. It's only good for a short distance: you need to memorise all of the obstacles. I wouldn't want to be under one while trying to cross this carriage, never mind the length of the entire rail-train, especially back in the Riccobanni Swamps."

"Meaning that when Yosec was killed, such an enchantment probably wasn't used," said Boz.

"I am a creation of wizardry," Batrix said with peculiar dignity. "Not a practitioner."

"Really?" I replied, as lightly as I could. "I never heard it said a heteromorph couldn't also be a Spook. Besides…" I pulled the hip flask of *chavet* out of my coat pocket and sloshed the contents around "…who was it supplied me with this stuff just before I was nearly poisoned by it?"

It was the second rude shock she'd had that day. I could see her practised detachment struggling to keep up.

"Very well," said Tork acidly. "You say you know one of us murdered Alva and the pilot. What do you intend to do about it?"

"No, Doctor, I didn't say that." I leaned comfortably back against the carriage side. "I said one of us is a murderer – and I meant the one who killed Professor Alva, of course. Sorry if I misled you."

That got them going again. "You mean, there are two murderers aboard?" Thryme squeaked, his rheumy eyes fidgeting.

"No, no, *Gosigné* Thryme. Don't worry. Just the one. I killed the pilot."

This time, for a moment, the silence was deafening. Then it seemed as though everyone was on their feet, waving hands, shouting. It was quite ugly. Only Batrix and Thryme remained sitting

– the old clock-maker was studying the carpet as though he'd never seen one before, the heteromorph still glaring intently at me.

I waited patiently until the uproar died. Then it just took a little wave of my gun to persuade everyone to retake their seats. This time, I definitely had their undivided attention.

"So much for all your clever arguments," Boz said. The words were spoken with little venom. His laconic exterior was as hard to crack as Batrix's.

"It's called guile, *Gosigné* Boz," I replied. "It's what I'm paid for."

"You murdered your closest friend," Batrix said, her tone level, like she was reciting a shopping list. "The man who you described to me as the closest you have ever had to a father."

"The Bureau weren't simply concerned that the Chrysomancers would launch some kind of attack on Alva's locomotive-train," I continued, ignoring her. "In fact, they knew perfectly well there would be one. Even where it would take place."

"A little late, surely?" remarked Boz. "With Alva dead, the whole project is finished."

"Hardly," I said, allowing a certain degree of anger to heat my voice. "With the good professor so blatantly murdered, the Philosophic Party's cause is almost certainly won!"

"How?" Nachollni looked close to tears.

Batrix answered for me. "Because Alva's death was so obviously murder, the Spooks will inevitably receive the blame. The people of Ramini will not take it well that a hero of theirs has been so cruelly slain. The fate of the wizards has been sealed for decades!"

"Then we have no need to worry!" the senator protested. "We need only reach Scana Carsofi."

"Your humanity does you credit!" sneered Tork.

"The *Novandik* has to reach Scana Carsofi first, Senator," I pointed out. "And we are already well on our way into the Drésdiracci Mountains."

Batrix's glare seemed to be even more piercing. "That's where the 'accident' is intended to take place?"

"And will do so still," I finished for her. "An unfortunate incident up in the crags ... no survivors ... the world none the wiser."

"Alva's locomotive-engine is perceived to be lethal," she said. "Too dangerous for his vision to be pursued further, and the Chrysomancers win after all."

"Exactly. For a heteromorph, you're frighteningly intelligent, Batrix."

"Thank you. Then indulge me and tell me why you killed the pilot. And who is the other Spook agent?"

I gave her my widest, most comfortable smile. "As I said earlier, the Bureau knew perfectly well that there would be an attempt on this train. I was placed on board, supposedly as an out of work, barely skilled wizard who could sniff out any magical skulduggery. You all thought it was Alva's idea – in fact, he received a gentle suggestion from someone so high up that such a 'suggestion' was more like holy writ. Sanej – Yosec – was appointed mission controller and came on board as the pilot. However, unknown to anyone in the Bureau, I've been working for the wizards for years. Sanej met me when he worked as a tutor at the Madrasaté Seminary, and 'recruited' me for what would one day be the new democratic government. He never guessed – brilliant agent though he was – that I was placed in the Seminary specifically for that reason. The wizards knew the Philosophics had a deep-cover agent planted there. It was up to me to ensure I was approached and recruited. Not to uncover their agent, but to beat them at their own game."

"And this is the fruition?" Boz asked. "If you destroy this train in the mountains, you'll die, too."

I shrugged. "I may be their best agent in the government, but if my death will bring down the Philosophic Party, the wizards are willing to pay that price."

"Are you?" Tork demanded.

I shrugged again. "What I want hardly matters, Doctor."

"Can we take it that Yosec, despite your masterful genius, had begun to suspect you," Batrix persisted. "And that is why you killed him?"

"Something like that."

"Then *you* have his abaston stone," Nachollni said, his eyes widening slightly.

"I might have, Senator. But you needn't worry yourself about it. We'll be in the mountains soon."

"And we're expected to just sit here until then?" Tork asked, his harsh face twisted in a humourless expression.

"No'once th'guards realise wha's happ'nin'!" Rengalet slurred. I noticed his gin bottle was dry.

"Sadly, Major, the guards now take their orders from me." I pulled out the slip of paper I'd shown to the sergeant earlier and tossed it towards him. Batrix caught it instead and rapidly scanned the few lines of copperplate, and the signature.

"I'm sure you recognise the name," I said.

"Where did you come by this?"

"It's quite genuine, I assure you. The President felt such a warrant might be needed some time. Very far-sighted of him, don't you think?"

"What is it?" Nachollni demanded, trying to read the paper.

"Presidential Warrant," said Batrix, throwing it at my feet. I made no attempt to pick it up. "Brevet-Colonel Wilonek Scilli. He effectively outranks us all."

"You said there was another Spook agent aboard," Tork reminded me. "One that you, rather hypocritically, called a murderer. You wouldn't happen to know which of us it is, I suppose?"

"What do you think, Doctor?" I asked. "And, yes, they are a murderer, since Alva's death was quite inexcusable. The result of panic, I imagine. In all likelihood, they were caught rifling Alva's carriage by the professor himself. Certainly, the signs of death don't indicate a sneak attack, but a full-scale assault by magic. Simple panic."

"And this person will die with us?" Tork asked.

"Of course. It is both their duty and their punishment. I wasn't appointed to correct others' mistakes."

"Then the's some j'st'ce." Rengalet raised the gin bottle and squinted stupidly at its emptiness.

I risked a glance out of a window. The rail-road was rising along a heavily wooded, steep incline. Even in the growing dark I could see that the trees – all conifers now – were beginning to thin out as the gradient increased. The track bed was little more than a ledge cut into the steep mountainside. A few hours would see us several thousand feet above sea level and into the highest mountains.

I turned back to my reluctant guests. "Well, gentlemen – and Batrix – we'll be here for quite some time yet. Would anyone care for anything to eat? Or drink? I'm sure Alva will have had a private supply. Or perhaps a game of cards?"

They all just glared at me. Batrix's stare was the harshest. There was no mercy in it. Just as she'd transferred all the hatred and loathing she felt that for the Chrysomancers onto Nachollni, my own fall from grace had left me even lower in her eyes than the senator.

"I am going to kill you, Scilli," she said after a while. I had no doubt she meant it.

"Finally experiencing the desire for revenge, Commander?" I asked, careless as a pupil at the start of his summer vacation. "How does it feel?"

"'T's you!"

Major Rengalet was suddenly half out of his seat, waving an unsteady hand towards Nachollni. He staggered alarmingly on bent knees. The senator looked back at him in astonishment. I watched them both, not convinced this wasn't some elaborate charade to catch me out.

"What's me?" Nachollni asked. His lips curled back in distaste, as though he'd opened a cupboard and found a fish which had been dead for several days.

"'S'you! You're th'one! Th'other spy!"

"You're drunk!" Not an astute observation, but I couldn't fault the senator's accuracy.

"Where were y'then?" the major prompted. "When Alva was bein' kill'?"

"I was trying to get that fool of a Sebite to speed the train up!" Nachollni snapped. "Ask Scilli – he sent me there."

"Now there's an intriguing character witness," remarked Boz lazily.

Nachollni rounded on the author. "Keep out of this!" He turned back to Rengalet. "If we want to open up enquiries into people's whereabouts, Major, perhaps you'd like to tell us where you were when the last two carriages became uncoupled."

Rengalet frowned ponderously and collapsed back into his chair. "Can' 'member," he muttered

"How convenient. If I recall correctly, you were on the platform, standing just above the couplings."

Rengalet shook his head. "Drunk."

"So you say—"

"Be quiet!" snapped Tork. He was glowering at me. "You're doing exactly what he wants. Turning on each other, throwing accusations without thought. He's had us doubting each other right from the start!"

"Hardly matters now," said Thryme morosely.

Batrix stood up suddenly. I raised my gun, but one look at her face and I knew she wasn't about to attack anyone. She was almost grey. Her skin was greasy with sweat, and huge bags had settled under both eyes.

She'd begun the change, a day early. Tomorrow was the night of the full moon. It had to be the stress and unpredictability of the past few days.

She took two steps and collapsed to the carpet. I almost dropped to her side, just catching myself in time. "Doctor!" I waved my pistol at Tork. He didn't need any more prompting.

"She's going into premature metamorphosis!" he said, kneeling at her side. He felt for a pulse and looked into her eyes before pulling back again. "I know nothing about heteromorph physiology!" It sounded as though he was berating himself.

"Get her back to her compartment," Thryme suggested. "Post one of the guards in with her…" He faltered, as though embarrassed by his own suggestion. "It's a natural process," he finished with a shrug. "Allowed to proceed naturally, she should come to no harm."

Not so natural this time. I looked down at Batrix, and Tork kneeling helplessly at her side. She was writhing in agony now. Her face seemed to be twisting and pulsing. I didn't want to watch any longer.

"There's already too much distraction in here," I said. "Senator, fetch in the two guards standing outside."

For a moment, I thought he was going to defy me. In the end, he meekly opened the door and summoned two Sharpshooters: the sergeant I had spoken with earlier, and a tall, thin corporal. I don't know what they made of Batrix's agonies on the carpet, but they were disciplined enough to wait for someone's orders.

"Corporal," I addressed the taller one, "carry the heteromorph back to her compartment. Then wait with her. Alert me if you think the situation warrants it." I switched my glance to the sergeant. "Give him a hand, then resume your post outside the door. Understand?" Both guards saluted sharply.

Tork stepped out of the way as they swung Batrix up off the floor. Taking as much care as if she was one of their own, they carried her out of the carriage. I shut the door firmly behind them.

"How very touching. 'Alert me if the situation warrants it'!" Nachollni mocked. "Premature 'morphing is fatal, Scilli. It'll not survive long enough to complete the transformation."

I was all out of cutting repartee. "Shut up, Nachollni," I said.

Chapter Twenty-One

Once the guards had carried Batrix off to her compartment I took the opportunity for another look around Alva's sleeping area. The few Sharpshooters we had left were keeping a good lookout at both ends of the professor's carriage. I didn't think anyone would actually try to leave, anyway, not at this stage. Rengalet was practically comatose, Tork and Thryme were sitting morosely together, staring out of the window when they weren't glaring at me, Boz was reading a book – probably one of his own, and Nachollni was alone, looking blindly across the apex of his steepled fingers. I think my confession had finally drained away whatever pioneering spirit they'd ever had.

The doctor had left the sleeping compartment dark, either out of respect, or because he didn't want anyone to see what was humped up on the bed, a stained sheet thrown carelessly over it. Alva's clothes had been left in a heap on the lush carpet.

I had no reason to think I was going to discover anything incriminating or otherwise in the compartment, not judging by the state in which the murderer had left it. Anything of vague interest would have been transported away in exactly the same way as the contents of Alva's pockets. But I'm methodical, when all else fails.

Trying to be neater than the previous searcher, I went through every drawer, every cupboard, looked under the carpet, inside the washbasin's U-bend, even around the privy. I didn't find anything I didn't expect to find. My only consolation was in figuring out Alva's killer hadn't been any luckier. That, and finally realising what it was we were both looking for.

Eventually, I dropped into the compartment's only chair and tried to think. If I'd been the professor – a genius, given to thinking far above the level of we mere mortals – where would I have hidden a crystal? While I pondered, I finished off what *chavet* there was left in my rinsed-out flask. This was no time to risk withdrawal.

The carriage lurched slightly. There was a mournful blast from the *Novandik's* whistle. The burial party must be back on board and Law was setting us all in motion again. At the same time, I heard the door to the lounge open – carefully, stealthfully – as though the rattle of the gradually accelerating carriage was meant to cover it. I waited a few seconds before speaking, until my silent visitor had closed the door behind them and was standing immediately behind my chair.

"Come in, Senator. I'd offer you a seat, but only the bed's free. I doubt the present occupant is in the mood to object."

"You did know, then?" Nachollni stepped around the chair to face me. He cast one glance towards the shape on the bed, then perched on a corner, fastidiously wrapping the tails of his coat across his lap. "When you took credit for the pilot's murder, I had my doubts."

I didn't bother replying, instead I just repeated what we both already knew. "The crystal isn't here."

He grinned, showing too many teeth. In the semi-darkness, his baby-face took on a different expression. Much harsher. "I know."

"I mention it only because you made such a mess of the search. You could have missed something. Anything. In fact, you've made quite a mess of everything so far, haven't you?"

"Quite sure of yourself, aren't you, Scilli? If that's your real name." He leaned forward, and my hand tightened on the grip of the pistol in my pocket. "Don't think you're just going to walk in and take credit for everything I've worked for! I'm not going to disappear in some god-forsaken mountain pass while you garnish all the praise! I don't care how favoured you are! I don't care if you're the Archimandrite's bastard son—"

"I've met him and there's no love lost, I assure you," I said, calm to the last. "But you're wrong if you believe anyone's going to walk away from this operation. It's too important."

His laugh was the perfect pitch of scornful. "Don't give me that! Who's going to report success, eh? Six months' time and you'll be back in circulation – different face, different name. What'll it be next time, Scilli? Infiltrating the Bureau? Or the President's office?"

"I don't think the Philosophics need to worry too much if the Chrysomancers are going to tear themselves apart like this, Senator. Perhaps if you'd thought less of yourself and more of the mission, we wouldn't be in this position—"

"More of myself?" He sprang to his feet, waving his hands threateningly in front of my face. I felt obligingly threatened. "All of my life I've worked for the Chrysomantic cause! Pulling myself up through the ranks of that damned political party! Using my last precious dregs of power to cloak this grey, ordinary frame in virtually irresistible charisma. Even if Thinos had won the forthcoming election, he wouldn't have been able to stand a fourth time, and I was the natural choice as successor!"

I leaned back in my chair, crossing my legs. "We know. But it occurred to us – suspicious creatures that we are – that becoming President might just be higher in your thoughts than the good of the Party."

He collapsed back onto the bed. Alva's corpse did a little jig as Nachollni disturbed it. "So that's it. I'm to die here. It didn't matter how I conducted the mission, did it? I was always going to die in the

Treniccni Pass. No wonder you knew about it. I thought the location was a secret known only to me."

"It was," I admitted. The butt of my pistol was growing slick with my sweat.

He frowned at me. I was going to have to make it easier for him.

"It never ceases to amaze me," I began. "All our lives we trust no one and nothing, so much so that eventually we become prepared to believe just about anything: cynically credulous, as long as it fits our preconceptions." I slipped my pistol out of its pocket carefully, not sure if he saw the movement. Not that it mattered. I had the gun – but what exactly did Nachollni have?

His face performed another complete change of expression. He looked stunned, incredulous. I think the truth was finally getting through to him.

"You mean...?" His slumped form straightened a little. He cocked his head, even more childlike. "You're not...?" He began to laugh, whole-heartedly, his entire body shaking as though he'd just been told the greatest joke in the world. Maybe he thought he had.

"I take my hat off to you, Scilli!" he gasped, finding his voice. He wiped tears from his eyes. "You were perfect. You had me believing... Hell, you had them *all* believing! Even that heteromorph. Not that they're so hard to fool." He appeared to relax again, which meant he was about to try something. I placed my repeater over my crossed knee, to make it obvious if it hadn't been before.

He scarcely glanced at the gun. "I'm intrigued, Scilli. Just how did you work it out. I'm assuming you didn't know at the start."

I tried to look as relaxed as he did. It wasn't easy. "The Bureau knew there was a Spook agent working close to the President," I said. "We even had it narrowed down to a handful of suspects..."

"Tork, Boz, Thryme, Rengalet and me?"

"Four of you, yes – but not Boz. Alva brought him along for the prestige. Besides, he's a foreigner, just arrived in Ramini. The agent had been working from within the Philosophics for years, even before the war began. Not that I trusted Boz, I admit. I still don't."

"So, it was one of us four. Which means our presence together on this trip is not merely a coincidence?"

"Of course not. The Archimandrite would move heaven and hell to sabotage this maiden run. Whichever of you it was, they would definitely try."

"Risky, surely? Almost inviting disaster."

"Desperate times, Senator. For both of us. It was a case of putting a loaded gun down, and watching who picked it up." I twitched my repeater, pleased with my analogy.

"So, one Bureau man poses as the train's pilot, while another is a barely-trained wizard – dregs from the gutter brought along to sniff me out." He smiled again. This time there was no genuine amusement.

"Masks, Senator. We all wear them. But actually, I was along just to draw the fire; get everyone looking in the wrong direction. Sanej was meant to uncover the agent."

"From his little hut on wheels, up at the front?" He didn't try to hide the sneer in his voice.

"There are ways, Nachollni, you know that. However, when Sanej was murdered, that muddied the waters considerably."

"I expect you believed that to be me." His smugness was growing irritating. I wanted to club it straight with my pistol.

"For some time. But since whoever killed Sanej also took his personal abaston stone, I couldn't understand why they never used it. *You* would have done."

Nachollni bobbed his head in assent.

"Then there was the frantic search through all the compartments, all except Alva's. At first, I thought that was just some crude attempt to throw suspicion on the professor. Then it occurred to me that perhaps whoever was searching didn't think Alva would have what they were looking for. Why was that?"

"Same reason as yourself, Scilli. I could think of no reason why Alva would murder his own pilot. It made no sense."

"But when you couldn't find the missing crystal anywhere else, you had to try."

"And the damn' fool came in, disturbing me. I had no reason to kill him – quite the opposite, as you reasoned – but he gave me little choice. Flying at me like a wild man. I touched him once, a full discharge. In anyone else it would have looked like a seizure, but his constitution was too weak. His over-stressed organs couldn't take the extra strain."

"But it still didn't get you the crystal."

"Don't fret, Scilli. I'll find it."

"That I doubt."

He shrugged. "How did you work out Alva killed your partner, out of interest?"

"Something Thryme said whilst Doctor Tork was doing the autopsy. He mentioned Alva had friends at the Madrasaté Seminary, ones who had been supplying him with the crystals for his machines. It occurred to me he might well have seen Sanej there, as a tutor. If he had recognised him, the professor probably assumed Sanej was the Spook agent, and did what he thought was a patriotic act."

"You mean your partner was still wearing the same face?" Nachollni was incredulous.

I nodded sadly. "Sanej was too set in his ways. He'd worn that face far too long. No one could persuade him to change it."

"And it killed him."

"Yes." I paused for a moment, taking in a deep breath. "Alva probably thought the crystal was a bonus. He could always find a use for it later."

"Whereas I would have used it sooner."

"Quite." I rubbed at my eyes, careful not to take my attention off the senator. "And Alva certainly went a funny colour when he found out what Sanej really was."

"Inspired guesswork, Scilli. You were lucky."

"That's how it works, Senator: luck. Bad luck finds us out; good luck finds the others out."

"Which brings us to how you found me out." He was playing me along, confident he could best me when it came to the final hand. I wasn't so certain he was wrong, either.

"Well, who was there? Thryme: an old man, suffering Javier's Palsy through Alva's impatience, maybe feeling eclipsed by his pupil. Jealous. But likely to side with the Chrysomancers...?" I shook my head.

"Stranger things have been known..."

"Rengalet: a drunk, racked with guilt over his irregular sexual appetites, and much too defensive about his humble origins. A prime candidate for blackmail."

"But you discounted him."

"Only in the final analysis. Rengalet's soaked up too much army pride with his gin. If it came to a choice between betraying his country or being the subject of a tawdry scandal, I think he'd damn his blackmailer to hell. Then kill himself."

"The honourable thing, eh, Scilli?"

"Not everyone's like you and I, Senator." He was much too calm. It was making me edgy. "Then there's Tork, used by the Spooks as an informant during his student days in Pyndria. He could have been recruited by them way back. But if so, why waste such a valuable asset wrecking a rail-train? He's been the President's private physician for years; such a position would have been perfect for an assassination attempt. He could have made it seem quite natural, then performed the autopsy himself, to be certain of covering himself."

"Intriguing analysis, Scilli. Out of all those rogues, why me?"

I tried on a smile, but my face felt too stiff to keep it there for long. "Well, for one thing, you seemed to have no motive. Nothing hidden away that could be used against you, or might be fermenting some resentment, somewhere. A politician with nothing to hide – it's unthinkable. Secondly, you came to visit me after I was charged with Sanej's murder. You mouthed a few platitudes, allowed me to goad you, and left. On the face of it, entirely pointless."

"I came to extend a helping—"

"You came to check if I had Sanej's abaston stone. You probably had your own crystal in an inside pocket. If there'd been another stone in my compartment, you would have felt the proximity warning when it reacted."

He twisted a hand in a dismissive gesture. "As you say..."

"Finally, there was that odd piece of theatre, when you bravely threw yourself at the Archimandrite's projection. Why do that, I wonder? You already knew what to expect, and, for all your brave oratory, Senator Nachollni has never been renowned for his physical courage. Something about a childhood disease leaving you weak, I believe. The cough, wasn't it?"

He twitched his lips but managed to hold back the comment this time.

"Besides, I don't believe Sendivogius would have wasted all that abaston power sending a projection just to mock Alva and his party. Even he's not that petty. There had to be a damn' good reason. I think that was the moment when you received your final orders: destroy the train at the Treniccni Pass."

"You're guessing, Scilli."

I shook my head. "You're here, Senator. That's general confirmation enough. Details don't matter, except to a Court of Treason."

"Politics is all about detail, Scilli."

"Indeed. Like the little touch of having you and Alva arguing about stopping the train – when neither of you were actually there."

He looked smug. "Not difficult. That Sebite's mind is so basic, it was childishly simple to enthral and glamour it."

"Not so simple that even he thought your 'argument' was repetitive."

"I had no time for subtleties, Scilli. So, tell me how I poisoned your *chavet*."

"Only three people took any interest in that filthy stuff: Alva, who was supplying it on Bureau orders; Batrix, who despised both it and me for drinking it; and you, who was all concern about my poor addiction and the effects it must be having on me, and was I careful to keep a bottle near me at all times because of withdrawal's notorious unpredictability..."

"Merely the goodwill of a grateful man. One who is in a position to do—"

"A man who seems to know an awful lot about a mixture which is proscribed by his own government, the recipe for which was suppressed even by the Chrysomancers. Been doing a little experimentation on the side, Senator?" I decided it was time to give him some of his smile back. On my face it felt as false as my features. "Your own hoard running low, perhaps? You suddenly find yourself needing to manufacture it?"

He wasn't smiling now. "Wait until you can't find a supply anymore, Scilli! In fact—" he seemed to find a little more composure at the memory "—the stuff that almost killed you was one of my failed experiments. You were wrong there, *Gosigné* Investigator. No one altered it from afar. It remains effective *chavet* for about six hours before deteriorating lethally."

"You simply switched bottles."

"Once I knew the heteromorph was supplying you from Alva's store. I didn't have enough time to find wherever the professor was keeping his supply, but the bottle Batrix had taken out for you was left on display in its compartment."

"During your diversion with the swamp-things."

"I knew *it* wouldn't have the crystal fragment—"

"But you turned her room upside down anyway."

"On general principal, if nothing else."

I shook my head. "That remark about winning the war without saving a single heteromorph was a touch rash, don't you think?"

He made an expansive gesture. "I was young, and more than a little drunk at the time. I'd managed to live it down, I thought. You see, I do have something embarrassing in my past."

"As well as nearly dying of infantile cough?"

His expression was ugly now. "Guessed right again, haven't you, Scilli? Yes, I almost died, and nothing any of your precious modern physicians could do would have saved me. It was a Chrysomancer. Within minutes he restored my health—"

"And you've been faithful to them ever since."

"Quite."

"Pity he didn't bring you back to full health, though, isn't it, Senator? He could have done, you know. But I expect he wanted another string to pull – along with the *chavet*." I half-laughed. "Maybe I should let you live, allow you to continue blundering your way through life. I think I'd be doing the Chrysomancers a favour by killing you. You're one of the best weapons our government has."

He chose that moment to strike. Leaping from the bed, he tried to lock both hands around my throat. We tumbled out of my chair. I clamped one hand around a wrist, vainly tugging. With the other, I clubbed at his face with my pistol. One blow landed squarely on his temple. His grip loosened and he half rolled away.

I came to my feet quickly, but unsteadily. Little specks were dashing crazily about before my eyes. Nachollni was still crouched on the floor, grunting. I kicked him in the face for the hell of it. He flipped over, collapsing onto his side.

Before he could move again, I began to search him for the familiar bulge of his crystal. I didn't believe for one moment he had it on him, but desperation makes you hope strange things. I found nothing.

A fist lashed out, grazing the tip of my nose as I danced back, out of reach. Nachollni stood, slowly, breath wheezing from a gaping mouth, like a beached fish. Not so sick as Alva, but he was telling the truth, at least.

"I can't beat you in a fight, Scilli," he panted, tired out of all proportion to the effort. "But I don't need to. You're nothing ... not even initiated. While I attained sixth *shakrat* many years ago..."

I sprang at him, ready to club that baby face some more – but found myself diving face-first into a stone wall. My head rang. What felt like a torrent of blood began to sluice from my nose, into my mouth. I spat and shook my head, stepping back carelessly, and fell across rail-road tracks.

I was outside the *Novandik*. He'd transported me.

I heard the roar of the locomotive-engine. It was growing louder. One glance to my left told me why. I saw the approaching glare of a huge oil-lamp. Nachollni had moved me to a point on the track a few yards ahead of the train. It was coming straight for me.

I leapt off the rails, hitting the steep downward slope on the other side of the track bed. Locomotive-engine and carriages thundered by above me, splattering me in flashes of light. I tried not to roll and slither down the slope towards a too-close cliff-edge. Flailing wildly, grabbing at loose stones and dirt, somehow I came to a halt, inches from the drop. I looked down into blackness. It was a hell of a long way. Instantly, I was drowning in waves of vertigo.

I clamped my eyes shut and turned toward the incline. Slowly, painfully, I clawed up the slope, sliding back as often as I crawled up, not stopping until I felt steel rails against my palms.

I needed to get my breath back, but I didn't have that luxury. I staggered to my feet. The train was a good many yards away now, steaming round another cliff-bend. Somehow, I was going to have to catch it.

I began to run, keeping my feet on the wooden ties between the rails. Only a lunatic would expect to catch up with the *Novandik*. Even ascending the gradient into the mountains, it was still moving faster than I could run. But I had to try. There was nothing else for me. Besides, I guessed Nachollni was going to have to stop the train eventually, even if he had to wreck it. The pass wasn't far away now. If I could keep going. If I didn't trip over the ties. If I didn't end up falling back down the slope towards the black drop...

I tried not to think about it.

The nearly full moon was shining on the cliff-side. The sky was clear and alive with stars. It was almost as bright as day, except where the occasional tree or deep crag created jagged areas of deep, impenetrable shadow. I could see where I was going, where my feet were. I didn't need to worry what might be hiding in the shadows.

My nose wouldn't stop bleeding. The exertion of running wasn't helping. I had to keep dashing away the endless stream with the back of my hand, spitting out any that made it into my mouth. It was all I could taste and smell. I wondered if it was possible to suffer serious blood loss through a nosebleed.

I rounded a bend and began to think I was either growing faint, or the blow on my head had been harder than I'd thought. My vision seemed to be fragmenting.

It wasn't my muddled brain; I couldn't be that lucky. The rail-road and cliff-face were slowly coming apart in small, brightly-coloured motes. Within seconds, all I could see was a flat, random pattern of rainbow dots. The entire cliff and track – as far as I knew, the entire world – seemed to have no more depth than a sheet of paper, one sprayed with a chaotic jumble of randomly swirling coloured points.

Chapter Twenty-Two

I stopped dead. My feet were listening to something smarter than my brain. Although reason told me the mountains hadn't vanished into a one-dimensional pointillist nightmare, my senses were saying something else entirely. I reached forward tentatively, as though I expected to touch rock. Naturally, there was nothing. Like a rainbow, the huge illusion was always just beyond reach, shifting as I moved my head or eyes.

Nachollni. It had to be. He had covered his flight with some kind of chaotic magic. I vaguely remembered being instructed about such a spell. As usual, I hadn't been listening. It was too late for regrets.

I stretched a hand to my left where I knew the cliff should be. After a few moments, when it seemed I was completely wrong and the world really had vanished, my fingertips touched gritty rock. It was there. So much for my visual senses.

What the hell was it that those damned tutors had tried to instil in me so long ago? Perception spells ... veiling perspective ... depth reversal. If only my head wasn't aching so much. I could barely think past the pounding, the blood dripping off my chin.

Concentrate. Always the main thing: concentrate. That, and keeping calm. No easy task under the circumstances. While I was calming myself and concentrating, Nachollni was probably burying the *Novandik*, rail-train, and all the passengers under a rock-fall.

And stupid panic wasn't going to get me anywhere, either.

I stood a few moments longer, generating as much calm as I could. I looked back over my shoulder. The winding cliff-face and rail-bed clinging desperately to it were clearly visible, but as the track reached a point just about where I was standing, the whole world fell apart into random flecks. Only my arm and hand looked solid. The rock wall I was leaning against was totally invisible. Or rather, hidden behind an infinite number of twitching dots and dashes.

I wondered what I could infer from the situation. The Treniccni Pass was only a few miles away, or at least, it should be. I could still feel the cliff under my fingers and the track ties under my soles. The mountains hadn't vanished, or fragmented – I simply couldn't see them. Or perhaps it's truer to say they no longer had a perspective. The entire range had been crushed into a one-dimensional illusion.

It was the perspective idea that kept nagging at me. Obviously, I'd been told something about this concept years ago, I just couldn't remember what the hell it was.

I mentally slammed my brain around, trying to beat something out of it. I raged and cursed. It just curled itself up into a frightened ball and let me bully it, mewling softly to itself. No help there.

Then an image popped up out of nowhere: a tiny piece of childhood I'd buried completely. It was the face of one of my tutors, Grax. May he rot in hell for all eternity. He was looming over me, an iron ferrule waving negligently over my hands, which were laid palms down on a desktop.

Welcome back to us, boy, Grax was saying, his harsh voice thick with honeyed malice. *Perhaps you'd like to share with us all whatever it is you are thinking. Hmmm?*

Nothing, sir, a voice replied, shaking with a fear barely held at bay. Me, no more than eight years old.

Indeed? Then perhaps "nothing, sir" would care to tell us just what I have spent half an hour explaining. Can you do that, boy?

I couldn't find my voice. The sight of that ferrule swinging idly over my knuckles occupied my entire universe. I was frozen with terror.

We're waiting, boy.

I opened my mouth. Perhaps if I allowed enough room for them, the words would find their own way out

The ferrule smashed down—

—and I jerked my hand away from the unseen cliff-face, yelling at the pain searing its way through my shattered knuckles.

And I fell quiet. There was no pain, of course. No blood – except all down my face – no bruised bones, no pulped flesh. It was only a memory, albeit a very intense, painful one. But with it, something else had been dragged up. Another memory, the actual lesson I couldn't repeat that day.

Displacement magic: all the depth, all the perspective a human eye could take in and interpret, flattened out into an illusory, single dimension. But not as a pretty, flat picture like a sketch or painting. Compressing all that depth into one plane causes overlaps, interference patterns. Everything becomes an insane jumble: swirls of colour that change shape as you move your head, the nearest the illusion gets to an actual change in perspective.

It's an effective spell, quite a labyrinth if you get trapped too deep inside since the affected area can stretch for miles. And if you wander away from any reference point outside the enchanted area, you're lost. No one less than a fifth *shakrat* should even attempt it. Nachollni had boasted he was a sixth. I believed it. But that didn't leave me any closer to penetrating the illusion.

Strangely, knowing even that much, little as it was, had a calming effect. I recognised what I was up against, and reasoned that I could think a way through. I certainly wasn't going to blunder forwards in the vain hope I'd bump into the stationary train. I'd be hopelessly lost in seconds and most likely walk straight off the track-bed and over the cliff. I needed to penetrate the illusion itself.

But how was I going to manage that? I wasn't even a first *shakrat*, and the only abaston crystal I'd attuned myself with was jammed inside the *Novandik's* steam generator, being drained of whatever power was left in it.

But if the *Novandik* wasn't moving...

I reached out with that small part which both crystal and I shared. It took a few moments, but I found it: weak, attenuated – and not so far away. It responded to my touch almost like a dog when its master comes home. I almost believed it was happy to sense me, which couldn't be right.

Were abaston crystals alive in some way? Sentient, at least? Had the Chrysomancers built their empire of power by exploiting yet another living creature?

I begged the crystal for power – and it came through. Not a flood, barely a trickle. Even so, I felt electrified. It felt as though every hair on my body was erect; that sparks danced among the creases of my worn suit. It was glorious. For a moment, I knew what it was to be a fully powered wizard – and I wanted more.

Nothing around me had changed. The coruscating flecks still clustered in seemingly random swirls and streaks across a one-dimensional landscape. But I'd expected nothing more. I had achieved the calm I needed, now I had to concentrate.

The problem was: on what, exactly?

I relaxed my body, finding its balance point so I could ignore it as much as possible. All that mattered was directly in front of me. I stared forward, allowing my eyes to lose focus, channelling the meagre power from the distant abaston fragment up through my spine and out along the optic nerves. Let the crystal focus. It knew what it was doing better than I did. Or so I hoped.

I thought I saw something. Instantly it was gone. I was trying too hard, not allowing the abaston power to lead. I took a deep breath and relaxed. Once more, my vision slipped out of focus; the chaotic scene before me blurred...

...and grew solid. Suddenly I could see the rail-road, and the cliff, and in the distance, the mountain tops. And yet, this wasn't what I'd expected. Instead of normality being restored, the perspective crushed behind the illusion showed through the confusion of colours and shapes, composed of that very chaos. The abaston hadn't dispelled the illusion – perhaps that was too much to expect – but had draped it across the solid reality, like countless paint-flecks sprayed over an invisible man.

It was disconcerting, to say the least.

I remained motionless a while longer. I was afraid that once I began to walk the three dimensions would collapse again, leaving me as blind as ever, and possibly too far within the illusion to escape.

I took a step forward and fell heavily across an unseen tie-bar. The world fell apart into chaos again as I went face-first onto the invisible track. Pain stabbed through my forehead. Fresh torrents of blood started flowing from my nose.

I rolled myself into a sitting position, swatting at the blood. Some had pooled on the ground I had just butted. It appeared to be floating: a surreal puddle hanging against a nonsensical background. The rail-road was just a few feet behind, still running away down the mountains, fading into the night. It looked so welcoming...

Carefully, I climbed back onto my feet. Once again I groped for and found the carved-out cliff-face. Again, I reached out and found the crystal presence. Reluctantly, almost painfully, solid images grew out of the multi-coloured insanity around me. I took a deep breath.

This time, steadying myself against the cliff-face, using it as a solid guide through the chaos, I began my climb towards the heart of lunacy.

I don't know how long I spent trudging through that nightmare. Time seemed to have gone the same way as depth and perspective. I had a watch in my pocket – or had before the night began – but I didn't dare try to look for it. There must be no distractions. All my efforts were spent on keeping the bizarre image in front of me sharp, which wasn't easy. As I followed the winding cliff-face, the apparently solid scenery shifted and flowed below its illusory mask, like mountains of glass in a tank of water shot through with a rainbow of colour. All that, added to the effort of keeping my eyes constantly unfocused, wasn't helping to make the pains in my head go away.

I only hoped the rail-track stayed on this particular mountain. If it crossed a bridge over the gorge to my right, which seemed to be growing deeper – although that may have been part of the illusion – I would never make it. Even if I could keep the image clear, my morbid fear of heights would betray me before I was halfway across.

After a measureless time, the crags seemed to be closing in. A solid wall of rock was rearing up before me, and the track was heading straight for it, which meant the Treniccni Pass wasn't far away.

I forged onward, with straining eyes that were already aching abominably. I wanted to see the *Novandik* ahead of me. I wanted to be sure the train was still intact.

Then, swimming out of the whirl of colour, there it was. Nachollni hadn't wrecked it yet, but how were the passengers? Still alive? There was one thing certain: if I stood wondering about it for too long, I'd have a brilliantly-coloured, surreal memory of whatever his plans for the rail-train were to dwell on for whatever remained of my life.

The *Novandik's* image shimmered bizarrely, shifting to one side as though I was watching it through a thick, uneven pane of glass. For a moment, I panicked, sure I was about to lose it. Then the image stabilised.

Keeping my eyes fixed on just the rail-train, ignoring the shifting images of cliff and gorge as best I could, I trod carefully forward. The *Novandik* and carriages remained comfortingly real, despite their strange, shifting coloration. Now it was the background lurching drunkenly.

It was fatigue. It had to be. Concentrating so intently for such a long period had tired my eyes. Not even the crystal's power could keep them fresh. They kept wanting to re-focus, settle on something hard and solid, a feeling which only grew stronger with each step closer I came to the train. If I took my eyes away, if I blinked, I was convinced I'd lose it.

I was drenched in sweat. If the abaston fragment hadn't been constantly feeding me I would have collapsed I'm sure. I was increasingly drawing on the power simply to keep me going, which meant I was devoting less to penetrating the illusion.

To make it worse, as I got closer, the image's sharpness began to break down. It may have been an effect of the particulate nature of the three-dimensional overlay, or a sign that the shape which looked like the train was, in fact, nothing of the kind. Whatever the cause, it made it difficult for me to tell with any certainty where solid surfaces actually began. The only way to find out was to grab hold of something.

Finally, I thought I was close enough to the last carriage to be able to get aboard. I reached out, almost losing sight of the carriage's image as my hand came into view. I needed to deliberately look beyond it, keep it blurred, which made seizing the increasing unsolid image of the end handrail even dicier.

Blurred fingers made several futile grabs for the iron rail. They seemed to pass through each time, and I was beginning to think there was nothing there after all. Then they closed around very solid, very cold metal.

The world snapped back into place around me. Abruptly, I was flooded with nausea.

I dragged myself up onto the carriage's balcony end, eyes tightly closed against vertigo. Only when I was on the platform did I surrender to the nausea, retching dryly. There was nothing to come up. I lost all contact with the crystal, and felt better almost immediately. The wrench from illusion to reality, whilst still being fed by the abaston's counter-magic, had been too much, too abrupt. I was lucky to be just left feeling sick and weak. I'd seen much worse back at the Seminary when some over-eager tyro had let their control slip. Directionless magic is not a forgiving force.

Weak, and not feeling in the least heroic, I got to my feet and peered through the carriage's end door window. There was no one in sight along the corridor, and I was sorely tempted to try and sneak along it. My already abused guts quailed at the thought of the roof again. But I needed to get to the locomotive-engine, and the crystal fragment – if Nachollni had left it there.

Keeping my hand in constant contact with the carriage, I half stumbled back to the ground. There was a good chance I could walk alongside the rail-train up to the *Novandik* as long as I didn't lose physical contact with it. I doubted Nachollni was going to let anyone off to see what he'd done to the surrounding world. On the other hand, there were several Sharpshooters around somewhere. What had he done with them? Spirited them off, like he'd done with me? Murdered them? Struck them blind? Perhaps both murdered them and transported them off the train?

This led to another question: what about Batrix? Going into lunar transformation so early is dangerously unpredictable. Even if she'd survived, she'd be vulnerable. Nachollni clearly didn't have much time for heteromorphs outside menial labour. Did that mean he'd overlook her? Or kill her anyway – out of general principal, as he'd so eloquently phrased it.

I couldn't hang around clogging my mind with unanswerable questions. Before I could think of something else to fret about, I began walking, trailing my left hand along the carriage side. I paused every so often, pressing an ear against the bodywork. But either there was nothing to hear, or the various materials used in its construction were a good sound insulator. If it was the latter, it improved my chances no end.

I reached the front of the rear carriage. I peered around cautiously. On the platform of the late professor's private carriage, standing rigidly on guard, was the sergeant I'd spoken to ... the gods knew how long ago. He was a little too rigid, I thought. I stepped into full view. He didn't so much as twitch a finger.

He was frozen. In a magical stasis, courtesy of Senator Nachollni, of course. I wondered how many of the guards were also immobilised.

I stretched for the rail at the end of the private carriage before letting go the passengers' one. My shoulders creaked. Maybe I was being too cautious, but I was too tired, aching and glued-up with sweat and blood to be thinking clearly. I couldn't afford mistakes. Overcaution was my best option.

I slid forward alongside Alva's private carriage, exactly as I had the passenger one, leaving the sergeant like some unusually realistic waxwork. There was no more sound coming from it than from the other carriage. I was anxious. Were my fellow passengers still locked in? How had the senator explained away my disappearance? Presuming I'd been missed, of course.

Too many questions.

At the front of the private carriage, I found two more guards. As immobile as the sergeant, pointlessly guarding the forward-facing door. A few moments later, climbing up into the *Novandik's* interior, I came across Law, just as lifeless. Was there anyone on this train still moving, I wondered? Apart from myself and Nachollni, obviously.

I crouched and threw back the lever which opened the door to the crystal's compartment. Carefully, I eased it away from the two rods holding it in place and dropped it into my left palm, probing it gently.

The fragment was close to exhaustion. It may well have contained enough raw energy to power the *Novandik* the rest of the way to Scana Carsofi, but from a magician's point of view there was very little left to tap. It would be no use to me that way.

I dropped the piece of crystal into my coat and climbed down to the still kaleidoscopic ground. Slipping past the water waggon, I clambered up onto the private carriage's front balcony and squeezed between the two immobile Sharpshooters. The door wasn't locked.

Inside Alva's sleeping quarters, nothing had changed. The body was still draped in the dirty sheet, none of the signs of our struggle had been tidied away. Nachollni obviously wasn't too worried about anyone discovering the truth, which probably meant I didn't have much time.

I eased the door through to the lounge open a fraction. Everyone was still seated pretty much as they had been, except Nachollni, who wasn't in sight. And that worried me. Where could he...?

I resisted the urge to slap myself. Everyone was in sight – except for Nachollni – including me. I was just where I'd been a few miles back, face unstained by blood, repeater pistol at the ready. My pistol.

Nachollni? A shape-shifting spell? My respect for him grew by another set of notches. It was perfect. They already knew I was the traitor, thanks to my confession. In the unlikely event of there being survivors – other than Nachollni – who would they name as the Spook agent? Me.

The Nachollni with my face was muttering to himself. He seemed distracted. But no one else was moving. They were all as motionless as the guards outside. The senator was being pretty reckless with his scarce resources. Placing the entire train under stasis would consume a hell of a lot of precious abaston power.

And his muttering bothered me. Maybe he was just talking to himself – since no one else was up for much in the way of conversation – but I had the horrible conviction he was laying the ground for some final, catastrophic spell. Time to stage my re-entrance.

I slammed the door open as hard as I could. Nachollni snapped his borrowed face up, an almost comical expression of astonishment on it.

"Surprised?" I said. "I must say you're looking devilishly handsome, Senator."

"Scilli?" He obviously hadn't considered my return. Another ill-considered choice. "Damn me but you look a mess."

"Well, thanks for that kindly observation." I walked towards him, carefully, keeping my hand on the crystal fragment in my pocket. "If it helps, I don't feel any better."

He raised my pistol, pointing it steadily at a point somewhere above my nose, which had finally stopped bleeding although it still throbbed abominably, and between my eyes.

"Not very magical, is it?" I asked. "Couldn't you teleport me outside again? Inside a rockface this time. Make sure."

He laughed. It was strange, watching myself laugh like that, hearing someone else's voice come from my mouth. "What an excellent idea, Scilli. Pity I didn't have time to think about that earlier."

I risked a glance towards the frozen group of passengers. I noticed they weren't entirely motionless. Nachollni had left them able to breathe, and their eyes were still capable of movement. In fact, four pairs of eyes were darting back and forth between the two Scillis before them. I wondered what odd thoughts were falling over themselves in each mind.

"Don't tell me," I said. "The only survivor of a terrible accident will be Wilonek Scilli. He'll return to the Bureau and report that Senator Nachollni was the villain of the peace after all. Happily, the traitorous senator will have paid for his crimes in the accident. Unhappily, he'll have taken everyone else with him."

"It was your own idea, Scilli. You, as a double agent, ostensibly working for the Bureau. In reality, a wizard operative. I'll just bring your elaborate fantasy to life."

I turned to the immobilised author. "I hope you're paying attention, Boz. If you wrote all this down in a book you'd make a fortune. So much more exciting than all your dry, socially worthy tomes. Then again, your critics would likely claim it was all too fantastical." I returned my attention to Nachollni. "So, what's it to be, Senator? A landslide? Bury the entire train under hundreds of tons of rock? Or simply drop the ledge carrying the tracks down into the valley below?"

His – my – face twitched. "Landslide, I think. So much harder to dig anything out afterwards. Especially with the glamour I'll leave saturating the surrounding area. It should be good for six months or so, during which time any potential investigators will become so confused they'll simply give up."

"No more locomotive trains..."

"No more trains, no more industrial inventions, and no more discredited Philosophics Party. Ramini will be too poor to afford any more elections, so the Chrysomancers will simply slide back into control once more."

It was my turn to laugh. Dried blood cracked around my mouth. "For how long, Nachollni? Abaston power is growing weaker all the time. You've all but exhausted both the supply of crystals and the energy contained in them. Each time a Spook like you wants to show off a little is another tightening of the screw."

He shrugged. "Perhaps. But we can still control the destiny of this country for another hundred years or more. Longer than my lifetime, certainly. Why should I care what happens after that?"

"As Doctor Tork so aptly put it, I admire your humanity, Senator."

The lounge's outside door was very slowly opening. Nachollni wasn't aware of it, not while he was facing me. Unfortunately, the way the door swung, I couldn't see who was behind it. Had a guard somehow escaped their stasis conjuration?

I tried not to react, give anything away. But I must have twitched my eyes or fractionally raised an eyebrow. Nachollni turned – still keeping the gun trained on me. He was in a much better position to see who was trying to enter than I was. For an instant he was surprised, then his composure closed around him and he was all charm. He even had my voice, now.

"Corporal! Come in. I'm glad to see you. It appears the senator is our man after all." He turned back to me. A tall, thin Sharpshooter appeared in the doorway, raising a musket.

"As you can see, he's had the nerve to—"

Nachollni never finished. Without breaking stride, the Sharpshooter sighted down his musket-barrel and fired.

Chapter Twenty-Three

I was already diving for the floor as the hammer flashed. Nachollni wasn't so lucky. With his back to the guard, he didn't see a thing. The musket ball took him in his left shoulder, spinning him round. He crashed against the carriage side – hard enough to shake the whole vehicle – and rebounded onto the floor.

A moment later, I snatched up the dropped repeater. Cocking it, I spun in a crouch to face the Sharpshooter. He was lowering his musket, a puzzled expression on his pale, thin face. Then he pulled a pair of blue spectacles from his green tunic and slipped them on.

"Batrix!"

The heteromorph reached into his ammunition pouch and reloaded the musket with speed and precision. I was impressed. "I take it you are the real Scilli," she – he – said as he worked.

I came to my feet and stood over Nachollni's hunched figure. Sadly, he was still alive. He glared up at me, his features starting to run like dirty water.

"I'm glad you could tell the difference," I said.

"I could only see that one." Batrix cocked his musket and levelled it in my direction. "I thought he was you."

I froze. Only my neck was working. I lowered my head to stare down the barrel's muzzle. It was unnervingly steady. "You were trying to shoot me?"

"I was more than simply trying. Aren't you a self-confessed traitor, after all?"

"This is no time to develop a sense of humour, Commander."

"I can barely stand, Scilli." The heteromorph certainly sounded weary. I noticed his face looked unnaturally pale, and gleaming with sweat. "My transformation is only just completed. It is a day early. I am hardly in the mood to joke!"

He meant it. Turning my stiff head to look down at Nachollni, I said: "You did me a favour, Senator."

He pulled his lips into a pained smirk. His own face had almost returned, but there was enough of mine left for the pain and anger so clearly etched there to give me an unpleasant feeling. It was like watching a close relative suffering.

"Don't bet on it, Scilli. I'm not dead yet."

I shoved my pistol into his face. It didn't impress him.

"You can't kill me with that toy..."

"You seemed to think it would work on me well enough."

"You're nothing, Scilli. An unfortunate sliver of history's flotsam. I'm sixth *shakrat*!"

"So you keep saying." I pulled my own fragment of crystal from my pocket. His eyes lit on it, and I knew exactly what he was thinking. "Sorry to disappoint you, Senator. This isn't the missing piece."

I felt him probing. The backwash was like freezing water along every nerve in my body. My spine went numb.

"The shard from the machine!" Nachollni's face – all his own now – showed mild contempt. "I hope you're not thinking of challenging me with that, Scilli – there's barely enough power left to light a cigar!"

"While your own crystal is bursting with energy, I suppose?"

"Judge for yourself."

Raw power slammed out of him. I was knocked off my feet. Nachollni came slowly upright, almost floating. Batrix seemed to be frozen in an attempt to reach the senator. The heteromorph had joined the others, immobile and impotent. I was on my own.

I pushed myself to my feet. It was like trying to stand erect under a waterfall. Everything was much too quiet. I thought there should be at least a hurricane blowing through the carriage.

Nachollni was standing little more than an arm's length away. I'm pretty sure his feet weren't quite touching the floor. I could feel the power coming off him in waves, but he didn't look like a man who'd be standing for much longer. His face was deathly, with a massive black bruise from the fall spreading across his forehead. I imagine the musket ball in his shoulder was hurting him pretty badly, too.

On the other hand, I don't suppose I looked much better.

Miraculously, I'd managed to hang onto my piece of crystal and revolver. The gun wasn't going to be any use, but the abaston fragment might. I clutched it tightly to my chest.

Nachollni saw it, and chuckled. "I admire your persistence, Scilli. But what exactly do you expect that poor, tired splinter to do?" The gloat in his voice was belied by its thickness. He sounded like a man on the verge of unconsciousness. It occurred to me that Nachollni no longer had any desire to survive. Perhaps he was already dying from his wounds. A man with nothing to live for has nothing to lose.

"Something I learned off you."

Hurling myself against the crushing force, I managed to stumble drunkenly into him. I threw both arms around his shoulders. We hit the floor together. This time it was my head which cannoned off the floor. Lucky for me the floor was carpeted. Even so, it awoke echoes of pain across my face.

Through blurred vision, I stared directly into Nachollni's face. His own eyes were darting maniacally, as though he was having trouble controlling them.

"Let's go on a little journey," I muttered and threw myself into my crystal, just as I had the day we became attuned.

Once again, I was a disembodied mote drifting through a golden, crystalline universe: thin, pink filaments stretched in all directions amongst the matrix, like a colourful spider's web. I passed through the filaments as though they were no more substantial than smoke. Each time, I felt a tiny thrill of energy. Once more, I was in the very heart of the crystal, the portion where both the stone and I co-existed.

But this time, I wasn't content to drift, to observe while the abaston stone led. I reached out, beyond the stone and the world outside. I could feel the presence of other stones, other semi-sentient shards of crystal. And one in particular: Nachollni's.

It was like a white-hot dagger through my mind, burning so hot and fast it couldn't survive for long. Its waves of power battered at the Scilli of flesh in the world outside and smashed against the crystalline matrix of my fragment. I imagined I could hear the groan of tormented rock, the agonies of mountains as implacable glaciers carved them apart.

At a command, my fragment opened and let that awful power in.

It howled through the matrix like a vengeful typhoon: the crystal shook; pink filaments trembled. But everything held, somehow. Raw abaston power surged about my drained crystal like a vast wind through an empty cavern. At another command, it was absorbed.

I came free in that instant, the gold and pink matrix becoming Nachollni's pallid face and darting eyes. He was hot and sweaty; his breath foul.

I pulled away. The crystal in my hand felt hotter than the sun, although I knew it was an illusory heat. What did burn was my mental contact with the abaston power. As Nachollni's stone hurled more power at me, my own crystal drank it greedily. Its matrix had been almost drained, there was plenty of room.

"You showed me how the crystal's force can work both ways," I croaked, my throat constricted. Nachollni rolled about the floor, trying to rise, but he couldn't find the strength. "If heat can become cold, then what one crystal emits, another can absorb."

"Clever..." Nachollni 's voice was even hoarser than my own. With an effort even I could feel, he rolled into a half kneeling position. "Then perhaps I'd better stop..."

There was a flare of light, and his own crystal was floating before him, its golden light giving his waxy features an illusion of health. Greedily he snatched it from the air, and a few moments later, visibly stronger, he strained to his feet.

"Now then, non-*shakrat*, we'll see!"

"Thanks, Senator," I said, raising my own crystal. "I thought you'd eventually have to physically summon your stone. I'm grateful."

I threw my abaston fragment as hard as I could, straight at his hands.

The tiny fragment drifted through the air as though it was forcing its way through cold molasses. Nachollni had plenty of time to get out of the way, yet he seemed no more able to move than anyone else in the lounge. Instead, his arms reached forward, as though to meet the nearing crystal. His eyes glared at the blazing stone trapped between his hands. I could have sworn they were full of hatred.

Then both crystals touched. I dived to the floor an instant before the blinding detonation. I felt the frigid gale as it sucked the air from my lungs. There was a moment of almost unbearable agony, then, blessedly, it was gone. Somewhere above the howling wind I heard the shatter of glass.

Everything went terribly quiet, except the racing thunder of my heartbeat.

I looked up. Nachollni was still standing, but his imploring arms and hands were empty. Most of the flesh was torn from his palms, pale bone nestled in what remained. Both crystals were gone, destroying each other in a final, glorious absorption. Glass littered the floor: every one of the windows had been sucked in. Yet nothing else seemed touched. Even Batrix was standing exactly as he had a few moments earlier.

The crystals' greatest impact had been reserved for each other.

"It's over, Nachollni," I croaked. My throat felt raw. I was dizzy. I wanted a drink – anything but *chavet*.

"Not yet!" He groped clumsily for the musket in Batrix's senseless fingers. As he fumbled to raise it with raw, fleshless hands, I fired the pistol still clutched in my hand. He staggered back, dropping the musket. He looked surprised. I fired again.

I kept firing, slowly and methodically – Nachollni's body twitching with each bullet – until the hammer snapped impotently on an empty chamber. Strangely, all five had fired.

I still couldn't convince myself that he was finally, justly dead. Not even a whole arsenal of pistols could have done that.

As I looked down at the corpse staining the carpet, pointlessly covering it with an empty gun, there was a huge sigh around the carriage. A collective, waking gasp. I felt, rather than saw, someone stepping close to me. I waved the empty repeater in their direction.

"Perhaps there are miracles, after all," I said.

An instant later, I was hurled to the floor as massive withdrawal hit me. As the cramps ripped my guts apart and cold acid pulsed through my veins, I had a moment to be grateful they'd waited this long.

Then I passed out.

Chapter Twenty-Four

"It would seem your appetite has returned."

I looked up from my plate of chicken and unidentifiable leaves, moving my head carefully. I'd cleaned the blood off my face, checking gingerly that my nose wasn't broken, but I was still stiff and sore. The inside of my skull throbbed and echoed.

The speaker was Batrix, now formally re-dressed in his blue Internal Bureau uniform. It fitted him perfectly. I wondered if he had a wardrobe filled with uniforms of every size and shape.

"Found it tucked away in a cupboard in Alva's carriage," I said, meaning the food. "Cooked meat, canned stuff, bottled drinks – the professor must have enjoyed the occasional midnight snack. There should be enough to feed us all until we get down from the mountains."

"Indeed?" Batrix folded his arms. "And have you forgotten, my dear Scilli, that both crystals have been destroyed? There is nothing to power Alva's locomotive-engine."

I took the opportunity to take my first really good look at the transformed, male Batrix. It was hard for me to believe this was the same person as the female Batrix. He was a little over six feet tall, and so thin he looked considerably taller. Behind the familiar blue glasses his eyes – still brown, I noticed – were sharp and piercing. A thin, aquiline nose gave his whole expression an air of hawkish alertness. I felt like I was being assessed by a gaunt bird of prey.

"No. What you're forgetting is Sanej's crystal," I said. "Nachollni never discovered it. And neither did anyone else."

"Alva hid it well."

"Of course. Never one to let something like that go to waste, was the professor."

"Then where is it?"

I pointed towards the front of the train, and the *Novandik*. "Try the exhaust stack on the front of the locomotive-engine. Sanej told me it was false, just something added to make the machine look like it was burning wood or coal. Alva would have had just about enough time to toss the crystal in there."

Batrix stared at me for a long while. At least I recognised that expression. "He simply threw it in?"

"I doubt he could have climbed on the roof and dropped it down the hole. Pretty obvious when you think about it." I wiped my mouth with the napkin and stood. There wasn't much left of the night, and I intended to sleep the day through. I was owed that, at least.

"You fooled me entirely, you know," Batrix said. "That double agent speech. Quite convincing."

I nodded. "I'm rather glad I did, under the circumstances."

"And what would have happened if Nachollni had not taken on your likeness?"

"He did, so it doesn't matter." I picked up a glass of excellent wine and swilled my mouth out. "Back at Madrasaté they taught us that the universe is just one of an infinite numbers of realms, and all worlds are possible. Which means that somewhere there's a Nachollni who didn't pretend to be Wilonek Scilli, and a Batrix who shot and killed Scilli instead. Resulting in murder and mayhem all around. Just be thankful you're living on this world."

"You are quite a philosopher underneath that coarse exterior, Scilli."

"Don't let it get around. I'll be blackballed from the guttersnipe's club."

I looked around the lounge. Except for Batrix and I, everyone had returned to their own compartments. To get drunk, write it all down, become morbid – whichever way they chose to escape. Pieces of the broken windows still littered the carpet.

Batrix followed my gaze, though I don't think he was seeing anything. "Do you believe it is finally over?" he asked.

"As much as it can be, yes."

"Then the government has won."

I looked at Batrix carefully. He couldn't help it, I suppose. He was too much a creature of the administration. "I have lost my oldest friend," I said. "The Republic's finest mind has been murdered, some miles back the bottom of a gorge is a graveyard for Sharpshooters and quite a few service staff whose only crime was to be posted to this train. And you say the government won."

"The wizards lost, then."

"No one lost, Batrix. Or won. This rail-road system will no doubt be in full use before the year's out. Who knows, now the principles have been demonstrated maybe other, lesser, minds will plan more rail-roads, expand and develop Alva's locomotive-engine concept. But we've lost Alva and his particular, undisciplined form of genius. And the new Ramini needs genius, Batrix. It needs vision. Anyone can follow – take a brilliant concept that's already been realised, and tinker with it. Thinos was a visionary – still is – but Sendivogius was right about one thing: he can only survive one more term in office. Who'll take his place? More visionaries? Or the grey followers with their incomplete, diluted understanding?"

I paused, embarrassed by my own rhetoric. I looked down at the scuffed toes of my boots. "No – maybe I was wrong. I think we all lost. Just a little."

"Quite a speech, Scilli. I feel I should applaud. Have you ever thought of running for Office yourself?"

"Speeches are for career men, Batrix. I'm just a novice wizard who couldn't even make first *shakrat*."

Batrix looked like he was about to say something, but his mouth pressed shut. After a while he looked down at the glass littering the carpet as though seeing it for the first time. "I will collect together what remains of the Sharpshooters. Clean up in here and then see if that abaston stone is where you say it is."

I turned my back on him and made for the carriage door. "As you wish; I'll be in my compartment. Wake me when we reach Scana Carsofi."

In the remaining carriage, the compartment doors were shut, all except one. Boz's. The writer was clearly framed in his open doorway, seated comfortably in an armchair, scribbling frantically on several sheets of paper. Well, what else would you expect to see a writer doing?

"Another novel, *Gosigné* Boz?" I asked.

He looked up sharply. A moment later, a languid smile surfaced through his expansive whiskers. "*Gosigné* Scilli. No, memoirs, more like. A diary of my experiences as I travel through Ramini. My publisher suggested that since I was here, I might as well use my time to advantage. There's an excellent chance such a journal will have an eager readership back in Pyndria."

I stepped into his compartment uninvited. He placed the papers on a small table beside him. Face down, I noticed. "Funny you never mentioned it earlier."

"Should I have? I was never aware you were interested in the literary world." The façade never cracked.

"Literary, no. But I do have a professional interest in international politics."

He frowned politely. "I'm afraid you've lost me, sir."

There was another chair. Clearly his status allowed him more than me. I pulled it closer and sat facing him. I made no attempt to reach for the papers. "Please, Boz, don't insult us both. The *Plytath a'Pyndr* isn't a club for disaffected middle-class Pyndrians any more than it's a pseudo-occult organisation looking back nostalgically to a golden, pre-wizard age."

"Your ever-expanding field of knowledge never ceases to amaze me, sir. Then perhaps you'd care to tell me exactly what we are supposed to be."

"Pyndria used to control a world-wide empire—"

"Common knowledge."

"Which fact pre-supposes there was an Emperor. What happened to him?"

Boz gave a puzzled laugh. "The last Emperor – Veyne XIII – died childless a century ago. His line died with him. Pyndria has been governed by a parliament since."

"Really? No remnants of aristocracy? No landless nobles behaving badly?"

"What exactly are you getting at, Scilli?"

"The *Plytath a'Pyndr*. That's where they went, isn't it, Boz? The Order's head is a direct descendant of Veyne – from the wrong side of the blanket, of course. The rest of the members are either from the Imperial families, or fierce royalists – like yourself. All biding their time. All dreaming of the day you can overthrow parliament and put an Emperor back on the Pyndrian throne. An Emperor and a Thaumaturge."

"Supposing all of this is true," Boz said with an affected wave of his hand. "What business is it of yours? Or does Ramini's Internal Bureau now consider the entire world its bailiwick?"

"Normally, I'd agree with you, Boz. Pyndria can do what the hell it likes. What concerns me – and the Bureau – is when possible subversive elements enter our country."

"Subversive? I?" He laughed loudly. Maybe just a little too loud. "I may have annoyed a few members of my government with my books, but even my worst enemies would never describe me as a subversive!"

"Maybe they don't know you well enough."

"I came on this journey through the direct invitation of Professor Alva himself, the gods rest his soul—"

"And who told him to invite you, Boz?"

"Told?" He looked back at me incredulously. "Maybe your President could have influenced him into inviting those other passengers along ... but me? Why?"

"Not the President. But Alva had several ... friends, shall we say ... at the Madrasaté Seminary. Dangerous place to have friends, that. Not everyone was who they seemed."

"You and your friend Yosec are proof of that." His tone was mildly spiteful.

I shrugged. "How hard would it be, say, for someone to suggest – just off the cuff, as it were – why not invite that Pyndrian writer to come along? Think of the prestige. Considering what a crashing snob Alva was, I think he would have embraced the suggestion with unbridled enthusiasm."

"And why should anyone make such a suggestion?"

I dropped a fingernail-sized oval of abaston crystal onto the table, next to his papers. An inert, exhausted fragment. There was the profile of King Menelik XIV of Steatal carved sharply into it. Boz barely glanced in its direction.

"Found in the destroyed meeting-place of a group of dissidents," I told him, though I doubt he needed anything explained. "Ancient crystal, ancient king – yet newly carved. So not supporters of the Chrysomancers – or the government. Yet possessors of some kind of magic. Maybe even more ancient than abaston power. Like thaumaturgy."

"Is that some kind of implication, sir?"

"Ramini also used to have an aristocracy. Before the Chrysomancers became the ultimate power and united all the various kingdoms under one tyranny. What remained of the nobility was absorbed into the wizards' ranks. But, as you know, blue-bloods have long memories. They consider themselves to be aristocrats first and wizards second."

"I still fail to see where you are driving us, Scilli."

"Of course you do. Consider this: the *Plytath a'Pyndr* realised that if they sit placidly and wait for the right time, it'll never come. What they needed was an ally, one who would also benefit from their help. And here is Ramini, across the sea, the Chrysomancers weak and failing – dreaming just as vainly about past glories and a return to power. Individually, neither they nor the *Plytath a'Pyndr* stand a chance of succeeding. But together?"

"And what am I, some kind of ambassador?" His expression said the idea amused him. His eyes told an entirely different story.

"Something like that. Someone who can go on a tour of the country legitimately, even keep a journal of everyone he meets, everything he learns. Although I doubt it'll be your publisher who reads it on your return."

"There you'd be wrong."

I shrugged. "It wouldn't be the first time. I still think what your publisher sees won't be exactly everything you record. The edited highlights, perhaps."

"All authors exercise self-censorship, Scilli."

I switched tack, wondering how much it would throw him. "Your travels won't be taking you anywhere near Dak Talini?"

"Dak Talini?" He frowned again. "Isn't that where the Archimandrite lives? I couldn't say, Scilli. I don't think I know exactly where Dak Talini is. My geography of Ramini is a little hazy."

"A bit late with the disingenuous act, Boz."

His frown dissolved into a wide grin. It wasn't a nice one. "You cannot prove a word of this, Scilli."

"No. But that doesn't make any of it less true."

"What do you intend to do?" The grin had vanished, replaced by a total lack of expression. If he was worried, he certainly wasn't showing it.

"You're not the only one who can make reports, Boz." I waited to see if his blank expression altered at all. It didn't. "So, will you try to kill me?"

"Kill you, Scilli? Whatever for? Even if I believed it would achieve anything, I have no reason to do so." The grin was back. "Do I?"

I matched him grin for grin. "We'll see, eh?" I stood. "I won't say goodbye. It might be premature."

Boz half stood. He bowed before dropping back into his seat again. "Then farewell, *Gosigné* Scilli."

"Be seeing you." I began to leave, then paused in the doorway. "Keep the cameo. And give my best regards to Sendivogius." I went into the corridor before he could pretend he didn't know who that was, either.

He wouldn't kill me. Of that I was certain. Like he said: he had no reason. I couldn't prove a damned thing. It was my word against a noted foreign visitor. And the Bureau wouldn't look kindly on an ex-Madrasaté pupil making unsubstantiated accusations, they'd think I was just trying to scare up work for myself.

The carriage jerked. It began to move. So Batrix had found Sanej's crystal and Law was getting us underway. The *Novandik* would get to Scana Carsofi after all – and not too adrift from schedule.

I walked down the corridor, past my compartment, and out onto the rear balcony. The view was spectacular: stark cliffs lit by the moon against an inky sky. The Treniccni Pass reared above us on either side, echoing back the rattle and shriek of wheels on metal. The rail-train was beginning its climb through the towering cleft, slowly accelerating, not far from the highest point of the pass. In an hour, maybe less, we would be starting the descent towards the dry Atchinor Territories, and in a day or two, steaming triumphantly into Scana Carsofi. Well, perhaps not so triumphantly, but with some sense of achievement, and loss, and not a little relief.

I looked up towards the needle-sharp peaks that were gradually dropping behind us. I sensed rather than saw it – black against black – perched on the highest crags. Winged, maybe multiple-winged – I was prepared to bet good money there'd be twenty-six – its form no more solid than dirty smoke. Somehow, without moving, it kept pace with us. The logic of dream, or magic.

The Chrysomantic Council, still watching over us. They certainly wouldn't be there just to enjoy the scenery.

"There you are, you old bastard," I said, almost to myself. I knew from experience I wouldn't have to shout. "I guessed you had to be following. So much easier to project via an attuned sending than all the way from Dak Talini."

There was no reply; I didn't expect one.

"So, will you attack from on high? Or have we won this round?" Or more likely, would a personal assault be too costly in abaston resources and expose the Chrysomancers to an unacceptable degree of risk? Especially the Archimandrite, who was certainly up there, part of that swirling winged thing, his essence combined alongside the rest of the Council.

Again, there was no reply – but after several seconds, the thing far above us ceased its movement, without movement. It remained perched on a thin, sword-like pinnacle of pallid rock, its many wings undulating and pulsing. Eventually, it was so far behind I could no longer even sense it. That was a response of sorts, I thought.

I stepped back inside the carriage, shutting the door carefully behind me. In my compartment, I threw my tattered coat to one side, after removing the flask of *chavet* and placing it close to the sofa-bed. I fell back, shutting my eyes and starting to list my various injuries. After a while, I gave up. I wasn't sure I could count that high.

I waited for sleep, feeling almost content. It was all downhill from here.

Batrix and Scilli will return in

Citadel of the Moon

So as an taster of that forthcoming novel,
turn the page and enjoy

Chapter One

The sky grew lighter. It had passed the night without boiling monsters; no wizard had rained magical destruction down from it. The house across the road had remained stubbornly silent. Another joyless vigil was over.

I slipped my watch out of its waistcoat pocket: dawn was just under two hours away. Good. Some other fool could waste his time staring at an empty mansion. I wanted sleep, food, and *chavet* – although not necessarily in that order. The persistent gnawing of withdrawal had begun some time earlier, and my bottle was empty.

Snapping the watch closed, I dropped it back into the pocket. I wanted to stretch, yawn, make those disgusting, early-morning noises most of us seem to feel so necessary, but I couldn't break cover. Just in case. I had to remain concealed in the wild stand of trees across the road from the mansion until my relief came. I prayed he wouldn't be late this morning – for once.

I'd passed the point where I believed we'd been misinformed about *Gosigné* Mawinnek's pretty, Scan Feta retreat days ago, now I was convinced the whole mission was simply an attempt by Under-Director Risnek to drive me mad. That yes-man's yes-man had never liked me.

The feeling was mutual.

There was a rustle of movement to my left. "Scilli!" a voice hissed. I relaxed, dropping my hand from the butt of the Alva repeating pistol tucked away in my topcoat.

Sadly, it wasn't my relief, just Krajicek Fochs. I recognised his less than cautious voice. Another Bureau employee caught up in a seemingly endless operation, and one of the Under-Director's non-favourites. Mainly because, like me, Fochs had the nerve to have been forcibly enrolled into a wizard's seminary as a baby, and the misfortune not to be a fully indoctrinated Chrysomancer when the war ended. Risnek never could tell the difference between the lost and saved. It was one of his more endearing qualities.

"Fochs," I acknowledged his foggy silhouette as it thickened out of the pre-dawn air. "I hope you've come to tell me it's all been a big joke, Risnek's laughed himself into a seizure, and the Director's signed my premature retirement with full pay."

Fochs' expression – permanently frozen in a fishy stare behind his thick eyeglasses – faltered. Looking like a stunned tortoise, he smoothed what remained of his thinning, pomaded hair. "That's not exactly—" he began. I stopped him before he could ramble on further in his pedantic way.

"Then we've got to hurry up and wait, yes?"

"No."

I sighed the sigh of a man doomed to eternal disappointment, and leaned against the half-dead tree at my back. "We're not going in?" I said, injecting as much pleading into my voice as I could. It was wasted on someone with Fochs' sensitivities.

"Up until four days ago, we were certain Deynah was still a member of the group." He forged on, regardless of how well I already knew. As project controller I was supposed to know better than he, but Fochs was not the kind of man to be side-tracked once he'd decided to impart whatever gem of information he'd been saving up.

"But you don't any longer," I tried to interject. I would have been better employed detouring an iceberg.

"Then we lost all trace of his signature. There was no indication that he'd been killed, just the loss of the abaston trace linked to his aura."

"Maybe he lost the crystal."

"You know perfectly well the cross-link has a range of several miles. No one has left or entered the house since we lost the trace."

"That you know of."

"We've been monitoring all this time, Scilli! No chrysomantic magic has been used!"

"And what if they don't use chrysomancy?"

He stopped long enough to take a breath. "The Bureau is fully aware of the suspicions both you and the late Sanej entertained about other forms of magic. But so far you've signally failed to produce any proof."

"Scan Leroth – bureau operatives killed in a bizarre explosion. Cause unknown. Instances of peculiar abductions and deaths in the Kant. Cause unknown. The assault on the Capitol last month: fifty Sharpshooters simply disappearing before as many witnesses. Three previously healthy senators dropping dead with unaccountable fevers. Causes unknown. How much more proof do you need?"

"They are not proof, Scilli, merely unanswered questions."

"You remind me of a heteromorph I used to know..." Fochs wasn't improving my mood any, and the mention of Scan Leroth had awakened unpleasant resonances. The similarities with this stakeout were uncomfortable and I didn't want it ending the same way.

Over six months had passed since Sanej and I – who'd been my partner back then – wasted similarly futile nights watching a deserted merchants' house in the eastern seaport. Eventually, Sanej had ordered a raid, and we'd lost over half our force in an explosion of no recognisable cause. All that was recovered, before the entire building collapsed, was an exhausted fragment of abaston crystal, recently carved with the profile of a long-dead king.

Then Sanej had been murdered during an undercover operation, leaving me with as many questions as theories and, as Fochs was so happy to point out, no proof.

I looked back at the house. Its pale sides were beginning to glow like dying coral in the increasing light. Three storeys high, with twenty half-moon windows along the visible, front wall, and a shallow, tiled roof. Its grounds were neatly laid out with lawns and parterres, and a grove of Cotechatlu palms beside the main, wrought-iron gate. Quite a picture. And like most pictures, most of it lay cryptically behind the pretty façade.

"We can't wait any longer," Fochs insisted, his tone fussy. I agreed.

"Get everyone into position." I sounded even more tired than I felt. "We go in on my signal."

He busied himself away, goggling face smug with the belief he'd forced me into an unpleasant position. It was half-true: what I was imagining was a whole lot worse than unpleasant, but a self-important ninny like Fochs would never be able to force me into anything. My devious conscience was all I needed, along with some personal, perverted sense of what was right and wrong. Deynah might still be alive in that villa, a prisoner, with just enough left worth saving. As long as a treacherous voice hiding in my mind kept insisting on that, I'd have to find out.

The Bureau knew me very well, and used its advantage to the hilt.

I slipped out my watch again. The minutes spun past as daylight grew stronger, the villa's front wall changing from coral to pale lemon to sharp white. If Fochs didn't get everyone into position soon there'd be no point in attempting the quiet, unobtrusive swoop I wanted. No mad charges like at Scan Leroth. Every conceivable outcome had been anticipated, we'd all been fully briefed. Seventy percent casualties had been declared well within the criteria of success.

Shows what kind of sick mind plans these ventures.

Fochs appeared again, batting aside a growth of ferns twice his height. Under his thick lenses, his eyes looked glazed and luminous. I hoped it was simply a distortion caused by the glass.

"All ready, Scilli," he gasped. He sounded on the point of collapse. What was he going to be like once we were actually inside?

"You lead the assault on the west side," I ordered. Then he'd still be in the shadows I reasoned, the safest position. Nothing to do with keeping him as far away from me as possible. "Your watch?"

He tugged a heavy, double-cased beast out of his waistcoat and flipped it open. Both our timepieces were synchronised to within fractions of a second. The Bureau never stinted when it came to equipment.

"We start in thirty seconds from—" I waited for the seconds dial to reach the top "—now."

Fochs vanished instantly. I wasn't wrong: he was drunk on taking such a major part in the operation. If he lived through it I promised myself to take him to Grif Ditya's for the best dinner he'd ever had.

The second hand swept round with uncomfortable speed. It seemed as though Fochs would never have chance to get to his men in time.

Thirty seconds passed. I shouted a command, and burst from cover. Silently, twenty men – all armed with Alva repeaters – followed. Uniformly clothed in unremarkable, charcoal suits, we were a band of freelance mourners, searching for business.

We dashed across the narrow road, stooping low – not that anyone in the villa could fail to see us. The gates weren't locked, and we were through in a moment. We were most exposed during the dash up to the villa's walls, but there were no yells of alarm from the building, no shots, no magical defences. It was unnerving.

All twenty-one of us slammed up against the west wall of the villa. I signalled north and south, and my group split into tens, as per their training, fanning out across the wall. Ground floor windows were the targets, open, preferably, although we all knew enough ways to force a locked window without alerting the household.

Rapidly, in total silence, we made it inside. There were three open windows and all twenty-one of us slipped through in a choreographed unit that made me proud. But the building's continual silence and lack of opposition rattled my nerves.

The villa was in darkness, except for the east-facing walls, now stained orange by the approaching dawn. It was decorated in classical style, with plastered walls, dark-varnished floors, open staircases, and a great deal of heavily embroidered furniture. The ceilings were ribbed with fake beams, and everywhere the rooms were filled with oil lamps in the latest style, brass and steel, polished to mirror-finishes.

And not one lit.

My group swept the ground floor without being told. Nowhere was left unchecked. Cushions were uprooted, cupboards and drawers opened, closets scoured. The only sounds were of rubberised boot-heels on polished floors. There was nothing. Nothing to hint the villa wasn't the retreat of a normal, everyday businessman with the time and money to indulge his tastes. Not even the signs of a mistress – yet it was a matter of record that *Gosigné* Mawinnek had several.

I hoped Fochs was having better luck.

The sun was two or three degrees above the horizon when our search came to a futile halt. Nothing in any of the above ground storeys, so there had to be a basement. Maybe several. Many fashionable villas across Ramini were built on the sites of old ruins; at one time it had almost been obligatory. I was betting Mawinnek had a maze of ancient, stone-built cellars under his highly-polished floorboards.

I was in one of the salons, thinking hard, staring at the floor as though I could force my vision through. I heard the rapid footsteps, and knew it was Fochs before I looked up. His fishy stare was disturbed; all the excitement had gone out of the chase. Mawinnek wasn't playing fair.

"Anything?" I asked, by way of something to say. I already knew the answer. He wouldn't be here, looking so upset, otherwise. But at least he was still breathing. That was a plus.

"Not a thing." He was trying to match his expression to the sulky tone, but on his face it didn't fit. I shoved my hands into trouser pockets, and tapped the floor with a boot toe. It sounded solid enough.

To give Fochs credit, he caught on fast. "Cellars?"

"It's all we've got left."

The pout vanished instantly, his goggling stare catching fire once more. "Then I'll find them!"

He was racing back to join his men before I could stop him. I hoped the older, more experienced heads amongst his team would stop him before he did anything terminally foolish. I shrugged and faced my own, disconsolate bunch. They'd been hoping for some action too, and Mawinnek had sorely disappointed them.

"Clean up and secure the place," I said. "We'll hand this whole sorry mess over to the relief. Whenever they deign to turn up."

"Scilli!" came Fochs' sudden, excited yell, "I've—!"

It wasn't much of an explosion, just a vivid, actinic flash that drowned the entire house in light. My ears popped in the displaced air. When I picked myself up off the floor, everywhere was soundless once again.

In a hallway, almost at the centre of the villa, a rectangle now stood proud of the floor. Residual energy sparked around its corners, a stark purple in the dawn light. Fochs was huddled nearby, folded in on himself like a newborn baby. He was dead, of course.

A member of Fochs' own squad gently turned the body over. It sprawled across the floorboards, hands charred lumps, clothing white with ash. Even the eyeglasses were buckled, the lenses warped and half melted.

"What happened?" I asked, more for clarification's sake.

"He spotted a groove, running at odds with the boards," said the one who'd turned the body over. "Before I could stop him, he tried to prise it open." He pointed at a molten splash against the wood. Up until that moment I hadn't spotted it.

"A knife?" I asked. The other nodded.

I found myself sighing again. It was a good day for them. "I think we can assume the spell's done its worst."

I stepped over Fochs and stooped to look at the raised piece of floor. It was a trapdoor, disguised just enough to fool anyone not actively searching for it. Probably explained the spell. Mawinnek would know the door couldn't stay hidden forever, so it was overlaid with a simple defensive spell; one that would certainly kill anyone who tried to open it. A trapdoor indeed.

Except there were more than one of us. Somehow, I didn't think that possibility would have passed Mawinnek by. "Which means there's something down there, waiting for us," I finished the thought aloud.

Nobody looked happy at those words. The number of volunteers to investigate didn't move me to tears, instead they were waiting for me to lead. One of the joys of being appointed controller.

Taking a firmer grip on my pistol – though I don't know what use I thought it was going to be – I nudged at the trap with the toe of my boot. Reluctantly, it flipped over into a fully open position. The hinges couldn't have been oiled in years: they screamed in outrage. Someone lit a match and tossed it into the hole. Several steps glared against the blackness before the match hit bottom and went out. Not far down, then. If an unseen someone chose to grab my ankles as I stepped down, at least I'd survive the fall.

Taking a match out of my own lucifer case, I stepped onto the top stair. The bottom was hidden by the dark so I wouldn't go all dizzy and lose what little respect I might have left among these men. I doubt any of them knew about my little problem with heights – it's not the sort of thing that comes up in polite conversation at staff dinners and I wanted it to stay that way. I had enough grief being known as a seminary boy, without letting on I get nose bleeds in tall heels.

I took two steps down. The darkness didn't grow any more revealing. I struck the match. The sphere of illumination was just enough to show me the floor, several feet below, but nothing else.

I descended quickly, eager to reach the bottom, not wanting to be framed in an open trapdoor filled by dawn's light. If anyone down there was going to take pot-shots with pistol or crossbow, the match was the only target I was willing to give them. And I wasn't fool enough to leave it close to any part of me I couldn't live without.

The match began burning my fingers. I dropped it and lit another. Holding the light up, I scanned my surroundings. The cellar appeared to start at the wall immediately behind the steps. From the echoes my scuffling boots raised, I guessed it was pretty large and open. I held the match out level as far as my arm would stretch. I wanted to see any obstacles, not find them with my face. I needn't have bothered.

I'd taken just a dozen steps into the void, shuffling warily, when a faint glow pulsed some distance ahead of me. I took another step, and it pulsed a little brighter. One more, and it grew brighter still. Whatever it was, my presence had activated it.

"What's that?" someone called from above. Must have seen the glow, too. But I wished he'd kept his curiosity silent.

"I don't know. I'm taking a look. Get everyone out of the villa – just in case."

Fearless, thoughtful Scilli. Always putting the lives of his men before his own. I noticed no one tried to argue with me before getting out.

With each step the light grew brighter. It was like racing towards a heatless furnace, whilst barely moving your feet. The walls of the cellar were growing clearer: dank, nitre-encrusted curves of ancient brick. As I'd guessed, the foundations of Mawinnek's villa were old ruins. Some other time I might have been impressed by the possible symbolism, at that moment I was more caught up in what I could see a hundred yards ahead of me, clearly blazing in a blue-white flame.

It was Llyscu Deynah, or had been, once. I hoped that whatever made Deynah the man he was – his soul perhaps, not that the government encouraged us to believe in such things – was long gone.

He was trapped in what looked like a skeletal, metal chair. His face was rigid, eyes glaring, hair standing erect from his skull, writhing like it had acquired all the life Deynah had lost. His hands were half-clenched against the chair's thin arms. All about him, sinuous as any python, were blazing coils of thick white light, undulating and writhing against his flesh and clothing. Wherever they crossed, there was another, brighter flash, and another coil was born. As I watched, a thin, new-born coil wriggled towards his face and slowly tunnelled up a nostril. His expression never wavered. I hoped it was because he'd gone way beyond pain.

A luminous tear oozed from his right eye. It was several moments before I realised it was another tendril – or maybe the same one – squeezing past the eyeball.

Raising my pistol, I fired: straight for the centre of Deynah's brain. If the bullet ever reached his flesh, I never saw it. Instead, a vivid purple spark flashed across the front of the blazing blue light. The coils began to whip furiously. Deynah's body twitched as new tendrils grew with frenzied speed.

I fired again. Another flash; ever more coils. Belatedly, it occurred to me that I'd just done the very thing Mawinnek had wanted. The trapdoor had been a warning: Deynah was the real trap.

I turned and ran. I'd done enough as a hero, now it was time to be practical. Getting further away from Deynah wasn't making the light any dimmer; quite the opposite. As I reached the steps two brilliant tendrils coiled themselves around the base of the handrail. I cleared the steps two at a time, kicking the trapdoor shut behind me. It bulged as something below pressed up.

Hoping everyone was clear of the house I ran for the front door, not stopping until I was past the gates. Everyone seemed to be watching, appreciating my athletic performance.

"Take cover!"

Maybe it was the panic on my face, because suddenly I was the only one around. I raced across the road and dived into the shrubbery. An instant later, a colossus behind me coughed.

I watched in awe as the villa came apart. It wasn't a vast explosion, in fact there was almost a sense of order to it. Walls shivered apart, throwing disintegrating windows across the grounds in precise arcs. The roof hurled tiles in a wide circle. I heard the smash of debris falling all around me, but the exploding villa was unnaturally quiet. Merely the softest of pops as it disassembled itself.

A spout of blue-white brilliance coiled upwards, detonating in a silent, sky-filling flare. For a moment, everything had two shadows.

I pulled myself out of the cover of a gnarled wasp-oak. On the opposite side of the trunk, at the same level as my cowering head, a hand-sized shard of tile was embedded three inches into the striped bark. I could hear the rustle of men getting to their feet.

"Anyone hurt?" I called out. There was a chorus of negatives. If anyone had done more than break a fingernail, they were being brave about it.

I spared the razed villa a sour look. Another Scan Leroth. That only two lives had been lost this time – one of them before the assault – didn't cheer me. Under-Director Risnek would want my head served with an apple in my mouth, bacon rolls, fried potatoes, and herb bread.

And to make life even more appealing, now the excitement was over the pangs of *chavet* withdrawal began to demand my attention again. I groaned and spat out a curse or two.

"The same old Scilli," came a voice from immediately behind me. I lurched about, raising my pistol. There was a single figure, small, rotund, with a neatly-clipped moustache and oiled hair. His barrel-like figure was neatly clad in the blue and gold uniform of a Lieutenant-Commander of the Internal Bureau. He stuck out a podgy, though immaculately manicured hand.

"A pleasure to see you again."

For a moment I was puzzled. I didn't know this person. My reputation wasn't that big, surely? Then I recognised the blue-lensed eyeglasses the man was wearing. Those, and the Bureau uniform, told me everything. He wasn't a man at all.

I stuck out my own hand. "Batrix. You're looking ... well."

The heteromorph squeezed my fingers briefly before dropping his arm. The smile was business like. "Thank you. I feel well."

I started to wonder how many reverses the heteromorph's peculiar, magically-created physiology had made since our last assignment together – how many changes of gender with each full moon – before a thought hit me.

"You brought that order! The one to go in!"

Batrix looked as though he might have felt a little uncomfortable, but I didn't know his present form well enough to be sure. "Indeed, Scilli. Along with a further order from Under-Director Risnek. You are to return to Wael Edra immediately."

Wael Edra: the Ramini Republic's new capital and home of the Bureau's headquarters. Quite a jaunt to Scan Feta. To send someone like Batrix such a distance – a heteromorph at that – meant Risnek had something serious on his self-absorbed little mind. Something more than roasting me over a slow fire.

"Immediately, eh?"

Batrix nodded, a smile tweaking at his moustache. He remembered me too well.

"As I recall, the next coach to Wael Edra doesn't leave until tomorrow, Batrix."

He produced a watch, the twin of my own. "At exactly this time tomorrow."

"Then there's no hurry. How about dinner at Grif Ditya's tonight?"

The heteromorph frowned. "I believe that is the most exclusive, and therefore expensive, restaurant in Scan Feta, Scilli. Might I enquire as to the occasion?"

"Let's just say I owe it to someone. What d'you say?"

Batrix continued to stare at me through the blue lenses. Finally, he nodded. "As I said: the same old Scilli."